Love
at
Lakewood
Med

Love at
Lakewood
Med

TJ Amberson

SWEETWATER
BOOKS

An imprint of Cedar Fort, Inc.
Springville, Utah

This is a work of fiction. The characters, names, incidents, places, and dialogue are products of the author's imagination and are not to be construed as real. The opinions and views expressed herein belong solely to the author and do not necessarily represent the opinions or views of Cedar Fort, Inc. Permission for the use of sources, graphics, and photos is also solely the responsibility of the author.

ISBN 13: 978-1-4621-2070-3

Published by Sweetwater Books, an imprint of Cedar Fort, Inc.
2373 W. 700 S., Springville, UT 84663
Distributed by Cedar Fort, Inc., www.cedarfort.com

LIBRARY OF CONGRESS CATALOGING-IN-PUBLICATION DATA

Names: Amberson, TJ, author.
Title: Love at Lakewood Med / TJ Amberson.
Description: Springville, Utah : Sweetwater Books, an imprint of Cedar Fort,
   Inc., [2017] |
Identifiers: LCCN 2017049164 (print) | LCCN 2017053325 (ebook) | ISBN
   9781462128228 (epub, pdf, mobi) | ISBN 9781462120703 (perfect bound : alk.
   paper)
Subjects: LCSH: Medical students--Fiction. | Man-woman
   relationships--Fiction. | LCGFT: Romance fiction. | Novels.
Classification: LCC PS3601.M363 (ebook) | LCC PS3601.M363 L68 2017 (print) |
   DDC 813/.6--dc23
LC record available at https://lccn.loc.gov/2017049164

Cover design by Priscilla Chaves
Back cover design by Shawnda T. Craig
Cover design © 2018 by Cedar Fort, Inc.
Edited and typeset by Hali Bird and Jessica Romrell

Printed in the United States of America

10 9 8 7 6 5 4 3 2 1

Printed on acid-free paper

For the teachers, colleagues, and mentors who made this possible

Other Books by TJ Amberson

The Kingdom of Nereth
Fusion

Chapter One

S leep. I need sleep.

But instead of hitting the snooze button, I'm frantically charging along a downtown city sidewalk, weaving through throngs of Monday-morning business types who seem to be walking in every direction but mine. Car horns are blaring from traffic-jammed streets as I yank my cell phone out of my bag to check the time. I gulp. It's already six thirteen. I only have forty-seven minutes before I need to be at . . . at . . . well, at wherever it is that I'm supposed to be going for my meeting.

I dash for a crosswalk before the light changes and then concentrate again on my phone, this time to access my email account. Hastily scrolling through the long list of unread messages, I eventually find the one regarding this morning's meeting. I click the email open.

"Savannah Drake: Your Introduction to the Medical Student Emergency Medicine Rotation at Lakewood Med," the email's heading declares in large black font. Underneath the heading, the message states that today's mandatory meeting will take place at seven o'clock a.m. in the Discovery Conference Room of Lakewood Medical Center. I skim the rest of the brief email, but there aren't any details about the meeting's agenda or even directions on how to locate the Discovery Conference Room within the humongous maze that Lakewood Med is notorious for being.

This type of ambiguity is not good for an exhausted medical student.

With a sigh, I open my bag to put my phone away but stop short. My white coat is missing. Telling myself not to panic, I panic anyway and take inventory of the contents of my bag again: water bottle, pens, hair elastic, stethoscope, antibiotic guide, wallet, and lip gloss. There's no question that my short medical student coat isn't there, yet I keep staring into the depths of my bag in disbelief. I'm sure that I grabbed the coat as I was flying out the door this morning. Or maybe I am starting to hallucinate from sleep deprivation.

Calculating how long it will take me to run back to my apartment, I catch my reflection in a store window as I pass and do a double take. My light brown hair, still wet from my one-minute shower, is a frizzy mess, my blue eyes are puffy from lack of sleep, and the scrubs I threw on remain as wrinkled as when I unburied them from a pile of clothes on the—

"Watch out!"

A gruff voice snaps me to attention. There's a guy in a suit heading swiftly up the sidewalk, and he's apparently determined to walk right through me if he must. I leap out of his way only to wind up crashing into a woman who is going the other direction. I stumble and lose hold of my cell phone, which falls to the sidewalk and is promptly stomped on by a group of people jostling by. An ominous cracking sound reaches my ears.

A gap appears in the foot traffic, and I dive ungracefully for the pavement to gather up what's left of my phone. Standing up straight again, I turn the phone over in my hand and make an initial assessment of the damage. The prognosis is not good. There's a crack down the middle of the screen, the case is nearly shattered, and something electronic that appears pretty important is sticking out from the inside. So I do the only thing that I can: jam stuff back into place and push the power button. The phone lights up but then makes a bizarre sound and goes black once more. I give the phone a shake. Nothing happens. My phone is definitely dead.

It's probably a good thing that I don't have time to stress about this at the moment.

Shoving my phone into my bag, I break into a run. As I fly up the next street, I spot Lakewood Medical Center past the skyscrapers, sitting atop a massive hill in the distance. It's far, but if I hurry, I can still make it in time. I press onward.

Soon, though, the delicious smell of baked goods begins filling my nose. I slow my pace, eventually coming to a stop outside of a coffee shop. Through the shop's windows, I can see fresh pastries on display and hot beverages being served. My mouth starts to water. I cast another glance at the hospital, which remains several blocks away, and then I gaze again through the shop window. My stomach growls.

It will only take a few minutes to get a pastry.

There's a soft jingle from the bell above the door as I enter the crowded shop. Mellow guitar music is playing, and the scents of hot drinks and freshly baked goods waft through the air. Behind the counter, a wiry teenage boy is taking orders while a girl with a nose ring is preparing drinks. I slide into the back of the line to wait.

"Do you recommend the coconut orange scone or the blueberry scone?" I hear the lady at the front of the line inquire of the boy behind the counter. Dressed in head-to-toe floral print, she adjusts her gigantic glasses and peers at him.

The boy seems to snap out of a sleepy haze. "Huh?"

"Which scone is better?" the lady repeats, louder and more slowly this time.

The boy behind the counter gives an indifferent shrug. "I dunno. They're both good, I guess."

"I see." The lady leans forward, analyzing the options in the display case. "I do not know how I shall make up my mind."

The line comes to a complete standstill while the lady continues deliberating over pastries. Shifting restlessly, I glance at the clock on the wall and then stare at the back of the lady's head, willing her to hurry up.

Brittany shifts her gaze to me. "Sounds fun," she replies dismissively, observing my wrinkled scrubs.

Erik turns away, but it's obvious that he's trying not to laugh. I lower my head and discreetly try to smooth the creases out of my scrub pants.

"So if not emergency medicine, what specialty are you planning to go into?"

It takes me a moment to realize that the question is directed at me. I raise my head. The question came from the coffee shop guy, who is now on the other side of the crowded elevator. I had nearly forgotten he was here.

"Pediatrics," I say to him with pride.

Out of the corner of my eye, I see Brittany and Erik exchange amused glances.

There is another chime from the elevator. To my relief, we've made it to the eighth floor. As soon as the doors open, I maneuver around Erik and Brittany to make my escape. Emerging from the elevator, I find myself standing at one end of a formally decorated foyer, which is otherwise unoccupied. A moment later, I hear the elevator doors close behind me. I shake my head and start brushing the scone crumbs off of my hands.

"You made it just in time, Doctor Kent. They're holding on the phone," a woman says.

I whip my head up at the voice. There is a short, trim middle-aged woman approaching from the hallway to my left. She is dressed in a cute blouse and slacks, and she's looking right at me. I stare at her in confusion, until I realize that her focus is actually on someone behind me. Someone right behind me. I quickly peer over my shoulder. It's the coffee shop guy. He must have gotten off the elevator, too.

The guy checks his watch and replies to the woman, "We've got time. Let's go."

With determination in his steps, the coffee shop guy passes by me and walks off down the hall, the woman nearly having to jog to keep up with his long strides. My mouth falls slightly open in surprise.

Doctor Kent?

The coffee shop guy was a doctor? I bet he's the only medical resident in this entire hospital who chooses not to wear a long white coat to announce the fact that he's a newly-minted MD. After all, any normal resident would want to wear his or her white coat, since being a resident is a pretty big deal, especially in a teaching hospital like this. Everyone knows that residents graduated from medical school, earned their MD, and got accepted into a residency program for training in their chosen specialty. Residents get to be the cool, young doctors who strut around with pagers conspicuously clipped to their scrub pants like badges of honor. Residents are responsible for patients. Residents run the show and—

Well, okay, residents don't really run the show. Residents work under the close supervision of attending physicians—doctors who have completed residency training. In the medical world, attendings are at the top of the food chain. But attendings are so high up in importance that they're like an entirely different species altogether, and so they don't even count. Anyway—

"Sav! There you are! Where have you been?"

I spin around. My best friend, Danielle Gillespie, is approaching from a hallway on the opposite side of the foyer. Her green eyes are wide.

"The orientation meeting is about to start!" She rushes closer, her red hair bouncing on her shoulders. "I thought you left our apartment early or something, but I got here and couldn't find you. I sent a bunch of text messages . . ." She halts when she gets to my side. "What on earth happened to you?"

I toss my napkin into a recycle bin. "I forgot to set my alarm."

Danielle claps a hand over her mouth. "Can you imagine if you had come late? I mean, this is our first day and—"

"I know, I know." I laugh wearily while yanking my hair up into a sloppy ponytail. Danielle always has a flair for the dramatic.

"I might have blown my grade and doomed myself to medical student purgatory forever."

She gives me one of her looks. "Well, come on. We'd better hurry."

Spinning on her heels, Danielle retraces her steps, leading me down the hallway from where she came. Eventually, we reach an imposing set of double doors, which are marked with a shiny plaque that reads, *"Discovery Conference Room."*

Danielle lowers her voice respectfully. "Okay, this is it."

She pushes the doors open with ceremonial gravitas, which causes me to snicker. When we step inside, though, even I have to pause to take in the grandeur. The conference room is big, bright, and richly decorated, with high ceilings and a dark wood floor—and somehow, the regal ambiance is also extremely intimidating. Eventually, my attention drifts to the long table in the middle of the room, which has fourteen somber-appearing medical students seated around it.

As I observe the other students I'll be on the rotation with this month, my stomach sinks. Everyone else remembered their short white coat. As the only coatless medical student, I'm going to stand out. And standing out is bad. When a med student stands out, he or she usually winds up getting asked a bunch of extra questions by the attending physician. It is like a subconscious hazing ritual that leaves the medical student looking like an idiot or a know-it-all in front of the others.

Resigned to my fate, I shuffle over to the table and drop onto one of the remaining empty chairs. I set my bag at my feet. Still, no one says a word. So I remain quiet and start staring at the tabletop like everyone else is doing.

In the calm, for the first time today, I finally have a chance to think. And then I start getting nervous. Really nervous. Although I am not going to apply to emergency medicine for residency, this rotation still matters a lot. My grade from this rotation will go on my residency application, impacting what pediatric residency programs offer me an interview. Where I'm invited to interview will determine my options for residency training. Where I go for residency training will basically affect my whole future.

In other words, I have to do extremely well on this rotation.

"The meeting hasn't started yet, has it?" Danielle asks the group, breaking the hush as she sits beside me.

A tall, thin guy at one end of the table shakes his head. I remember him from the family medicine rotation that we did together last year. His name is Austin Cahill.

"And we're sure that this is the right place, right?" blurts out a petite girl with short, dark blonde hair.

Austin gives the girl a look. "I doubt we would have all come to the same wrong place, Rachel."

"You're right. You're right." Rachel exhales. "I just can't screw this up, you know? I *need* an honors grade."

"Let me guess: you're gonna apply to emergency medicine residencies?" inquires a guy who's wearing a cool pair of glasses. He has a dark brown complexion, short curly hair, and a friendly grin.

Rachel sits bolt upright. "Yes."

"Nice." The guy with the glasses smiles again. "So am I."

Rachel's face blanches. "How many honors grades can they give out per rotation?"

He shrugs. "Hopefully, at least two."

Rachel stares at him, horrified.

"Hey, you'll be fine," the guy assures her. "My name is Tyler, by the way. Tyler Warren."

Before Rachel can muster a response, the doors to the room open behind me, and everyone falls quiet. I turn around. To my surprise, into the room steps the same woman who was talking to the coffee shop guy in the foyer a few minutes ago. She is now carrying a large stack of papers and folders, which she sets on the table.

"Hello, everyone," the woman begins warmly. "Welcome to your emergency medicine rotation."

There is a murmuring of respectful replies, until Rachel springs to her feet.

"My name is Rachel Nelson. It is a great pleasure to meet you."

The woman reaches out and shakes Rachel's offered hand. "Well, hello, Rachel. I'm Lynn Prentis, the rotation coordinator."

Rachel's face falls slightly. "Oh. You're not one of the attendings?"

"Goodness, no." Lynn lets out a pleasant laugh. "I'm not a doctor. I—"

"She keeps this medical student rotation running smoothly, is the coordinator for the entire emergency department, and is an invaluable right-hand woman," comes another voice from the doorway.

A voice that is familiar.

As everyone else sits up at heightened attention, I can barely bring myself to look toward the door. It's the coffee shop guy again. Doctor Kent. The coatless medical resident.

What is he doing here?

As Doctor Kent strides into the room, I notice that he now has an ID badge clipped to his shirt pocket. I squint to read the words under his photo:

Wesley Kent, M.D.
Emergency Medicine Attending

Oh no.

No.

No, no, no.

The coffee shop guy is no resident. He's an attending physician. An *emergency medicine* attending physician. He's at the very top of the food chain. And the only reason that an attending would be here right now is because he's in charge of this med student rotation.

No. Just. No.

Though I manage to keep it together on the outside, I'm starting to lose it on the inside. If Doctor Kent is in charge of this rotation, his evaluation will go on my residency application. His impression of me will dictate my entire future. In other words, the guy who caught me running late this morning and heard me express no interest in emergency medicine is the same person I am supposed to impress.

Wake me up from this nightmare.

"I'm sorry for the wait." Doctor Kent joins Lynn at the head of the table. There is not a hint of emotion on his face. "There was a phone call I had to take."

I sink low in my chair and try to hide behind Danielle. Maybe if I don't move, he won't notice me.

"We're glad to have you joining us in the emergency department—the ED—for the next four weeks," Doctor Kent continues. "I hope you're glad to be here, too."

And I am hoping that the earth will open up and swallow me right now. Is it possible that I will still be able to graduate from medical school after I fail this rotation? Or will I be condemned to some sort of remedial course for students who are stupid enough to express a lack of interest in their attending's specialty?

Doctor Kent sits down. "The Emergency Department is unlike any other place where you have practiced, or will practice, medicine. No matter who checks in, what her issue is, how he's behaving, or what time of day or night she may arrive, from the moment that person walks, rolls, or stumbles through the doors, he becomes your patient and your responsibility. You must be ready to handle anything and anyone at any time."

Rachel is bobbing her head with every syllable that is coming out of Doctor Kent's mouth. The rest of the students are clearly awed as they listen to him. I just slide down even farther in my chair, attempting to stay out of Doctor Kent's line of sight.

"We don't have the advantage of being in long-term relationships with our patients." Doctor Kent sounds like he has given this speech a hundred times. "Most will be strangers to you, and you will be strangers to them. But within seconds of going to the bedside, you must figure out how to build rapport with patients

I act more nonchalant about it than I feel. "I think so."

"Well, if you get bored, you can always come find Doctor Godfrey and me in the Fast Track area, caring for thrilling low-acuity stuff like ankle sprains and infected ingrown toenails," Danielle quips.

We emerge out of the stairwell on the ground floor, and Danielle leads me down a corridor to a large, unmarked door.

"This is the shortcut," she explains.

I raise an eyebrow. "Let me guess: you memorized the floor plan of the hospital before this rotation?"

"Didn't you?"

"Must have slipped my mind."

Giving me an I-don't-know-how-you-even-survive glance, Danielle holds her badge up to a scanner on the wall. The door slowly swings out toward us. Stepping through, we find ourselves in another vacant hallway. There is a sign on the wall with colored arrows pointing the ways to the radiology suites, Fast Track, the main emergency department, a consultation area, front triage, and the operating rooms.

Without needing to consult the sign, Danielle starts down a hall to our right. "Bye, Sav! I hope that you have a fabulous time working with—"

"Goodbye, Danielle," I cut her off pointedly.

With a laugh, she strolls around a corner and is lost from view.

Alone in the quiet, I start walking in the other direction, following the red arrows that lead the way to the main emergency department. As I move deeper through the labyrinth of empty halls, I begin hearing overhead pages, phones ringing, someone shouting, and ambulance sirens in the distance. I'm passed by a man who is dressed in patterned scrubs and casually pushing an unoccupied stretcher that has a squeaky wheel. Still tracking the red arrows, I go right and continue down another hallway. Two residents in long white coats are hurrying in the other direction, talking fast while reading their pagers. Meanwhile, I can hear the noise up ahead getting louder. When I round yet another corner, I suddenly come to a halt as an unexpected rush comes over me.

I have entered Lakewood Medical Center's emergency department.

The place is huge. The lights are glaringly bright. Commotion is everywhere. I see secretaries on the phone, nurses darting in and out of exam rooms, EMS crews arriving with screaming patients on their stretchers, techs rushing past with ECG machines, and doctors working on charts. Accompanying the tornado of activity is a soundtrack of unrelenting noise: pumps alarming, conversa tions, overhead announcements, phones ringing, pagers going off, babies crying, and more ambulance sirens outside.

I stare upon the scene, dumbfounded. It is complete pandemonium in here—and I have to survive for four whole weeks.

As the initial shock gradually starts wearing off, I realize that I am actually standing near the back of the emergency department. The long walls on both my right and left are lined with curtained entrances into the exam rooms—there has got to be at least twenty exam rooms on each side. On the opposite end of the department from where I'm standing is a designated entrance for ambulance crews, which is adjacent to three large resuscitation bays. And in the center of the department, an area sectioned off by a half-wall contains the workstations for the doctors, nurses, techs, and secretaries.

Once I've gotten my bearings, I start venturing father inside. But I soon stop again, taken aback, when I see ill-appearing patients lying on stretchers in the walkways. I glance around, counting several more occupied stretchers that have been shoved into every possible inch of free space in this place. Dressed in faded hospital gowns, the patients who are on these stretchers are connected to portable cardiac monitors and most have medications infusing through their IVs. Meanwhile, the emergency department staff members are rushing past them as if oblivious to the fact that there are a bunch of sick patients out in the open instead of in exam rooms.

"Excuse me? Excuse me!"

It takes me a second to realize that someone is trying to get my attention. I spin around. Resting on a stretcher that has been jammed between a drinking fountain and a rack of clean linens is a frail, elderly woman. She is waving for me to come to her side.

I approach. "Can I help you, ma'am?"

She reaches over the stretcher railing and places her shaking hand upon my arm. "Can you tell me how much longer it's going to be?"

"Going to be?" I repeat, leaning closer to her. "Going to be until what?"

"Until they let me go home," she whimpers.

I stand up straight, hoping to spot someone who might have a clue about what is happening with this woman. But the ED team is now clustered at the far end of the walkway, busy with a critical patient who has just arrived by ambulance. I'm going to have to wing it for now. So I smile down at the elderly lady and speak to her again:

"I don't know, ma'am. But I can try to find out, okay?"

"Hey! I need help!" someone else bellows.

I jump at the noise and face the patient who is on the next stretcher over. The obese man unsteadily pulls himself up to a sitting position and puts his bloodshot eyes on mine. A trauma collar has been placed around his neck to protect his cervical spine. There are multiple oozing abrasions on his forehead, he's wearing nothing but boxer shorts, and he reeks of alcohol and sweat.

I stay where I am, keeping my distance. "What do you need, sir?"

"I said that I need your help!" His speech is slurred from intoxication. "Come over here! Come over here! Help me!"

"Don't you know how much longer it's going to be, sweetheart?" The elderly woman is still clinging to my arm. "Can you tell me? I want to go home."

"Are you a nurse?" I hear another patient call from a few stretchers farther down. "I need a urinal, please!"

The drunk guy starts yelling obnoxiously. "I need you to come over here! I need help! Help! Help! Help! Help! Help!"

"I really need that urinal!" The other patient sounds more anxious this time.

The elderly woman tries to sit up. "Do I get to go home soon, sweetheart? Can't you tell me?"

"Help me!" The drunk guy begins rattling the stretcher railing like he wants to tear it off. "Help me! Help! Help! I need your help! Help me right—"

"Okay! But you need to stop yelling, sir!" I order him over the noise. I then quietly address the elderly woman while gently prying her hand off my arm. "I'll find someone who can answer your questions. I promise."

I do my best to cover the elderly woman with the flimsy hospital blanket that was hanging off of her stretcher. Then I approach the drunk guy.

"Alright, sir, what do you—"

He lunges at me. Before I can react, his grimy hand has clamped around my wrist and he yanks me toward him. My cry of alarm is cut short as I stumble forward, striking my head hard against the stretcher railing. Everything starts spinning as I drop to my knees. The guy continues to hold my wrist in his vice-like grip with one hand while grabbing at me with the other. I flail to get free. Our arms tangle. The guy tugs my head back by my ponytail, and my hair falls loose and gets in my face, making it hard to breathe. Over the guy's intoxicated shouts, I think I hear other people yelling now. I make another desperate attempt to free myself from the guy's sweaty, suffocating hold.

Footsteps approach fast. An instant later, the drunk guy is ripped off of me by a person who is wearing dark scrubs. I collapse to the floor, shaking from adrenaline. Havoc continues directly above where I'm cowering. I crawl away from the stretcher and stagger to my feet. Turning around, I am met by the sight of

Doctor Kent pinning the drunk guy down on the stretcher. Lying on his stomach and fighting violently to get loose, the drunk guy turns his head and tries to bite Doctor Kent's hand. I bolt forward to assist Doctor Kent with holding the patient until more help can arrive.

"Stay back," Doctor Kent barks at me.

I halt halfway to the stretcher. Doctor Kent looks past me and tells a secretary:

"Call a Code Strong."

The secretary picks up a phone, pushes a button, and starts speaking. "Code Strong to Walkway Thirteen!" Her voice blares out from the overhead speakers. "Code Strong to Walkway Thirteen!"

The drunk guy attempts to spit at Doctor Kent, who doesn't even flinch. Giving up on his fight to get free, the drunk guy then proceeds to threaten Doctor Kent with a long string of profanity-laden death threats. Still Doctor Kent's demeanor remains unchanged—almost as if he's used to this kind of thing.

There is another escalation in noise as security personnel weave through the other patients and the staff, push past me, and surround the stretcher. In one coordinated maneuver, they grab the guy by his arms and legs. Doctor Kent steps away, allowing the security team to flip the patient onto his back and place him in restraints. The drunk guy is locked to the stretcher within ten seconds. It's oddly disturbing and impressive at the same time.

"Well, I think his c-spine is cleared," Doctor Kent quips in the transient silence that follows. He scoops up his stethoscope from the floor, and then he stands up straight and addresses me. "Savannah, are you alright?"

I can't respond. My head is aching. Woozy and stunned, I reach out to the counter to steady myself. Meanwhile, the drunk guy starts belting out an intoxicated rendition of the Culture Club song, "Do You Really Want To Hurt Me?" He's actually not that bad of a singer.

"Savannah?"

The sudden sharpness in Doctor Kent's voice jars me to awareness. I see him coming toward me.

"I'm okay," I say, exhaling slowly. I gesture to the drunk guy's stretcher. "I'm gonna go out on a limb and guess that you've done that whole Code Strong thing before."

Doctor Kent stops. For one moment, I think I see a hint of a smile on his face. Then it's gone.

"Once or twice," he answers.

The drunk guy finishes the song's chorus with an enthusiastic, "Woo hoo hoo!"

"Woo hoo hoo!" comes a melodic response from a patient who is shut inside a nearby psychiatric containment room.

"Woo hoo hoo!" the drunk guy sings again.

I slowly look around. Yes, this is really happening. Yes, there really is a drunk guy happily singing eighties ballads while he's strapped down, half-naked, to a stretcher in the middle of an emergency department. Yes, there really is a locked-up psychiatric patient performing backup vocals. And yes, this is the weirdest thing that I have ever experienced in my medical school career.

Before I realize it, I've started laughing. I can't help it. It may only be my first day in here, but there's one thing that I think I can already say for certain: this place is totally different than a clinic or an inpatient floor.

I'm still chuckling as my eyes fall again on Doctor Kent. He's not laughing. He's not even smiling. Instantly, I fall silent and my amusement is replaced by dread.

Medical students aren't supposed to make fun of patients. Medical students are not supposed to do anything that even remotely resembles making fun of patients. Medical students are expected to convey respect, understanding, and professionalism toward every patient, no matter what. In other words, medical students aren't supposed to laugh about a patient in front of their attending—especially when that attending happens to run the rotation.

Doctor Kent is still saying nothing. I wonder if he'll flunk me right now. I'll probably get sent home in disgrace. I heard that happened once when a med student—

"He might get a recording contract if he keeps this up," I hear a different guy say who then adds his own, "Woo hoo hoo."

Surprised, I glance to my right. The comment came from a nurse who is working at a computer a few feet away. The nurse is about the same age as me, he's wearing a t-shirt and scrub pants, and he has a grin on his face.

"Possibly," I hear Doctor Kent reply. "This is certainly his strongest musical performance to date."

I whip my head back toward Doctor Kent, not hiding my surprise. Was Doctor Kent trying to be funny?

Doctor Kent faces me once more.

"Hey, thank you, by the way," I tell him, running a hand through my hair to try to fix the mess that used to be my ponytail.

Doctor Kent blinks. "You're welcome. Let's go see some patients."

He walks off, clearly expecting me to follow. But I don't.

"Doctor Kent?" I call out before I can catch myself.

Doctor Kent stops and peers at me over his shoulder. And he waits.

I point at the elderly lady on the walkway stretcher. "She's wondering how long it'll be before she gets to go home."

"I see." Doctor Kent faces me squarely and crosses his arms. "Anything else?"

"Well, yes, actually." Like an idiot, I gesture toward the patient on the stretcher farther away. "That person really needs a urinal."

Doctor Kent does not reply, but it doesn't matter. I know what he's thinking: he is an attending, and I am a med student. He has things under control around here, so I should shut up and not try to tell him how to do his job.

The nurse at the computer chimes in. "I'll take care of that urinal."

The nurse heads away. Without another word, Doctor Kent passes by me and goes to the stretcher where elderly lady is resting. Left by myself in the walkway, all I can do is watch while Doctor Kent crouches down beside the lady's stretcher and begins speaking quietly to her.

"How's your head?"

I glance back and see the nurse returning to his computer.

I brush the sore spot on my forehead. "I think I'll survive."

The nurse sighs. "I'm really sorry that happened. That patient is one of our frequent fliers, and he's a jerk." He extends his hand. "I'm Hadi, by the way."

"I'm Savannah." I shake his hand in return. "I'm a med student. I'll be here for the month."

"Cool. We like having med students around here. If you need anything, let me know."

"Thanks," I tell him sincerely.

Hadi motions beyond me. "So I take it that you got assigned to work with Wes this month?"

"Yeah."

Hadi lowers his voice. "Let me tell you a little about working with him. Wes is—"

"Savannah, are you ready?"

I jump and spin around. Doctor Kent is heading my way.

"Yes. I think so." I glance past him to observe the elderly woman on the stretcher. "So when does that lady get to go home?"

Doctor Kent adjusts the stethoscope around his neck. "She isn't going home. She has dementia, and she has no family to take care of her. She's coming into the hospital for treatment of her pneumonia, but she doesn't understand what's going on."

I pause, struck by his words. As I keep gazing at the elderly woman, I somehow begin seeing her more distinctly—as a weak, confused, frightened person who is alone and lying on a stretcher in the walkway of a chaotic emergency department. Then something starts to burn inside of me. It isn't right for that woman to be left out in the open. She deserves better. At the very least, she deserves some privacy.

"Why isn't she in an exam room?" I inquire, looking up at Doctor Kent.

Doctor Kent's expression stiffens. "Because every exam room is currently occupied by a patient who is even sicker than she is," he tells me in words that are measured and deliberate. "If I had an available exam room to put her in, I certainly would do so."

"Sorry. I didn't realize that—"

"Currently, there are about twice as many patients in the ED as there are available rooms," Doctor Kent goes on unrelentingly. "It will only get more overcrowded throughout the day."

"Is it always like this?"

"Always."

"So how come no one is working to solve the overcrowding problem?"

Hadi lets out a strange cough. I peer at him. Eyebrows raised, Hadi lets his gaze float meaningfully in Doctor Kent's direction before becoming extremely engrossed with whatever he's typing on the computer.

Hang on. Hadi isn't trying to tell me that—

"I have spent more than two years trying to convince hospital administration to fund an emergency department renovation." Doctor Kent sounds as though it is taking every ounce of his willpower to remain polite. "But as you have so astutely noted, Savannah, I have yet to be successful."

I cringe. I'm done for. In the last twenty-four hours, I have insulted Doctor Kent, his specialty, and the way he does his job.

I look away. "Sorry, Doctor Kent."

"It's Wes."

I take a moment before shifting my eyes back to his. His expression has not changed.

Our conversation is interrupted when a nurse approaches fast. "Doctor Kent, we've got a code coming in."

Doctor Kent immediately starts walking toward one of the large resuscitation bays. He's almost inside before he halts and peers back at me.

"Aren't you coming?"

My jaw drops. "In there?"

"You're here to do emergency medicine, right?" He jerks his head toward the resuscitation bay. "You can't get more emergency than this."

I continue to stand there, gaping; he continues to wait. So I unglue my feet from the floor and rush to join him, my mind spinning so fast that I'm getting another headache.

A code. A cardiac arrest. I am about to participate in the attempt to resuscitate someone whose heart has stopped beating—someone who has *died*. So what am I supposed to do? Epinephrine? Defibrillate? Do I use atropine anymore? And isn't there something about amiodarone? I think I've forgotten the H's and T's of PEA! What—

"Code Blue. ETA five minutes." The announcement comes from the overhead speaker. "Code Blue. ETA five minutes."

Trembling, I enter the resuscitation bay, where I'm instantly struck by a quiet, fiercely powerful energy that permeates the room—it's unlike anything I've felt before. My heart begins beating fast as I slide into a corner to observe the team work. Doctor Kent has already gone to the head of the empty stretcher, and he's swiftly donning gloves and a mask. Hadi and two other nurses are preparing the cardiac monitor and IV starts. One tech wheels the code cart into position while another brings the portable ultrasound to the bedside. Someone from radiology arrives with the x-ray machine and goes to the corner opposite me to wait.

There is another disturbance in the doorway as an army of people in long white coats storms inside. The tension in the resuscitation bay seems to quintuple when they appear. I start backing up to give the army room, until I notice that Erik is among the group. He has a bunch of pagers clamped to the waistband of his scrubs. As he charges toward the middle of the resuscitation bay, I take the chance to peek at his ID badge:

Erik Prescott, M.D.
Orthopedics Intern

My stomach somersaults with this little piece of new information. Greek God Erik is an intern—a first year resident. He's going into orthopedics, and I'm guessing that he's on a trauma surgery rotation for the month.

"We're from the trauma service," Erik declares, confirming my suspicion. "What's coming in?"

Doctor Kent stops what he is doing, as if only now aware of the white coat onslaught, and looks at him. "Cardiac arrest. ETA five minutes."

Erik doesn't hide his exasperation. "That's all the info you've got?"

One of the other white coats sighs with annoyance. It's Brittany Shiny Hair, who is standing near the back of the group. Before she spots me, I sneak a glance at her ID badge:

Brittany Chen, M.D.
General Surgery Intern

"Charge is currently on the radio getting an updated report from the medics," Doctor Kent is telling Erik steadily. "Presumably, we'll have more information soon."

Erik crosses his arms across his broad chest. "Alright, we need to have the code cart ready, two large bore IVs, cardiac monitoring—"

"It's all ready to go, man," Hadi cuts in without bothering to look up.

Erik seems flustered for only a moment and then throws his head back. "Okay. So who's doing airway? Who's pushing medications? And who—"

"I take it you're intending to run this code, Doctor Prescott?" Doctor Kent asks calmly.

There is a distinct break in the hubbub. I look at Erik. So do the rest of the white coats. For only an instant, I think I see something like hesitation—or was it fear?—on Erik's face.

"I'll be here doing airway, should you need anything," Doctor Kent adds in a tone that is unchanged.

Erik wets his lips and moves to the foot of the empty stretcher. "Of course I'll run this."

Doctor Kent resumes readying the laryngoscopes and endotracheal tubes that are on the small tray beside him. Then he raises his head and scans the resuscitation bay. He stops when he spots me. "Savannah, when was the last time you intubated someone?"

Everyone's gaze shifts to the corner where I'm hiding.

"Intubated someone?" I cough. "It was a little over a year ago. In simulation lab. On a mannequin."

I hear a few of the white coats chuckle.

Still concentrating on me, Doctor Kent motions to the equipment beside him. "This tube is yours, Savannah."

I feel the color drain from my face. Doctor Kent cannot be serious. There is no way that he's asking me to do a critical care procedure that I have never done before on a real human—especially one that needs to be done while the patient is coding. Not on my first day. Not in front of him. And not in front of Erik, Brittany, and everyone else in the entire emergency department.

"Grab some gloves," Doctor Kent adds.

I stare at him. He's serious. He is actually expecting me to intubate the patient. Or is he setting me up to fail on purpose? Is this his sick way of getting revenge for insulting him?

Wiping my clammy hands on my scrub pants, I make my way to Doctor Kent's side. I feel tingly and slightly sick as I peek at the tray of airway tools beside him, wondering if I even know what each piece of equipment is for.

The door of the resuscitation bay is swung open. The same nurse who first told Doctor Kent about the code walks inside.

"Fifty-one-year-old male," the nurse reads loudly from her notes, which are written on a scrap of fluorescent green paper.

"Found unresponsive at home. Estimated down time at least thirty minutes prior to EMS arrival. Asystole."

"And how long have medics been running the code?" Erik is sounding confident again.

"Twenty minutes."

With a decisive air, Erik addresses Doctor Kent. "Asystole for almost an hour. This guy is long dead. We don't need to run this code."

Doctor Kent looks at Erik without saying anything and then faces my way. "What size of endotracheal tube are you going to use to intubate?"

I promptly open my mouth to reply, but no sound comes out.

"A seven-point-five is often used for an average-sized male," Doctor Kent goes on for me. "But I always have a size up and a size down accessible, in case."

I clamp my mouth shut in disgrace. I knew the correct answer, but I cracked under the pressure. As far as Doctor Kent is concerned, not only do I fall apart under stress, I don't understand the basics of airway management, which is a fundamental part of emergency medicine. Averting my gaze, I curse for the millionth time that I wound up paired with the head of this rotation as my mentor.

Suddenly, the resuscitation bay door is slammed open again, and it's like I am hit with a bolt of lightning. The patient is here.

The EMS crew rushes in pushing a stretcher, which has someone lying motionless upon it. One paramedic is riding on the side of the stretcher while pumping on the patient's chest. Another medic is jogging alongside, bagging to push oxygen into the patient's mouth and lungs. A flurry of activity ensues all around me as the patient is transferred over to the ED stretcher and the team begins to work.

"Fifty-one-year-old male." The lead paramedic wipes sweat from his brow while an ED tech takes over chest compressions and a respiratory therapist starts bagging the patient. "Found by family. Down time at least thirty minutes prior to our arrival.

Asystole throughout the twenty minutes of resuscitation on scene and the ten minutes of transport. Two large-bore IVs in place. Normal saline wide open. Status post four rounds of epinephrine."

Erik says to Doctor Kent, "Sixty minutes of asystole. I'm going to call this."

Doctor Kent looks at him again. But this time, he does not stay silent. "Have you confirmed his rhythm, Doctor Prescott?"

Erik grins while he casually reaches for one of his pagers. "No need. The guy's been dead for almost an hour."

Doctor Kent continues watching him. "And as you know, Doctor Prescott, we need to establish an airway, confirm his rhythm, and address any correctable causes for his cardiac arrest."

Erik's smile dissolves away.

Doctor Kent motions to me. "Alright, Savannah, tube this guy."

I pick up the curved laryngoscope with my left hand, but I'm shaking so badly that I can barely hold onto it. Before I'm ready, the respiratory therapist moves the mask away from the patient's face.

That's my cue.

My heart is pounding so hard that my ears ring as I use my right hand to open the patient's mouth. I dip closer and change my stance. Then I have the horrible realization that I am not sure what to do next.

"Advance the blade into the vallecula," Doctor Kent reminds me.

I insert the laryngoscope into the patient's mouth with the jerky movements of nerves and inexperience. I have no idea what I'm looking at, but I don't think it's vocal cords. I feel a rush of panic. I should not be trying to do this on a coding patient.

"I don't see anything." I stand up straight so Doctor Kent can take over.

But he doesn't take the laryngoscope from me. "Sweep the tongue to the left and out of the way."

"Great," Brittany remarks, not softly. "We're wasting our time on a dead guy so this can be a med student teaching case."

I glance self-consciously around the resuscitation bay. Everyone is witnessing me mess this up. I hate today. I hate emergency medicine.

"Savannah, lift the blade up and forward."

Doctor Kent's instructions jar me back to what I am doing. While CPR continues, I grip the laryngoscope so tightly that my knuckles go white and maneuver it like Doctor Kent described. The patient's epiglottis moves out of the way, and two tiny white stripes pop into my view.

"I see them," I announce breathlessly.

"Don't take your eyes off of them." Doctor Kent slides closer. "Hold out your right hand."

I obey. Doctor Kent places the endotracheal tube onto my sweaty palm. My heart is punching my chest as I guide the tube into the patient's mouth and between the vocal cords.

"It's in," I tell him while removing the laryngoscope.

The respiratory therapist skillfully takes control of the top of the tube, pulls out the stylet, and begins to bag. "There's good color change," she reports.

I step aside in a daze. I did it. I actually intubated a real patient. And it was incredible.

"Savannah." Doctor Kent holds out his stethoscope. "Confirm tube placement."

In my excitement, I didn't do the final, crucial step of intubation. I grab the stethoscope from Doctor Kent and use it to listen over the patient's lungs. There are bilateral breath sounds every time the respiratory therapist squeezes the bag to supply oxygen. I give Doctor Kent a nod.

Doctor Kent takes his stethoscope back. "Doctor Prescott, your airway is established."

Erik is eyeing him with obvious irritation. "Airway established. Confirmed asystole. Now can we call this?"

"What's his temperature?" Doctor Kent inquires.

Erik stares, as if he cannot believe what he is hearing.

"Twenty-eight degrees Celsius," Hadi calls out.

"Doctor Kent, with all due respect, this guy has been dead for at least an hour," Erik points out. "He's cold because he's been dead for a long time. He's not going to come back to life if we warm him up. We can call this."

The room goes quiet. The tech who is doing chest compressions slows his effort. Everyone faces Doctor Kent, waiting.

"No one is dead unless they're warm and dead," Doctor Kent says.

Erik mutters something while scrolling through a message on one of his pagers. Then he speaks to the team. "Alright. Doctor Kent would like to spend some time warming this guy up. So let's warm him up."

The controlled chaos resumes at full force as warming efforts commence. Still at the head of the stretcher, I observe the body. The unnamed man is mottled and stiff. There's no question that he is dead. Really dead. As in, beyond-able-to-resuscitate dead. Looking up, I catch Brittany and Erik speaking to each other. They are obviously unhappy, and I can kind of understand why: working on someone who is so clearly dead seems like a complete waste of time and resources, especially when there are other patients who need to be seen. Yet Doctor Kent is still guiding the resuscitation with an air of calm authority. Curiosity strikes me. Does Doctor Kent know something that we don't? Is it possible that this patient actually has a chance?

Intrigued, I watch in silence as the resuscitation keeps playing out before me. How much time passes, I can't say anymore—I'm so focused on this patient that it's like there is nothing else happening in the whole world.

"The patient is at thirty-three degrees Celsius," Hadi announces.

"Hold compressions," Erik immediately orders.

The tech stops pushing on the patient's chest. Everyone peers at the monitor. I realize that I am holding my breath as I wait to see it blip with signs of life.

But nothing happens.

"Asystole," Erik states pointedly.

If Doctor Kent is surprised, he certainly doesn't show it. "So what do you want to do, Doctor Prescott?"

"I would like to call the code." Erik seems to be doing all he can to remain composed.

Doctor Kent addresses the rest of the group. "Does anyone have objections to ceasing resuscitation efforts?"

No one answers.

Erik checks the clock. "Time of death: nine-fourteen."

"Thank you, everyone," Doctor Kent adds.

And just like that, the energy that filled the resuscitation bay evaporates, replaced by a mood that is respectfully subdued. Some of the team begins cleaning the patient's body, while others quietly slip out the door. I peel off my gloves and take a last look at the body on the stretcher. That was a living person only a few hours ago. I will never know his story. I'll never even know his name.

Lost in my thoughts, I step back and bump into someone. It's Erik.

"Hey," he says, showing a hint of his stunning smile.

Though still dazed, I manage a smile in return. "Hey. Nice job with the code."

"Thanks," Erik tells me before he proudly leaves the resuscitation bay with the rest of the army, his long white coat flowing behind him like a slow-motion movie moment.

"Savannah?"

I pull my eyes from the door and see Doctor Kent coming my way. No longer wearing the yellow gown over his scrubs, he has his stethoscope again around his neck, and his hair is slightly disheveled. I feel a little rush of anticipation as he draws near. It will be gratifying to hear my attending congratulate me on doing my first real intubation, particularly since that attending happens to be Doctor Kent, who probably rarely gives compliments at all.

Doctor Kent comes to a stop right in front of me. There is not a hint of warmth or praise on his face. "Savannah, if you take anything away from this, remember one thing: they're not dead unless they're warm and dead."

That's it. No kudos. Nothing.

"I will." I try not to show my disappointment. "Thanks."

Doctor Kent motions to the exit. "Time to go see another patient."

He leaves the resuscitation bay. I watch him go and roll my eyes. Was it really too hard for him to take an extra five seconds to give me a little bit of positive feedback?

Reminding myself that I only have to deal with him for three weeks and six-and-a-half more days, I head after Doctor Kent to join the fray.

Chapter Three

"There's going to be a what?"

"A retreat." Danielle holds up her cell phone to show me the email that she's reading. "An educational, team-building thing. It's for all of the med students who are currently on the emergency medicine rotation. Lynn's email says that the retreat is happening this weekend, which is why none of us are scheduled to work." She puts her phone on the table. "They do something like this for the students every rotation. Didn't you read that in the welcome packet?"

I can only shake my head.

A sly smile starts to appear on Danielle's face. "Maybe this retreat will give you and Doctor Kent some quality time together. You know, a chance to move past the slightly rough first shift that you had and get to know each other better?"

"Danielle," I moan. I look over at her boyfriend, Joel, for help. "Can you do something about her, please?"

Joel holds up his hands. "Me? No way. I'm not getting involved. This girl stuff is way over my head."

Danielle giggles and gives Joel a loving peck on the cheek. Joel gazes adoringly at her. I resume eating my dinner, not sure if the two of them make me want to take their picture or throw up.

"However, I will say one thing in Savannah's defense," Joel adds while the waiter refills our drinks. "If this Doctor Kent guy is as aloof as she describes, I don't blame her for not wanting to spend any more time with him than she has to already."

"Thank you!" I say. "That's what I've been trying to explain to Danielle. Doctor Kent didn't give any positive feedback during our first shift. I could never tell what he was thinking. It was so *aggravating*."

Danielle props her chin in her hand. "Once again, Sav, you're diverting the conversation away from romance."

"We weren't talking about romance," I remind her curtly. "We were talking about my attending."

Danielle shrugs. "Well, I still think that you're exaggerating about him. Doctor Kent isn't cold or unfriendly. He's—"

"Unemotional? Frustrating? Cryptic?" I suggest.

"A bit *serious*," Danielle offers. She takes a drink of her water. "But what did you think about the fact that he faced your side of the room the entire time he taught during didactics today?"

I sit up. "What? No, he didn't."

But even as I respond, I think back to this morning. We had the first of our weekly classroom lectures for the rotation, which were taught by some of the emergency medicine attendings. Doctor Kent spoke the first hour about the management of hemorrhagic strokes. His presentation was pretty interesting, especially the part about—

I break from my thoughts when I notice Danielle watching me with an annoyingly smug gleam in her eye.

"Okay, yes, Danielle, Doctor Kent faced my side of the room a lot," I concede. "But only because Rachel was sitting in front of me and answering every single one of his questions. Doctor Kent had no choice."

"She might have you on that one," Joel remarks to Danielle, who immediately shoots him a look. Joel wisely shuts up and starts eating his dessert.

"Besides," I can't help going on while jabbing at my salad a bit more forcefully, "I am most certainly not—and never would be—attracted to Doctor Kent."

Danielle tips her head. "Sounds like you've put some thought into this."

"Only because you repeatedly insist on bringing it up." I set my fork down with exaggerated patience. "Just because I'm not interested in the one guy you arbitrarily pick out doesn't mean that I'm avoiding all men."

"Alright, then why did you refuse to go out with that guy from Joel's work when we tried to set you up a few months ago?"

"I was on my general surgery rotation at the time, remember?" I point out calmly. "I was waking up at, like, three in the morning. Who would feel like going on a blind date when they're running on no sleep?"

"Well, how about we have Joel set you up with him now?" Danielle leans into Joel expectantly.

Joel adjusts his glasses. "That might not work."

"Why not?" Danielle demands.

"He's dating someone else."

"Shucks. That's a real shame," I interject with heavy sarcasm.

Undeterred, Danielle addresses me again. "Okay, Sav, if you're not avoiding romance, then tell me one thing that you've done regarding this Erik Prescott intern whom you claim to be so interested in. Besides reading his ID badge, that is."

"That's not fair," I protest. "It's only been two days and—"

"Mm-hmm." Danielle lets the waiter clear her plate.

I decide it is not worth arguing, so I resume munching through the remnants of my salad. If I didn't love Danielle to pieces, I would find her the most frustrating person on the planet.

Thankfully, Danielle changes the subject. "I thought today was pretty cool. I'm going to like Wednesdays during this rotation. A couple hours of lecture in the morning, a procedure lab, a written assignment, and—"

"The assignment!" I blurt out. "I forgot to turn in my assignment!"

Danielle's mouth drops. "Are you sure? Didn't you give it to Lynn?"

"No." I start digging through my purse. "I left my jacket in suturing lab and ran back to get it, remember? I was so distracted that I forgot to hand in my paper." I pull out the wrinkled page of completed multiple choice questions as proof.

Danielle checks the time. "It's only seven-thirty, and the assignment technically isn't due until midnight. You could slip it under Lynn's office door, and she'll find it in the morning. Leave a note explaining what happened. I'm sure she'll understand."

"Good idea." I shove my things into my purse. "I'll go to Lakewood right now."

"Let me give you a ride." Joel reaches for his car keys.

I peer out the restaurant window into the early evening light. I can see Lakewood Medical Center perched regally atop the mammoth hill in the distance. I hate that hill.

"Thanks, but I'll be alright," I tell Joel with a sigh. "This is my fault. You guys stay and enjoy dessert. After being cooped up in class today, I could use a good walk, anyway."

"But it'll be dark soon." Danielle seems worried. "What about getting home?"

I shrug. "I'll grab a bus. Thanks for the offer, but you two stay here. I insist."

Before they can argue, I toss money for my meal onto the table and scurry outside. Slinging my purse over my shoulder, I commence walking down the street. And the next. And the next.

Alright, I may have slightly underestimated how long this little stroll of mine would take.

It's past dusk by the time I finally arrive at the base of the hill. Above me, I can already see the lights of the hospital beginning to glow against the twilight sky.

"Alright, Hill," I mumble, "I don't like you, and you don't like me. But I need to get up to the hospital, so we're going to get along this evening, okay?"

Deciding that the hill and I have come to a reasonable understanding, I begin the hike upward. I remove my jacket and sling it over my arm, thankful for the July evening breeze that's keeping me cool. Soon, though, I become aware of a different problem: my slip-on shoes are rubbing mercilessly against my bare feet with every step that I'm taking. While the shoes might look cute with my jeans and blouse, they most definitely were not meant for mountain climbing. I'm not even a third of the way to the top before I start feeling blisters forming.

Stupid hill.

The raw, stinging pain in my feet gets so bad that I finally peel off my shoes altogether. But things don't improve much as I waddle barefooted the rest of the way up the cracked and rocky sidewalk. By the time I reach the top of the hill, my feet are covered in scratches as well as the blisters, and they're throbbing horribly. I throw my shoes on once again and limp with curled toes toward the hospital's entrance. Since it's after-hours, I have to scan my badge to get the doors to open. I step inside and find the lobby vacant, dimly lit, and eerily quiet. It's like a completely different place.

My unsteady steps echo through the lobby as I move past the unmanned information desk for Elevator Two. I get inside and press the button for the eighth floor of Prescott Tower. It ascends directly to my destination. As the doors slide open, I exit into the foyer, which is also strangely dark and still. To my right is the familiar corridor that leads to the Discovery Conference Room. But instead of going in that direction, I face the vacant hall on my left, which, as Lynn explained during orientation, leads to the offices of the emergency department's administrators, attending physicians, and support staff.

But I don't move. The thought of venturing into attending-land has me a little intimidated—especially since it's nighttime and I'm sneaking around like a spy in a low-budget television show or something. However, considering that there's no one else actually here, I decide it's pretty unlikely that I'll be captured and tortured by an international spy ring. So after a Hollywood-esque check over my shoulder, I start down the hallway toward the attendings' offices. And that's when the comparison to a television show swiftly ends—the way that I'm hobbling is anything but sleek or sexy.

As I continue forward, I glance out the floor-to-ceiling windows on my right, which give an impressive view of the city skyline and the congested streets far below. I can see the entrance to the emergency department directly across the road, and so I stop to observe what proves to be a continuous parade of ambulances rolling through the drop-off zone; it's a striking reminder of how busy the ED remains, day or night.

The burning in my feet brings me to attention. Wiggling my toes in an effort to alleviate the discomfort, I resume my way down the corridor. Eventually, I reach a long row of closed office doors on my left, which spans the rest of the length of the long hallway. Each door is marked by a name plaque. I begin to read them as I go by:

Tammy Sanders, M.D. . . . Ned Godfrey, M.D. . . . Leslie Yamada, Assistant Coordinator—

An unexpected noise from up ahead shatters the quiet, causing me to jump. The door at the very end of the hallway has been propped open from the inside, and now light from the office is spilling out into the corridor. I'm not the only one up here tonight, after all.

I consider abandoning my plan. If I have to explain to someone that I'm here because I forgot to submit my first assignment of the rotation, word would surely get around to Doctor Kent. But, I then remind myself, this assignment is due by midnight. Either I turn it in now, or my grade will suffer. So after another second of deliberation, I choose the lesser of the two evils. I resume moving forward as quietly as I can.

Wilma Fox, M.D. . . . Jesse Santiago, M.D. . . . Gary Priest, M.D.

I pass the last closed door without finding the one with Lynn's name on it. Cursing the bad luck that continues plaguing me during this rotation, I slide toward the open office, keeping myself pressed up against the wall so I can't be seen by whoever might be inside. Once I'm close enough, I check the names on the door:

Wesley Kent, M.D.
Lynn Prentis, Coordinator

Okay, Lynn is here. And now that I think about it, this is a good thing. I'll be able to explain to her in person what happened and—

"Don't talk around the issue, Rick," someone inside the office suddenly says. "You and the rest of hospital administration have decided to spend an enormous amount of money on renovating a part of the hospital that doesn't need it. Meanwhile, the emergency department remains atrociously outdated and undersized."

I freeze. That was not Lynn's voice. That was Doctor Kent.

Now all I hear is muffled silence. I think he's talking on the phone.

"Of course I understand how much money outpatient surgeries bring in for the hospital," Doctor Kent snaps. "But you need to understand that there are patients with life-threatening illnesses in the ED, and we don't have the proper space to care for them. You can't keep ignoring that."

More quiet.

"The elective surgery center doesn't need to be remodeled." Doctor Kent has an edge to his tone that I have never heard before. "That money should go to the ED."

Another long break, and then Doctor Kent states:

"This discussion isn't over yet, Rick. We'll be talking about this again before August second."

I flinch when I hear the phone get slammed down hard. I glance at the wrinkled paper in my hand. I need to submit this. But it's not like I want to go waltzing in there, announcing to the head of the rotation that I failed to get my first assignment turned in correctly. Especially since Doctor Kent sounds like he is in an even worse mood than—

Loud, strange-sounding music suddenly starts blaring through the corridor. I yelp in surprise and spin around, trying to figure out where the obnoxious noise is coming from. It sounds like a mutated pop song is being played backward and underwater at maximum volume. Yet, in a way, the music is also familiar. It kind of reminds me of my ringtone.

Hang on. It *is* my ringtone.

It takes me another split-second to realize that the warped music is coming from my busted cell phone. The phone that I thought was dead. Whipping open my purse, I snatch out the phone and frantically begin pushing buttons. Cracked and deformed, the screen flashes an array of colors while the distorted ringtone stubbornly continues to play. Growing desperate, I hit the phone against my knee, and it finally goes dark. The music stops.

There's a stunned pause.

"Hello out there?" Doctor Kent calls from his office.

I don't move.

"Hello?" he says again.

I am about to sprint back to the elevator before Doctor Kent comes out and finds me, but with my torn-up feet, I realize that the chance of a successful get-away is essentially zero. So instead, I drop the phone into my purse and poke my head around the doorframe.

"Hi, Doctor Kent."

But I see no one.

I am actually peering into the first of two offices, which are joined by a connecting door. The front office must be Lynn's. Framed photos are on neatly organized shelves, a stack of file folders is atop her desk, and a few reminders scribbled on sticky notes are taped to the computer monitor. On the wall opposite me is a connecting door that leads into a second, larger office. The door is partially open, and all I can see is the edge of a desk on the other side.

"Savannah? Is that you?" Doctor Kent's head comes into view as he leans forward and peers past Lynn's office and out at the hallway.

I keep the assignment hidden behind the doorframe. "Yes. I'm dropping something off for Lynn."

He says nothing and leans back so he's again out of sight. I hear him starting to type on a computer keyboard, and I sigh with relief. I can't see him, and he can't see me. If I'm quick, I can get this taken care of without Doctor Kent ever knowing what happened.

Hiking my purse onto my shoulder, I scamper into Lynn's office and toss my homework onto her desk. I snatch up a blank sticky note and one of her pens, and I start scribbling down a message.

"So I assume that you can tell me what that unearthly noise was just now?"

Drat.

I turn to face the connecting doorway. Doctor Kent is coming into Lynn's office. His tie is loosened and slightly crooked, and he's got a hint of facial scruff. He begins rolling up his sleeves as he sets his inquiring eyes on mine.

I stuff the half-written note into my pocket. "It's my ringtone. I mean, it *was* my ringtone. I dropped my cell phone a couple of days ago, and it hasn't quite been the same since."

He just stares at me. So I reach into my purse and hold up the phone for evidence. As if on cue, the phone makes a weird blipping noise, flashes purple, and then goes dark again.

"I see," Doctor Kent remarks. His attention shifts to my wrinkled assignment on Lynn's desk.

I rush to explain. "About that. I forgot to turn it in this morning, but I swear that I had it done. I left my jacket in suturing lab, and then—"

"Did you come all the way back here tonight just to hand in that assignment?"

I open my mouth to respond, hesitate, and then glance between him and the paper. "I suppose it was an OCD-med-student type of thing to do, wasn't it?"

"It was, yes."

Our eyes meet, and the silence that follows makes me restless. Fidgeting with the pen in my hand, I hear myself blurt out:

"I'm sorry the hospital won't give you money to remodel the ED."

He raises an eyebrow. "Do you habitually eavesdrop on your attendings' private phone calls?"

"Yes," I answer immediately. "I mean, no. I mean, I wasn't eavesdropping . . . well, I guess I was, but I didn't try to."

Doctor Kent scratches his chin and peers at me for another moment. Then he picks up my assignment from Lynn's desk and heads through the connecting door into his office. Apparently, our conversation is over. Not sure whether to be relieved or offended, I trudge the other way toward the exit. I'm almost out the door before I hear Doctor Kent call after me:

"You came all the way up here tonight for this, Savannah. Are you going to give me your student identification number so I can log it in as completed on time?"

I come to an ungraceful halt. "What? Oh, yes. Thanks."

I head for Doctor Kent's office. But I stop in the connecting doorway, daring not to go any farther. His office is painted light gray. The wall to my right is lined with shelves that are filled with medical textbooks. There is a window opposite me and a well-used reading chair beside it. To my left is Doctor Kent's desk, which has nothing on it but a computer monitor, a notepad, and a fancy-appearing frame that displays a picture I can't quite see.

With my homework in hand, Doctor Kent goes around behind his desk. I remain where I am, my eyes drifting around the office until I notice the spreadsheet that is open on his computer monitor. I do a double take. The spreadsheet is filled with calculations, and at the top it says forty-three million. With a dollar sign next to it. As in forty-three million dollars.

I realize that Doctor Kent is watching me. I avert my gaze, but it's too late.

"To satisfy your apparent curiosity, Savannah, yes, this is what that phone call was about." He points at the computer monitor and goes on, "This is how much money the hospital administrators are going to allocate toward remodeling part of the hospital this year."

Hiding my limp, I take a few steps into his office. "That's a lot of money," I remark, not sure what else to say.

"And do you know where the hospital administrators are planning to use that money?"

"Um, no."

Doctor Kent sits, reaches for the mouse, and clicks on a window that had been minimized on his desktop. When the window fills the screen, it reveals an architect's rendition of a modern building that has big windows and a fountain near its stately entrance.

I lean in for a better view. "That's beautiful. Would that be the new elective surgery center that you were on the phone fighting, er, talking about?"

"No, that's not the proposed new elective surgery center. That is the schematic of the current elective surgery center. It was completed five years ago."

I don't hide my confusion. "But that's still practically brand new. What's there to spend forty-three million more dollars on? Are they gonna have cold drink dispensers in the bathroom stalls? Chartered jet flights up to the second floor?"

The tiniest of smiles shows on his lips. "I hadn't thought of that. Maybe."

I almost smile back but catch myself and glance away. After a moment, I add, "So the hospital administrators have forty-three million dollars to put toward a remodel, and they're choosing to upgrade that already-gorgeous building—"

"Instead of the place where sick, injured, and dying people are regularly being cared for in overcrowded walkways," he finishes, the trace of his smile disappearing.

I adjust the purse on my arm. "But that doesn't make sense. They're really going to use forty-three million dollars to renovate a building that's only five years old? Are you sure?"

Doctor Kent gets a strange expression on his face.

"Right." I clear my throat. "You've, um, spent two years working on this. You probably have your facts straight."

He crosses his arms. "I'd like to think that I do, yes."

Once more, I see a hint of an amused grin on his lips. I start to snicker. Doctor Kent breaks into a laugh, which catches me so off guard that I stop in surprise. He, too, falls quiet. For one moment, we look at each other. But I blush and then hastily go on:

"So how come the administrators didn't decide to remodel the emergency department? It obviously needs it far more than the elective surgery center."

He sighs and rubs the back of his neck. "Certainly seems straight forward, doesn't it? But things are not that black-and-white. Hospitals care for patients, but hospitals are businesses, too. Hospitals have to make money, and well-insured patients who are undergoing elective surgeries are a great source of revenue. So there's a very strong incentive to cater to those patients—to give them the best of the best—in the hopes that they will bring their business."

"But the ED is way busier than any elective surgery center. What about all of the money that the ED patients bring in?"

"Most of our ED patients have no insurance, meaning that the hospital absorbs a huge portion of the cost of their care. Although the ED is the busiest place in the hospital, it is ironically a source of income loss. Plus, the truth is that even when an ED is old and outdated, people still need emergency care. They'll still come." He gestures toward the monitor. "So you can see why, from a business standpoint, there is little motivation to put even more money toward it."

I take time to think this over. It's hard to absorb that a place as insanely busy as the emergency department is actually struggling to make ends meet.

Doctor Kent is silent for a while before he continues. "Anyway, on August second, the administrators are going to formally announce their plans to renovate the elective surgery center. In honor of their grand proclamation, they'll be holding a massive PR event on the hospital grounds. There'll be media coverage, local dignitaries in attendance, speeches, ribbon cuttings, family activities, hospital tours, the works." He tugs on his tie, loosening it further. "Unless, of course, I can persuade the administrators and their donors to fund the money-sucking emergency department rather than the highest revenue generator in the entire hospital."

"You don't sound optimistic."

"I'm not." He shrugs, though his eyes have fire in them. "The decision really has been made already. The money isn't going to the ED." He minimizes the image on his desktop again, as if he's sick of seeing it.

"I'm sorry, Doctor Kent."

He looks right at me. "It's Wes."

I feel a disconcerting flutter in my chest. It's time for me to leave. STAT.

"Well, good luck with all of that," I say with forced cheeriness. I move for the door, trying not to wince from the pain in my feet. "Goodnight."

"Savannah?"

I stop.

"Your ID number?" Doctor Kent motions to my assignment. "For your grade?"

I blink. "My ID number. Right."

Reaching into my purse, I find my student ID card and hand it over to him. While Doctor Kent proceeds to enter the information into his computer program, I can't help thinking about what he told me. Then into my mind appears the image of that elderly woman who was lying on the stretcher in the ED walkway. I can vividly see her still, fearfully confused as the chaos of the emergency department swirled around her.

"You've still got time!" I suddenly declare.

Doctor Kent jerks his head up, seeming as taken aback by my outburst as I am. But now there is a weird momentum building inside of me, and so I walk right up to his desk, waving my hands animatedly as I continue talking:

"You could still sway the hospital administrators to change their minds. Get a social media campaign. Interview ED patients and make a video to post online. Break the story to local news channels. Organize a protest outside the hospital. Or—"

As I make a broad gesture, my hand whacks into the picture frame on his desk. I have just enough time to realize what I've done before the frame tumbles to the floor. It lands face-down amid the horrible sound of shattering glass.

Then I remember that I am standing in the office of my attending.

"I'm so sorry," I whisper, kneeling down to clean up the mess.

"Stop," he orders. "You'll cut yourself."

I obey and stare miserably at the carpet.

Doctor Kent comes around the desk with a manila envelope in one hand and a trash can in the other. Crouching down opposite me, he starts using the envelope to sweep the glass into the garbage. I carefully pick up the frame and flip it over to get the glass off the photo. As I do so, I find myself staring at a picture of Doctor Kent and a beautiful woman. The woman, who appears about his age, is wearing a fancy gown, and her blonde hair is cascading in perfect curls around her shoulders. Dressed in a dark suit and tie, Doctor Kent has an arm around her waist. The picture looks like it was taken at an outdoor wedding or some other type of fancy party.

I have no idea how much time it takes me to notice that Doctor Kent has stopped what he was doing.

Blushing again, I hand over the broken frame. "Thankfully, your picture didn't get scratched."

Doctor Kent takes the frame from me, stands up, and goes back to his desk. He sets the frame beside his monitor without saying anything.

"I'll buy you a replacement." I get to my feet. "Where'd you get it?"

He raises his eyes. "My girlfriend got it for me in Paris."

Girlfriend. Paris.

"Don't worry," Doctor Kent adds. "She lives in D.C. She'll never find out."

I now detect something like pity in his voice, which is more than I can take. I reach into my purse and fish around for my wallet.

"No, I want to make this right. At least let me pay you so—"

My hand bumps my cell phone, which promptly starts playing another sick-sounding ringtone. I pull the broken phone out of my purse and slap it until the music stops.

Doctor Kent lets a few seconds go by before suggesting, "Maybe there's something else that you should put your money toward."

"No. I want to—"

"I said don't worry about it." He holds out my student ID card in a way that makes it clear our discussion is done.

I take my card from him, humiliated. "Then I'll see you later, Doctor Kent. Again, I'm really sorry."

I leave his office as fast as my torn-up feet will allow. I move through the connecting door and around Lynn's desk to reach the empty hallway. Then I break into a pathetic attempt at a run. Everything is a blur as I charge past the other offices for the elevator, which is mercifully open and waiting. Hurling myself inside, I push the button for the lobby repeatedly until the doors shut. As the elevator starts going down, I don't know which hurts more: my feet or my pride.

The elevator gently bounces to a stop. There is a chime as the doors open on the ground floor. I trudge by the information desk and continue outside into the cool, nighttime air. I manage a couple more steps before pain finally forces me to take a break. Using one arm to brace myself against the building, I use the other to strip off my shoes. Some of the blisters on my feet are starting to bleed. I lift my head. There is not a bus stop in sight. It's going to be a long walk to the apartment.

"How are you getting home?"

I wonder for a moment if I'm hearing things. Then I spin around. Doctor Kent is coming out of the hospital. He's wearing a jacket, and he has car keys in his hand.

I slap my shoes on. "I'm going to walk."

He continues approaching. "No, you're not. It's nine o'clock at night. Not to mention, this isn't exactly the nicest part of town."

"It's already nine? I . . ."

I go quiet when I realize where this conversation is going. There is no way—*no way*—that I am going to let him drive me home. I am supposed to be a responsible adult who is capable of caring for others, not someone in need of a babysitter.

I gesture vaguely toward the road. "I'll grab a bus."

"You mean the bus that leaves from halfway down the hill and only comes around every ninety minutes?" He looks at his watch. "The one you just missed and won't be around again until ten-thirty?"

I remain defiant. "Okay, I'll call Danielle."

Out of habit, I take my phone from my purse. Immediately, the phone proceeds to play another warbling ringtone while red and yellow lights flash on the screen. Grumbling under my breath, I stuff the phone away and peek at Doctor Kent. Once again, I swear he's trying not to laugh.

Defiant, I point over his shoulder at the hospital entrance. "I can go inside and call Danielle from the phone at the information desk."

"Do you know her number?"

"Of course I do." I scoff. "Danielle's my best friend. We've known each other since junior high. We live together."

Doctor Kent coolly removes his own cell phone from his jacket and holds it out for me to take. "Great. Call her."

I snatch the phone from him. Then I pause. I have no idea what Danielle's number is.

"It's the curse of having a contacts list, isn't it?" he remarks.

Twisting my mouth in frustration, I slap the phone back into his hand. "Thanks for the offer, but I really don't need a ride. I'll—"

"You'll what?"

Trying to come up with an answer, I shift my weight to my other foot, which causes me to gasp with pain.

His focus immediately shifts to my lower legs. "What's wrong?" he asks, his tone changed.

"Nothing serious. I walked too far in these crappy shoes. That's all."

He draws his eyebrows together accusingly. "But you planned to walk all the way home?"

I decide not to answer.

He motions past me as if the decision has been made. "My car is in the garage. I'll bring it out to pick you up."

"No. I can walk to the car at least," I insist, trying to salvage a bit of my dignity. "I'm fine."

"You're fine."

"Yes. Fine."

"Alright. Do what you like."

And the next thing I know, I'm walking—or more like tottering—beside Doctor Kent toward the parking garage. I stumble once, causing him to reach out to steady me by the arm. Once I gather my footing, he lets me go and continues walking. I breathe out and go after him.

We enter the garage, and Doctor Kent raises his arm and pushes a button on his key fob. There is a chirp from a black Toyota at the end of the row. Doctor Kent picks up his pace and heads toward it. He opens the passenger-side door and waits for me to catch up. I reach the car and slide inside without making eye contact.

"Thanks."

He shuts my door without a reply. I fumble with my seatbelt as he goes around the car, gets in on the driver's side, and starts the engine.

"So where is this taxi going?" he inquires after pulling out onto the main street.

"Taxi!" I exclaim. "I'll call a taxi. Stop and let me out."

He gives me a look and keeps driving. "Do you really expect me to stop the car, dump you on the street, and leave you with a broken phone to call a taxi?"

"I . . ." I sigh. "I live in Heritage Meadow Apartments."

He does a double take. "The complex on the other side of town? You were going to walk there?"

"I guess I hadn't thought that far ahead."

"Clearly not."

I sit up, affronted. "Pardon me for having a lot on my mind, alright?"

He tips his head. "You are officially pardoned."

I realize that I am again starting to smile, so I face away from him and watch out the window.

"I guess I can't complain to you about being busy," I state after a while. "I mean, you care for patients, you run the medical student emergency medicine rotation, you're in the middle of a battle with the hospital administration, and you've got your girlfriend on the other side of the country. That's a lot to have on your plate."

When he doesn't say anything, I face him.

He glances my way. Flipping on the turn signal, he seems to choose his words carefully. "It has, unfortunately, been an unexpectedly uphill battle with the administration regarding the ED. It's been particularly discouraging, since getting involved with an ED remodel was a major reason that I moved out here and took this job."

"It was? So if the administrators aren't going to fund an ED remodel, are you going to leave?"

"It's complicated."

I get the message. I should shut up and stop prying into his personal life. I stare out the windshield and don't say anything else. Neither does he. As the drive drags on, Doctor Kent flips on the radio to mask the quiet. By another stroke of bad luck, it's apparently nineties night on the radio station, and so "As Long As You Love Me" and "MMMBop" torturously fill the void until my apartment complex finally comes into view. Doctor Kent has not even brought the car to a complete stop in front of the building's entrance before I open my door.

"Thank you for the ride."

He motions to my feet. "Are you sure that you can get inside okay?"

"I'm sure, Doctor Kent."

I slide out, slam the door, and start limping toward the entrance. Behind me, I hear the passenger-side window being rolled down.

"Savannah?"

I look over my shoulder. "Yeah?"

"It's Wes."

Chapter Four

Pulling my stethoscope from the pocket of my short white coat, I enter Fast Track, the low-acuity area of the emergency department. Courtesy of Danielle, I'm walking almost normally this morning—she diligently bandaged up the wounds on my feet before we left our apartment, and she loaned me a pair of her comfortable shoes. So I suppose it was worth telling her about what happened when I went to Doctor Kent's office last night, even if it did mean having to listen to Danielle babble for an hour about what a gentleman Doctor Kent was for driving me home.

Danielle just doesn't get it.

Since it's my first shift here in Fast Track, I pause in the entryway to survey the place. I count a total of fifteen exam rooms. Some of the rooms' curtains are partly open, giving me glimpses of well-appearing patients who are seated on stretchers, eating food, watching ancient-looking televisions, and talking on cell phones. I break into a relieved smile as I observe the scene. I'm grateful that I was scheduled to work in here today. Not only will this shift entail less walking, which my feet will appreciate, but I'll be able to take care of these uncomplicated patients without needing a lot of help from my attending. That will be good for my grade and— after humiliating myself last night in front of Doctor Kent—good for my morale, too.

I stroll farther inside. I spot two nurses working here today: a middle-aged guy who appears bored as he gives a pill to a patient in Room Three, and a younger girl who's dressed in colorful scrubs and surfing the Internet. The relaxed atmosphere makes a striking contrast to the chaos and high acuity of the main ED just down the hall.

Yet it doesn't take long for me to note one thing about Fast Track that does resemble the rest of the emergency department: the overcrowding. In addition to the patients who are waiting in every exam room, there are more people seated on old chairs that line the corridors. Fast Track is already packed beyond capacity, and it's not even seven o'clock in the morning.

With patients starting to glance hopefully my way, I finish looking around and confirm that Doctor Kent hasn't arrived yet. Perfect. I can start seeing patients independently, and by the time he arrives, I'll be ready to present to him my assessments and plans for care. There is no way that he won't be impressed.

I stash my bag underneath the empty attending's desk and sit down in front of the computer. After logging in and the patient tracking board pops up on the monitor, I count the number of patients who are waiting. It's worse than I thought. Using the mouse, I try to open the first patient's chart, but a few unsuccessful clicks reminds me that this place still does notes and prescriptions on paper—no doubt the lack of funding has prevented a complete transition to electronic medical records. So I get up and go to the nursing station, where a bunch of charts are piled in a wire bin, which is labeled by a hand-written sign that reads, "*To be seen.*" I pick up the chart of the first patient and head to Room Seven.

"Hello," I say with a courteous smile on my face as I push aside the curtain and step into the room. "My name is Savannah Drake. I'm a fourth-year medical student, and I'll be caring for you today. What brings you in this morning?"

"I'm a hiccup."

I stop, letting the curtain swing closed behind me. The patient is a woman with stringy, disheveled hair. She has on a stained turtleneck, purple leggings, and tinted glasses. I peek down at her chart and read the note from triage. It states that she is forty-eight years old and her chief complaint is "*Other*."

I look up again. The woman is sitting extremely still on the edge of the stretcher, with her hands folded in her lap. And she's staring at me. No, actually, I think she is staring through me.

I clear my throat. "I'm sorry?"

The only thing that moves is her mouth as she repeats, "I'm a hiccup."

"You have hiccups?"

"No. I am a hiccup."

I shift slightly. Maybe I missed it, but I don't recall any medical school lecture about managing patients who think they are involuntary spasms of the diaphragm.

"I see," I finally remark, trying to sound as though I know what I'm talking about. "And, um, when did this start?"

"A long time ago."

"Okay. Great. And why, exactly, do you think that you're a hiccup?"

She has yet to blink. "It's obvious, isn't it?"

"Yes." I pretend to write something on the chart. "You're right. I understand."

"Can I go home?"

I lift my head. "But don't you want—"

"I don't want anything. I got a sandwich from the nurse already. Now I want to go home."

I start backing up. "Okay. But could you at least wait for the attending physician to hear about you?"

She doesn't move, so I assume that means she is going to stay put. After giving the patient another uncomfortable smile, I spin around, push the curtain out of my way, and dart from the room. I can't help wondering if this is some sort of Fast Track hazing ritual for new med students. I mean, this place is bursting at the seams with patients who have straight-forward ankle sprains, sore throats, and lacerations, and yet I somehow wound up with a woman who thinks she is a hiccup. I have no idea what to do with her, and yet I'm going to have to try explaining this to—

"Good morning, Savannah."

I nearly drop the chart when Doctor Kent walks into Fast Track. Instead of scrubs, today he's wearing another button-up shirt and dark jeans. He has his stethoscope hanging casually around his neck, and he still hasn't shaved off the facial scruff from yesterday. I stay where I am, watching as he heads to the attending's desk and sets his bag down beside it. When he turns to me again, his eyes astutely drop to the chart in my hands and then to the patient tracking board before shifting to Room Seven.

"You've already seen a patient," he notes, not sounding impressed in the slightest.

"Um, yes."

Doctor Kent sits on the corner of the desk and puts his laser-like attention fully upon me. "Alright. Tell me about her and what you want to do."

I stare down at the chart. A lady who thinks she's a hiccup. A hiccup.

Doctor Kent notices my hesitation and motions toward the room. "If you'd like, I can go and help—"

"No," I cut him off. "No, I've got it."

He studies me for a moment, and then he sits back, crosses his arms, and waits.

I exhale sharply. Hiccup lady may be all I've got to work with, but I'm determined not to embarrass myself in front of Doctor Kent again. Focusing on the chart, I launch into my most professional-sounding patient presentation mode:

"The patient in Room Seven is a forty-eight-year-old female who presents today with a chief complaint of 'Other.' She—"

"Other?" Doctor Kent interrupts.

I raise my head.

"*Other*, as in triage speak for *crazy*?" he clarifies.

My mouth falls open. We can't say that about patients . . . can we?

"Sorry." He sits up straighter. "Please continue."

I prepare to start my full presentation again, but I can tell that Doctor Kent is trying not to laugh.

I give up.

"The patient thinks she's a hiccup," I announce.

Doctor Kent scratches his chin. "She *has* hiccups?"

"No. She believes that she *is* a hiccup, and she states that she has been a hiccup for a long time. Oh, and she would like to go home."

He arches an eyebrow. "I see. Does she have any signs and symptoms of someone who is a hiccup?"

I'm hit with a pulse of alarm. Doctor Kent isn't kidding. Did I miss a class about patients being hiccups? Or is there a different meaning of '*hiccup*' that I'm not thinking of? How—

"I'm only messing with you." Doctor Kent gets to his feet.

"What?" I'm not sure whether to laugh or kill him. "You . . . you were . . ."

"I'll go give her my blessing so she can go home."

Doctor Kent heads off to Room Seven. I gaze after him with an expression of feigned exasperation. Despite the fact that he nearly caused me to have a panic attack, I have to admit that what he did was kind of funny. Actually, it was really funny.

"Excuse me, can I help you?"

I realize that the female nurse has just addressed me. She's observing me curiously—and, frankly, I can't blame her. I'm just staring at the closed curtain of Room Seven with a goofy half-smile on my face.

"I'm good, thanks." I show her the chart in my hands. "My name's Savannah. I'm the fourth-year medical student who's working in here today."

"Cool! I'm Cassie!" The nurse gives me a bubbly wave before prancing away to see the new patient in Room Two. As soon as she's out of sight, I head to the desk and begin writing Room Seven's chart note in my nicest medical student handwriting.

"Yes, Hiccup can definitely go."

I glance up and see that Doctor Kent has reemerged from the patient's room. I watch as he strides my way. But when I realize that I've started smiling at him again, I duck my head and resume writing the chart note. Now my face feels warm, like I'm blushing. What is wrong with me?

Cassie pokes her head out of Room Two. "Doctor Kent, could you come over here?"

Doctor Kent changes course and heads into the room. A minute or so passes before I hear him call out:

"Savannah?"

I peer over my shoulder. Doctor Kent has pushed the curtain of Room Two aside, and he is motioning for me to join him. I set the chart on the desk and hurry over.

"Nineteen-year-old male who fell off his skateboard," Doctor Kent reports, closing the curtain behind me. "He has left upper quadrant pain and some bruising of his left flank. What are you concerned about?"

I consider the young man lying on the stretcher. He appears uncomfortable but not in acute distress. Cassie is putting an IV into his right arm while Doctor Kent examines him.

Trauma. Left upper quadrant abdominal pain.

"Splenic injury?" I answer.

"Exactly," Doctor Kent replies. "He's kindly given the okay for you to examine him, too. I want you to feel what a peritoneal abdomen is like."

I place my hand lightly on the patient's abdomen, which feels unnaturally rigid. The patient grimaces in pain.

I yank my hand away. "Sorry!"

"It's okay." The patient shifts with obvious discomfort. "It just hurts."

"Blood in the abdomen is irritating, which is why there's so much pain," Doctor Kent explains to both of us. He turns to me. "What are we going to do?"

There is deliberateness about Doctor Kent's manner that catches my attention. I understand what he is trying to tell me: this patient needs care, and he needs it now.

"An IV," I say, my thoughts seeming to focus. "No, wait. Two IVs. And IV fluid. And monitoring."

"What else?" Doctor Kent presses.

"Labs, including pre-op stuff."

"Anything else?"

"Imaging to evaluate for a splenic injury?"

"Yes." Doctor Kent keeps the questions coming. "And what are you going to do while you're putting those orders in?"

I realize that I don't know. I wonder if I should use the tried-and-true medical student technique of spouting off some long-winded remark that is only tangentially related to the attending's question. It's a classic way to sound smart while stalling, since attendings usually interrupt and answer their own question.

But instead, I just meet Doctor Kent's gaze and shake my head.

"You're going to call trauma surgery," he states. "So while he's getting his IVs placed and labs drawn, let's go do that." Doctor Kent gives the patient a reassuring pat on the shoulder. "We'll get you some pain medication, and I'll be in here again soon."

"Okay," the patient says. "Thanks."

Doctor Kent motions for me to go first, and then he trails me out of the room with the patient's chart in his hand. When we reach the attending's desk, Doctor Kent picks up the phone and pushes the zero button.

"This is Wes Kent in the ED," he tells the hospital operator. "I need the on-call resident from the trauma service paged to this number please. Thanks."

Doctor Kent hangs up and gestures to the triage note on the chart. "The patient was tachycardic when he arrived. With a heart rate so high, he should never have been put in Fast Track, but they were too full in the main ED to take him. And he still sat in the waiting room for almost three hours." Doctor Kent drops the chart onto the desk. "Had he come during a busier time of day, who knows how long he would have been left out there, undiagnosed. Another near casualty of this overcrowded ED."

The male nurse interrupts us. "Doctor Kent, there's a new patient in Room Ten."

But before Doctor Kent can reply, the phone rings. Doctor Kent picks it up. "This is Wes Kent in the ED. Yes. I've got a nineteen-year-old male who . . ."

While Doctor Kent talks the trauma surgery consultant, the male nurse shifts focus to me.

"Are you the med student on today?"

"Yes."

"Great. Can you check the new guy in Room Ten? Sounds like he only needs treatment for a small skin tear. If you do a quick eval and give the okay, I'll do the wound care. We'll have him discharged in ten minutes."

I glance at Doctor Kent, who remains on the phone. I am definitely not going to interrupt him for something as minor as glorified bandage placement. In fact, if I get a patient out of here, it would probably be the most helpful thing that I could do.

"Sure," I tell the nurse. "No problem."

"Awesome. Thanks."

The nurse heads off to give medication to a patient in another room. Leaving Doctor Kent at the desk, I march for Room Ten. After announcing that I'm outside, I push the curtain back and step into the room.

"Hello, I'm Savannah Drake. I . . ."

I don't finish. The well-groomed man who is seated on the stretcher is wearing a green-and-white striped prison jumpsuit, waist chains, and ankle shackles. There are three armed corrections officers standing around him. I notice the officers exchange glances as I enter.

"I'm sorry, what did you say your name was?" the inmate asks me politely.

"Savannah Drake."

I take a deep breath, applauding myself on my recovery. My medical school instructors would be proud. As they taught us, we are not here to judge. We are here to help. The fact that this man is a prisoner doesn't mean that I should treat him differently than any other patient. This man deserves my complete respect.

"Are you the doctor, Savannah?" the patient goes on gently.

With a professional air, I return his smile. "I'm the fourth-year medical student who is working with the attending physician today. Now, I understand that you have a—"

"I didn't expect to get such a pretty helper. Lucky day for me," the patient interrupts, sounding eerily pleased.

I pause and clear my throat. "Well, anyway, Sir, I hear that you—"

"So, Savannah, may I ask how old you are?" the patient cuts in again.

Although I'm trying not to show it, the way that the patient is now eyeing me is making me extremely uncomfortable. But would I have this same creeped-out vibe if the patient wasn't in shackles? My own question strikes me with guilt. Here I was, priding myself on overcoming social stereotypes, when I'm actually harboring the exact type of closed-minded judgments that my instructors taught us to shun.

I keep my voice steady and answer him almost apologetically. "I'm twenty-six."

Now the patient's smile is gone, and he's observing me from head-to-toe with an intense, chilling stare. "That's a nice age. You said your name is Savannah Drake? Do you live near here?"

I have to avert my eyes away from his as I motion to a wound above his wrist. "How about we take care of—"

Behind me, I hear the curtain get torn open. A hand clamps around my arm, and before I realize what's happening, someone starts pulling me away from the bed. Stunned, I look up. It's

Doctor Kent who is practically dragging me from the room. Once we get outside, Doctor Kent whips the curtain shut behind us. Jaw clenched, he keeps his secure hold on me while continuing to lead me away.

"Pete!" Doctor Kent barks.

The male nurse comes out of another room. "Yeah, Doctor Kent? What's up?"

Doctor Kent's eyes flash furiously. "Why did you send Savannah into Room Ten?"

I shudder when I hear Doctor Kent's enraged tone. What is going on?

Pete seems equally confused. "It was for a quick wound assessment. I was going to clean the wound and apply the dressing myself."

Doctor Kent releases his hold of me. He's fuming. When he speaks again, his voice is low. "Did you not bother to read the warnings that are all over his chart? The ones that state that no female staff—ever—should go near him?"

Pete goes pale.

"He has drugged and raped several women. He's considered extremely violent." Doctor Kent's voice catches as he says the words. "His triage note states that he was being transferred to maximum security prison and tried harming himself along the way. That's why he's here."

"Geez, I had no idea, Doctor Kent." Pete seems about as shell-shocked as I feel. He says to me, "Hey, I'm really sorry."

"It's okay," I respond.

But to be honest, I'm not sure that it is okay. That man now knows my name and how old I am. He could easily do some online research and find out more about me and where I live. Or where my family lives. It's haunting.

"I'm going to get that guy treated and discharged." Doctor Kent sounds business-like again, but his brow remains furrowed. "Savannah, one of the residents from trauma surgery will be coming to see our patient with the presumed splenic injury. If I'm still tied up when the resident arrives, would you mind updating him or her on that case?"

"Sure." I hope that Doctor Kent doesn't see how much I'm trembling. "No problem."

Doctor Kent walks off to Room Ten, and I take a seat at the attending's desk. The hairs on the back of my neck are standing up. I can't get that prisoner's stare out of my head. I shiver again. I was just standing a few feet away from a man who has intentionally harmed innocent women—women like me.

A quiet moan of pain breaks through my thoughts. The curtain to Room Two is partly open, allowing me to see the nineteen-year-old inside. He is lying stiffly on the bed, and his breathing is shallow.

"Hey, are you okay in there?" I call to him.

He barely lifts his head. "Yeah."

I get up and go to his bedside. "Is your abdominal pain getting worse?"

He attempts a stoical shrug. "Maybe a little."

"I'm going to call the trauma surgery team again, okay?" I explain. "I'll—"

"No need," says a recognizable, smooth voice. "I'm here."

Erik Prescott steps into the room. As always, everything about him is movie-star perfect.

"Hey," he says to me. "It's Sarah, right?"

I try not to sound completely crushed. "Savannah."

"Savannah." Erik nods and then addresses the patient. "My name is Doctor Prescott. I'm from the trauma team. I understand that you fell off your skateboard, and you have abdominal pain. As a precaution, we'll be sending you to get a CAT scan in a little while to make sure that you don't need surgery, alright?"

Erik moves to leave the room without waiting for the patient to reply. I peek over at the patient, who has actually started shaking from pain. My eyes dart between the patient and Erik's departing figure. I bite my lip. Surely Erik wouldn't knowingly leave a patient in this condition. I bet Erik just didn't see how uncomfortable the patient is—after all, the lighting is pretty dim in here. I open my mouth to say something but catch myself. Erik doesn't need my advice. He's the doctor, not me. He understands what we're concerned about.

Doesn't he?

"Wait!" I exclaim.

Already halfway beyond the curtain, Erik stops and peers at me with both impatience and surprise.

"His abdominal pain is getting worse," I point out as deferentially as I can. "Do you think we should get him over to radiology for the CAT scan now?"

Erik adopts an aura of exaggerated patience. "We'll get him over there eventually. Don't worry."

Great. Erik clearly thinks I'm one of those over-zealous med students who incessantly hounds residents and attendings about everything. And Erik is probably right. I haven't handled a lot of trauma before. I have no clue how to manage this stuff. Yet as my eyes fall back on the patient, I can't help noting that he is paler than earlier, and he definitely seems to be in more pain. Trauma guru or not, I know that is not good.

"I could call radiology and ask them to scan him next," I offer.

Erik sighs. "I said we'll get him over there in a little while."

"No, he's going now." Doctor Kent enters the room, looking between us.

I have no idea how long he was listening to our conversation.

Erik is about to say something but seems to change his mind. Instead, he shrugs. "Fine. I've got to answer a page from my attending, anyway."

"Then I recommend that you tell your attending about this patient," Doctor Kent advises as Erik walks out. The hard lines in Doctor Kent's expression fade as he speaks to the patient. "I've called over to radiology, and they're ready to do your CAT scan. I'm going to drive you there myself."

"Alright. Thanks."

Doctor Kent hooks the patient up to the portable cardiac monitor and begins wheeling the stretcher out of the room. As he passes me, Doctor Kent leans in and drops his voice. "Do you mind remaining here and keeping an eye on the place? I'd like to stay in radiology with this patient until the scan is completed."

I try not to notice how close Doctor Kent's face is to mine. "Sure."

"Thanks. Call me if you have any questions."

Doctor Kent picks up his pace and wheels the patient out of Fast Track. I head to the attending's desk and sit down. Staring at nothing, I inhale deeply, trying to collect my thoughts.

"No, the skateboarding kid with the belly pain is fine," I overhear someone say.

Shifting in my chair, I peer around the corner. Erik is at the nursing station, talking on the phone. He must be speaking to his attending.

"Yeah. His exam is normal." Erik leans casually against the counter. "His abdomen is benign."

I sit up, confused. I don't recall Erik examining the patient. Did I miss that part?

Erik adjusts the phone against his ear with a laugh. "The ED attending actually rushed the kid over to radiology himself. It's Kent . . . yeah, I know."

Erik chuckles again but stops abruptly when he notices that I'm watching. I look away, warmth creeping into my cheeks while I pretend to pore over a chart that is open on the desk in front of me.

"Hmm?" I catch Erik state into the phone after a pause. "Yeah, I'll call with an update."

I hear Erik hang up. Keeping my head down, I continue acting as though I am engrossed in the chart of an eighty-year-old woman with external hemorrhoids.

"Hey, Savannah?"

I look up. Greek God Erik is coming toward me.

I shove the hemorrhoid chart aside. "Yes?"

"Could you log in and see if that skateboarding patient's CAT scan is up yet?" Stopping beside the desk, Erik might as well be posing for a magazine cover. "I just need to tell my attending that it's alright."

As I reach for the computer mouse, Erik takes the seat next to me. I catch a whiff of his cologne. Incredible.

"So what do you think of Kent?" Erik inquires while the CAT scan images start loading on the monitor.

"What do you mean?"

Erik laughs as though he feels sorry for me. "I know, I know. You can't say anything bad since he's your attending, but I totally get it: he's a pain."

"A pain?" I echo, still not following.

"Yeah. Being all dramatic and rushing that kid off to radiology, as if he has a surgical emergency. Or forcing everyone to run the code on that asystolic patient the other day. Or complaining non-stop about the need to renovate this place." Erik shakes his head. "Doctor Kent loves to be in the spotlight, and everyone is sick of his antics."

I face him. "Why would anyone fault Doctor Kent for drawing awareness to how undersized and outdated this place is?"

Erik is clearly amused. "Wow, has he already got you brainwashed, or what?"

"I'm not brainwashed," I retort and gesture around us. "This place is a disaster. Old technology. Small working areas. Patients being treated in walkways. Seems pretty obvious that renovations are needed. Doctor Kent is only trying to get patients better care."

Erik snorts. "Or he's paying lip service to a cause that he knows will generate a lot of positive press for himself—press that will land him a certain high-profile administrative position at a fancy hospital in D.C."

I have to stop while that sinks in. "What are you talking about?"

As if pitying my ignorance, Erik slides his chair nearer to mine and drops his voice. "Kent only came to work here to make a big name for himself. Once he gets all the accolades he needs, he's going right back to D.C. He's gunning to be a top administrator at some big hospital out there but has to pad his resume first. Trust me: Doctor Kent has one goal in mind, and it has nothing to do with this place or patient care."

I try not to reveal how bothered I am by what I'm hearing. "And exactly how do you know all of this?"

Erik seems to deliberate before replying. "There were stories in the news about him after he moved here. Doctor Kent applied for that big administrative position in D.C. a few years ago, but he was deemed too young and early in his career to take on such an important position at the time."

"Well, that doesn't mean he's not sincerely interested in improving the situation here, and—"

"Come on, it has nothing to do with the situation here. It has everything to do with the fact that Kent needed more leadership experience before he'd be able to play ball with hospital administration bigwigs on the national level. This job opportunity became available, and Kent jumped on the chance to get a few easy years in the spotlight. And he's been putting on the show ever since."

I fight the sense of disappointment—even betrayal—that is welling up inside of me. "You're making some pretty big assumptions. Maybe Doctor Kent actually wants to help Lakewood Medical Center."

"Right." Erik doesn't bother masking his sarcasm. "Maybe he's just so altruistic that he chose to abandon his life and established career in D.C. and move to the other side of the country because he wanted to renovate some random emergency department."

I want to come up with a good retort, but I can't.

One of Erik's pagers goes off. As he begins reading his new message, I notice that the rest of the skateboarding patient's CAT scan images have loaded. Glad for the diversion, I scroll through the images of the patient's abdomen and pelvis. Then I scroll through them again, and my stomach tightens.

"Hey, look at this." I point to the monitor.

"Hmm?" Erik distractedly puts his pager on the desk and glances at the images. "That's some fat stranding. It's nothing."

"Really? It looks more like—"

The phone on the desk rings. I pick it up.

"Um, hello, this is the Fast Track. How can I—"

"Savannah, it's Wes," he says. "Is Doctor Prescott around?"

"He's sitting next to me."

Out of the corner of my eye, I notice Erik perk up with interest.

"I see." Doctor Kent pauses. "Well, can you please ask him to pull up the patient's CAT scan? There's something I'd like him to look at."

"I've got it up already." I start talking faster. "I was scrolling through the images, and I think there's a bleed."

Erik chuckles and returns his attention to his pager.

"There's definitely a bleed," Doctor Kent confirms. "Please inform Doctor Prescott that I've already spoken to his attending about the patient's splenic laceration. I'm taking the patient directly to the OR. As soon as I transfer care to the surgical team, I'll get back to Fast Track."

"Got it. I will."

"Thanks, Savannah."

Doctor Kent hangs up. I slowly set the phone down.

"So what did Kent say?" Erik is lounging in the chair. "Does he still think it was worth radiating that kid to prove nothing was wrong?"

I play with the phone cord. "He said that the patient has a splenic lac, and he's taking him to the OR right now."

Erik's eyes flick to the monitor, and then he jumps to his feet. "I'd better go. They probably need me in the OR too."

His pager, which is still on the desk, goes off yet again. I glimpse the message:

OR covered. Stay on floor and write chart notes. Thnx.

I'll pretend I didn't see that.

Erik picks up his pager, gives me a last glance, and then charges off down the hall.

As soon as Erik is out of sight, Cassie bounces over to the desk. "Please tell me that Doctor Prescott will be coming back!"

I brush a loose piece of hair from my face. "I'm not sure."

"Well, that's a bummer." She adopts a playfully disappointed expression. "He's so gorgeous. I'm pretty much in love with him."

I force a laugh. "Oh, really?"

"Yeah. Who isn't? I mean, he's beautiful! Not to mention, he's a *surgeon,* which makes him even more attractive." She bats her eyes mischievously. "And it doesn't hurt that he's got an entire wing of this hospital named after him, either."

I do a double take. "What?"

She giggles. "Yeah. Erik Prescott's grandfather was a famous surgeon here years ago. That's why part of the hospital is now named—"

"Prescott Tower," I interrupt incredulously, making the connection.

"Uh-huh. Plus, Erik's father is a famous businessman, and he's the hospital's president."

I allow my attention to float again toward the hallway. "I had no idea."

"Anyway, do me a favor and find an excuse to consult trauma surgery again before my shift is over, okay?" Cassie winks and then practically skips off to another patient's room.

I continue staring down the hallway. Erik's grandfather has an entire tower of the hospital named after him, his dad is at the top of the hospital administration, and—

Hang on. Hospital administration. Erik's dad is head of the hospital's administration, which means that he is one of the people whom Doctor Kent is fighting with about the ED remodel. It also means that—

"Savannah? Earth to Savannah?"

I jump at sound of Doctor Kent's voice. He's reentering Fast Track.

"Is everything alright?" he adds, coming toward the desk.

"Yes. Everything is alright."

He picks up a new patient's chart. After scanning the triage note, he hands the chart over to me. "Good. Because here's something that is really going to test your skills."

Intrigued, I take the chart and read the note:

31-year-old male who states that he is a "space cowboy" and wants to eat electrical tape.

I peek up at Doctor Kent. "Let me guess: I should go ahead and call for the psych eval?"

"Might be wise."

Chapter Five

Hypothermia occurs when the body is unable to maintain adequate thermoregulation in the face of a cold stressor, resulting in a drop in body temperature."

"That's correct, Rachel," Dr. Tammy Sanders tells her, and then she turns to the rest of us. "And what's the temperature at which we begin to say someone is hypo—"

"Below ninety-five degrees Fahrenheit," Rachel adds without delay. "Equivalent to thirty-five degrees Celsius."

Dr. Sanders smiles. "Once again, you're right. Excellent job."

Beaming proudly, Rachel sits up as tall as her petite frame will allow. Danielle, who is sitting on the edge of the dock behind her, peeks my way and rolls her eyes. I drop my head and bury my face in my tank top to hide my laughter. I know what Danielle is thinking: it has pretty much been The Rachel Show all afternoon.

Earlier today, Danielle and I—along with the rest of the med students who are on the emergency medicine rotation this month—arrived at a beautiful, big cabin up here in the mountains for the weekend retreat. For about the past two hours, we've been at the nearby lake, listening while attendings give short lectures on various wilderness medicine topics. Thus far, Rachel has managed to talk about as much as the attendings.

"As body temperature drops into the range of mild hypothermia, one of the body's first responses is to generate more heat by shivering," Dr. Sanders is explaining. "And if body temperature continues to fall, blood is shunted away from less vital organs to preserve the heart and brain."

A few students unexpectedly burst into obnoxious applause. I look behind me and see one guy clumsily attempting to fish his baseball hat out of the lake. Nearby, Austin is observing the scene with his usual expression of disdain, which causes me to start snickering myself. After the hat is saved and everyone quiets down, Dr. Sanders resumes what she was saying:

"The heart and the brain are particularly sensitive to cold. When body temperature drops, the heart slows down. ECGs on a hypothermic patient will show—"

"Osborne waves!" Rachel declares.

Dr. Sanders nods. "And as the body gets even colder, the heart becomes susceptible to arrhythmias. Eventually, the heart will brady down and finally . . ."

I don't hear the rest. With the sun warming my skin and the lake water lapping soothingly against the dock, I feel myself pleasantly zoning out. I toss my braided ponytail over my shoulder and tip my head to the sun. My gaze soon wanders over to the steep, forested mountainside that rises high above the lake's far shore. I mindlessly watch the trees sway in the breeze until, out of the corner of my eye, I spy Danielle inconspicuously composing a text message, no doubt to Joel.

Shifting positions, I let my attention drift over to where most of the other ED attendings are congregated beside the dock. Taller than the others, Doctor Kent is easy to spot. Standing beside a canoe with his arms crossed, he's wearing a t-shirt, shorts, and flip-flops, and his eyes are hidden behind sunglasses that reflect the water. He turns his head toward the dock, and I look away, attempting to refocus on what Dr. Sanders is saying:

"As the body's core temperature drops below thirty-three degrees Celsius, brain activity also begins to become abnormal. Once down to about twenty degrees Celsius, an EEG may appear as though the patient is brain dead."

Tyler raises his hand. "I've heard about people who were super hypothermic for a long time—like trapped under ice or something—and survived. How come?"

There is no question about it: Tyler is definitely getting an honors grade on this rotation. Maybe he can put in a good word for me.

Dr. Sanders seems impressed, too. "Great question. At normal temperatures, when the heart stops and blood doesn't circulate, the body quickly suffers from the decreased oxygen supply. The window of time that someone can survive is short. However, when a body is hypothermic, its need for oxygen is decreased. This means that the body can theoretically go for longer periods of time with less oxygen before suffering permanent damage."

I suddenly recall when Doctor Kent explained the whole "warm and dead" thing to me in the resuscitation bay the other day. I glance his way again, but he doesn't notice.

"In fact," Dr. Sanders is adding, "hypothermia is so beneficial that patients who are resuscitated after a cardiac arrest are often maintained at—"

She is interrupted by a shriek of surprise and a huge splash. I spin around. One of the students has tossed Rachel into the lake.

Dr. Sanders chuckles. "I think this concludes our talks for the afternoon. We'll have dinner for you guys at six. And don't forget about the night hike—we'll be leaving from the cabin at nine p.m."

As several students jump into the lake to join Rachel for another round of water volleyball, I make my way to the end of the dock and sit beside Danielle.

She sets her phone down in frustration. "We don't have good coverage out here."

"Hey, it could be worse." I dip my feet in the water. "Your phone could look like it was crushed by a steamroller."

Danielle snickers. "You should probably splurge on a new cell phone sooner versus later."

I stare distractedly out at the lake. Doctor Kent told me the same thing when I was in his office the other evening.

"Sav?" Danielle nudges me. "Hello?"

"Huh?"

She peers at me over the top of her sunglasses and then casts a long, deliberate glance over toward the shore. "Your glazed-over expression wouldn't have anything to do with that hot, well-built, intelligent man who is standing over there, would it?"

"Don't be stupid. As I've told you already, I'm not interested in Doctor Kent. I'm interested in—"

"Erik, the buff Orthopedics intern," Danielle finishes for me, using her hands to make air quotes. "Yes, you've only mentioned a hundred times that he talked to you during your Fast Track shift. But I don't get what you see in him. Erik is not the right guy for you."

I laugh. "Oh, and even though you've never met Erik, you nonetheless determined that someone else is the right guy for me?"

"Of course." Danielle jerks her thumb a bit too obviously toward the shore. "It's Doctor Kent."

I sigh.

"The next time they suggest 'a little night hike,' they need to clarify that they mean a two-hour expedition around the entire lake," Danielle grumbles, bending forward to dig another rock out of her shoe.

I swing the beam of my flashlight away from the narrow trail in front of us and shine it at her feet so she can see what she's doing. "Don't worry. I think I spotted the lights of the cabin. We're almost done."

"Really?" Danielle raises her head hopefully. "How far?"

"Not too far," I lie.

"Listen up, everyone!" Dr. Godfrey calls through the darkness from the front of the group. "Be sure to keep close together. This next portion of the trail ascends steeply for a while before it winds back down to the lake's shore."

Danielle moans. "Is he kidding?"

I peer through the blackness, barely able to see Dr. Godfrey far ahead of us. He starts walking briskly up the inclining trail while motioning enthusiastically for everyone to follow. I have to admit, I never would have pegged Dr. Godfrey as a spry mountain climber.

I shake my head. "He's not kidding."

Danielle mutters something and continues digging around in her shoe.

"Better hurry," I say to her after a while. "We'll be abandoned out here if you don't speed things up."

"My shoelace just broke."

"What?"

Danielle makes an annoyed sound. "It wasn't like I brought hiking boots!"

"Can you go barefoot?"

"On this ground? Are you kidding me?"

I reach into my jacket and pull out a hair elastic. "Do you want to try using—"

"Hey, are you two coming?"

A blinding beam from another flashlight is shone in our faces. Squinting, I identify Austin's tall, lanky figure in the distance.

Danielle shouts to him, "We'll catch up with you in a sec!"

"Do you want some of us to wait?" Austin asks.

Snickering, Danielle whispers to me, "Tell him to have Doctor Kent wait for you."

"No, we're good!" I quickly yell while nudging Danielle with my foot.

The light swings away, and Austin hurries off to join the rest of the group. Soon, Danielle and I are alone.

"One more sec . . . okay . . . got it." Danielle stands up. "I'm not sure if my shoe is gonna hold, but here's to hoping."

"And here's to hoping we don't get lost out here."

Danielle laughs at me as we resume hiking. "There's only one path, Sav. I doubt we'll get lost."

I say nothing and direct my flashlight toward the rocky terrain in front of us. Other than our footsteps, all I can hear is the wind and the faint sounds of our group farther up the path. Before long, as Dr. Godfrey warned, the trail begins taking us along a steep incline.

"Why couldn't we have toasted marshmallows tonight? Or taken a night swim?" Danielle adjusts the bandana on her head. "I'd even take listening to Doctor Godfrey read us bedtime stories about the Krebs cycle over this."

I chuckle until I notice how steeply the trail drops off the mountainside to my right. I slide closer to Danielle to get away from the edge.

"Or why couldn't the team building activity be something like a car wash or bake sale?" Danielle continues venting. "At least we wouldn't have to be wandering around in the woods in the middle of the night."

I stop. "Danielle, you're a genius!"

"What?"

"That's how we can convince the hospital's administration to fund a remodel of the ED instead of the elective surgery center!"

Danielle observes me strangely. "Exactly how will wandering around in the woods do that?"

"No, not the woods! A car wash or a bake sale! We could hold a fundraiser to attract attention to the issue! And we could do it right outside the hospital administrators' offices!"

"Right." Danielle begins walking again. "When did you become interested in fighting hospital administrators or remodeling the ED? More importantly, when did you start caring about emergency medicine at all?"

I have to admit, it's a good question. When did I start to care?

Danielle comes to another halt. "My shoe is loose again."

As Danielle hunches over to resume operating on her footwear, I shift the flashlight to take another peek up the path. I see no one; I don't even hear our group anymore. I then make the mistake of glancing over at the steep drop-off on my right. It is a really long way down. I nervously start moving even closer to Danielle, and she stands up at the same time. We collide hard.

"Ouch!" she exclaims.

I stagger backward and suddenly feel my heels hovering right on the edge of the drop-off. My stomach leaps into my throat. I swing my arms in a frantic attempt to regain my balance, but as the ground crumbles away from beneath my feet, I have one crystal-clear thought:

I am going to fall off a cliff.

I don't even have a chance to yell before I topple over the edge. Danielle screams. My hand smacks a tree branch, knocking the flashlight from my hand and throwing me sideways onto the rocky, hard earth. Then I start sliding down the mountainside. Dirt is flying into my face as I thrash about, trying to break the momentum of my fall. My head strikes something hard, I see white, and my body goes limp. Plummeting downward at increasing speed, my legs tangle in tree roots and get twisted painfully. Something rams into my side. Now it hurts to breathe. I feel my skin getting scratched and torn. Another scream from Danielle reaches my ears. An instant later, everything comes to an abrupt stop. It takes me a few seconds to process that I'm lying in a crumpled heap on the cold ground.

"Savannah!" Danielle's horrified cry echoes through the night from somewhere high above. "Sav? Can you hear me? Sav, are you alright?"

I blink a few times, totally stunned, and try to assess the situation. My airway is still intact. I'm breathing. I can feel my arms and my legs. I have no midline cervical spine pain. I think it is safe for me to move. So I gingerly roll onto my back. In the darkness, all I can see is the glow of my flashlight lodged in a tree way above me. Then I become vaguely aware that my left ankle is hurting. With a groan, I push myself into a sitting position and scoot back so I am resting against the side of the cliff.

85

"Savannah! Sav! Are you dead?" Danielle is hysterical.

"No," I do my best to shout despite terrible pain in my ribs. "I'm not dead."

"I can't see you!" Danielle shrieks. "Where are you?"

I carefully turn my head from side to side, trying to make out what I can in the moonless night. "At the bottom, I guess."

I spot another faint light overhead. I think Danielle is using her cell phone to try and see better.

"Can you climb up here?"

I actually laugh. "Doubt it."

"Alright. Don't move, okay? I don't have any reception, so I'm gonna run get the others!"

"Don't move. Got it."

I hear her scamper away. With a busted shoe and no flashlight, though, I know that her rescue mission will be slow-going. So I rest my head back, settling in to wait. Another gust of wind stirs the trees. An owl hoots.

My left ankle is killing me.

Okay, I think the numbness of the initial shock is wearing off, because I am suddenly shivering even though it's not that cold outside. And in addition to my throbbing ankle and agonizing rib pain, I am becoming aware that my right wrist is also sore. I change my position, trying to get comfortable, but every movement feels as though someone is stabbing me in the side. Groaning miserably, I start to feel something trickling down my face. It must be blood. I might have a huge gash in my head. My brains could be splattered all over the place.

It's also possible that I could be starting to panic.

I attempt to keep myself preoccupied with evaluating my injuries. I reach my left hand over to my aching right wrist. I don't feel any bone deformity. Hopefully, it's only a sprain. Next, I try to lean forward to palpate my left ankle, but another excruciatingly sharp spasm in my ribs causes me stop and hold still until the awful sensation subsides. I then clumsily slip my good hand into my sweatshirt pocket and dig out a tissue, which I use to blot whatever is bleeding on my forehead. I exhale.

This sucks.

The night air and the ground beneath me are growing cooler. I shiver again. I hurt everywhere. I feel sick. My mind is growing foggy, making everything go in-and-out of focus. I know time is passing, but I have no idea how much.

My head jerks up with a start. I must have drifted off. For a moment, I'm not sure where I am. Then the terrible pain in my side reminds me that I'm stuck at the bottom of a cliff. Alone. At night. Injured.

My thoughts swirl. I need to get one more letter of recommendation for my residency application. I can't forget to mail Dad his birthday present. Dinner tonight was really good, but I didn't like the salad dressing. I've got to water the plant by the front window in our apartment. Did I tell Danielle that I really liked that new shirt she wore the other day? I—

A soft, repetitive noise catches my attention. I squint to see what it is, but the blackness reveals nothing. Eventually, I recognize it as the sound of lake water lapping up onto the shore, which must be nearby. Listening to the water's rhythmic noise, I feel myself drifting off once more. I really want to sleep. I—

A rush of nausea wakes me. I begin dry heaving, the harsh motion jarring my injured ribs as though someone is thrusting a hot poker into my chest. I cry out. I need to distract myself. I try recalling the cardinal signs of compartment syndrome. Pain, paresthesias, pallor and . . . I can't remember the other one.

Speaking of remembering, I need to remember to go shopping for a new cell—

"Savannah?"

Was that Danielle's voice? Or am I hallucinating?

"Savannah? Sav? Where are you?"

I strain to listen. Somewhere above me, I hear what sounds like people running along the trail. I try to call to them but am in

87

too much pain to yell. Thankfully, my flashlight is still stuck in the tree and shining brightly, marking where I wait.

"Sav?" Danielle sounds as though she is directly over me now. "Are you still down there?"

I manage a weak reply. "Still here."

A new light is shone down. "Savannah, it's Doctor Godfrey. Are you breathing alright?"

"My ribs hurt, but I'm breathing."

"Do you have any neck pain?"

"No."

"Will be able to stand?"

I attempt to range my left ankle and nearly shriek. "I might be able to stand on my right foot."

More flashlight beams sparkle in the darkness overhead. Then I start catching faint bits of people talking.

"Savannah, don't move yet," Dr. Godfrey instructs loudly enough for me to hear. "We're going to finish assessing the situation and figure out the best way to get to you, alright?"

"Sure."

There are more conversations above as flashlights continue shining down at me. I know they'll come to the same conclusion as I already have: it is going to be impossible for me to get up there.

Dr. Godfrey eventually calls out, "A couple of us are going to try and get down there. Remain still until we reach you."

Before I can respond, I hear a noise only a few feet away. I nearly scream that I'm about to be attacked by a bear when someone says, "Savannah?"

A blinding light shines in my face. Then I discern a familiar figure coming toward me. Doctor Kent crouches at my side and adjusts his headlamp so the beam is angled off to one side.

"Wes?" Dr. Sanders shouts from the trail above. "Sounds like you made it alright?"

He peers upward. "Yeah. I went back to the cabin and canoed over from the dock. We can definitely access this spot from below."

"Great. I'll send a couple more people to the cabin to wait there, in case you need assistance. The rest of us will remain here to help."

"Sounds good." Doctor Kent drops his head and refocuses on me. "Savannah, talk to me. What's going on?"

I stare blankly at him. I know he said something, but my brain has become so hazy that I can't process anything. I don't reply.

Doctor Kent's expression changes. He places a hand on my left shoulder. "Savannah, can you—"

"I have a great way to make money," I announce brightly.

His eyebrows go up, as if I'm not making any sense. "What?"

"A bake sale," I repeat deliriously. "Actually, it was Danielle who came up with the idea. Isn't it great?"

I see his jaw clench. He lets go of my shoulder, gets to his feet, and positions himself so he is right behind me. "How about you lie down," he suggests, although his tone makes it clear that it's actually an order.

I feel him put his hands on my shoulders from behind, so he's securely bracing my head and neck between his forearms. Keeping his arms in position, he kneels down and slowly lowers me back so I'm lying flat on the ground. Still stabilizing my head and neck, he leans forward and peers down at me.

"What hurts?"

"Hurts? Let me think." The words spill sluggishly from my mouth. "My right wrist is either sprained or has a non-displaced fracture, my left ankle is really busted, and my ribs are hurting so much that it's hard to talk. Oh, and I might be concussed because I have a headache and was thinking about online shopping a couple of minutes ago."

A wave of pain shoots through my body, which makes me grimace. Doctor Kent's intense gaze remains on mine as I work to catch my breath. Then, with my thoughts becoming more foggy, I resume babbling:

"I'm pretty sure that my cervical spine is cleared, but since I have distracting injuries I can't say for sure. Oh, and there was blood on my forehead. For a while I thought my brains were splattered all over the place. I really liked dinner tonight, didn't you?"

"Dinner was fine." Doctor Kent seems even more serious than his usual as he starts to press his fingers along the bones at the back of my neck. "Is this uncomfortable?"

"Nope."

He breathes in and out. "Savannah, I want you to stay exactly as you are. Don't move."

"Sure. But then we should get working on the bake sale."

He comes around to my side, and I notice that he's been wearing a backpack, which he takes off and sets at his feet.

"Even if you don't make enough money from a bake sale, you would still get really good publicity," I hear myself go on. My teeth are chattering. "Be sure to tell the local news channels to come. That'll get a bunch of attention."

Remaining quiet, he pulls something out of his backpack and walks toward my feet. Then he becomes very still.

"What?" I raise my head to see what he is doing. "What is it?"

"Keep your head down," he orders before kneeling and placing a hand on my left ankle.

I comply and resume staring up at the few stars that I can see through the trees. "Sure. Okay, Doctor Kent. I know that you told me to call you by your first name, but I can't. I mean, you're an attending, and I'm only a med—"

A terrible searing pain suddenly explodes from my left ankle and shoots up my leg. I scream in agony, which causes my chest wall to feel as though it is being cut by daggers. My breathing grows shallow, and my vision develops gray blobs floating across it. I can't think. I feel sick. I want to die.

"Wes?" comes Dr. Godfrey's anxious voice. "What's happening?"

"Had to reduce her left ankle. Dislocated fracture," Doctor Kent yells.

The horrific pain in my ankle subsides into an ache, allowing my breathing to slow down. My nausea dissipates. When my vision clears, I see Doctor Kent kneeling next to me. He looks really upset.

"Savannah, I'm sorry."

I blink away tears. "Do . . . do you think it's a good idea to have a bake sale?"

His clenched jaw relaxes, and he reaches again into his backpack. "We'll put that on the list of options. But for now, let's stabilize your wrist and get you out of here."

Doctor Kent takes my right hand in his and begins wrapping it in a bandage. As I lie there, I begin feeling utterly exhausted. Sound is fading. Everything is growing dim.

"Savannah?" Doctor Kent gently shakes me by the shoulder.

I set my eyes on him.

"Are you still with me?"

"Uh-huh."

He rests my wrapped arm on the ground. "I'm going to pack my stuff and then get you to the canoe. Which side is your rib pain on?"

"What?"

"Where do your ribs hurt the most?"

"The left."

He steps away into the darkness and soon reappears without his backpack. He speaks up to the others. "I think we're going to be alright down here. I'll see you at the cabin."

Dr. Godfrey replies, "Very good. We'll head out now and meet you there."

"Savannah?" Danielle's unexpected shout carries down through the darkness.

I manage a reply, "Yeah?"

"I hope you're having a good time down there!"

And I hope that I'm the only one who could detect the sassiness that was beneath the relief in her tone. Either way, for her sake, it's a good thing that I'm stuck at the bottom of a cliff with one arm in a bandage, or I'd probably smack her.

Next to me, Doctor Kent remains all business. He moves to my right side and carefully lifts me to a sitting position. The next thing I know, he has slung my arm over his shoulder, picked me up, and begun to carry me. At first, I'm too shell-shocked to do anything. But as I get rocked by the steady motion of his steps, weariness overcomes me, and I drop my aching head against his chest.

I open my eyes with a start.

"How are you doing?" he asks.

"I'm fine."

We reach the canoe, and Doctor Kent sets me down beside it, bracing me so I only have to bear weight on my good leg.

"Still doing okay?"

I shakily hold onto his upper arm. "Yup."

He guides me into the canoe and helps me onto the front seat. Then he shuts off his headlamp, leaving us in the dark.

"It'll be a bit of a ride. Are you sure you'll be alright like that?"

I shift to alleviate some of my pain. "I can make it."

"Okay. Let's go."

The canoe rocks as he pushes it into the lake. I hear splashing as he wades in behind it. Then the canoe tips slightly as he gets into the back. Soon, the sound of him paddling begins carrying over the water. For a moment, everything is weirdly serene. Then, without warning, I'm overcome again by nausea, and my head feels as though it has filled up with cotton. I groan, and my chin falls forward onto my chest.

"Savannah." Doctor Kent's voice is sharp.

"What? Huh?" I raise my head. I see cabin lights getting closer. For a few seconds, my mind seems to clear. "Thanks, Doctor Kent, for helping me."

"You're welcome," he replies as we float up to the dock. "And it's Wes."

People are running from the cabin to meet us. Doctor Kent gets out of the canoe and drags it up onto the shore. Deciding that I am well enough to get out on my own, I stand up. But immediately, I realize that was a mistake. I become lightheaded from debilitating pain. There is a rushing sound in my ears. I stagger. I see Doctor Kent right beside me. Then everything goes black.

Chapter Six

Savannah Drake is a twenty-six-year-old female on hospital day two and post-op day one. She is recovering from a fall down a mountainside, in which she sustained a scalp laceration, right wrist sprain, non-displaced fractures of left ribs six and seven, and a displaced left ankle fracture that was reduced in the field and then surgically repaired."

I stir slightly in bed. I think I hear a familiar voice, but I'm so groggy that it's hard to be sure.

"Post-operative course has been uncomplicated," the familiar voice continues. "No events overnight. The patient remains hemodynamically stable. Pain has been well controlled. No signs of infection. Labs remain within normal limits."

Groggy or not, there is no question about it: I know that voice.

"We anticipate that she will be discharged later today, pending a successful PT and OT evaluation."

I force myself to open my heavy eyes. Through blurry vision, I see a group of people gathered at the foot of my bed. They're all wearing white coats. And they're staring at me.

I sit up with a start. "What's going—"

My ribs surge with pain, forcing me to lie back. Panting and panicked, I scan the unfamiliar room. Where am I? What is going on? Why—

"Sav, it's okay. It's okay," another person says. "It's me."

I turn my head and feel a rush of relief. Danielle is here.

She has gotten up from a nearby chair and come to the bedside. She places a hand reassuringly on my shoulder. "You're in the hospital. You were admitted to the trauma service. Do you remember the fall, Sav? On the night hike?"

I stare back at her while flashbulb memories start popping up in my mind. Hiking the trail with Danielle, the terrifying sensation of plummeting downward, something about bake sales, horrible pain, Doctor Kent carrying me in his arms . . .

I break from my thoughts and nod. "I remember."

"Well, we're glad you're feeling better," a different person remarks.

Oh yeah. The army. The white coat army.

I focus again on the approximately one billion people who are observing me like I'm part of a zoo exhibit. I spot Brittany near the back of the group and Erik standing at the end of the bed—he was definitely the one I heard doing the bedside presentation. And the paper that Erik has in his hand undoubtedly contains every not-so-glamorous detail about my hospital course. I groan silently, very aware that I'm wearing almost nothing but a hospital gown, my hair is probably a tangled mess, and I haven't showered in who-knows-how-long.

"We're pleased that you've been making so much progress," the other person goes on.

I shift my attention to the older, extremely somber woman who spoke. She is standing off to the side of the others. Even without an introduction, it's obvious who she is—everything about her just *looks* like a trauma surgery attending physician. In fact, she's the most intimidating person I have ever seen. Except for my junior high PE teacher.

"Th-thanks," I stammer.

"It was fortunate that your dislocated ankle was reduced so quickly after the accident," the attending adds crisply.

"Yes," is all I can say.

She continues firing questions. "I understand that you are currently a fourth-year medical student?"

"Yes."

"Very good." The attending then addresses Erik. "Anything else, Doctor Prescott?"

I notice Danielle perk up when she hears Erik's name. Her eyes dart to Erik's badge, and a glimmer of realization appears on her face.

Erik is shaking his head. "No, nothing else, Doctor Briggs. I'll do her post-op exam and notify PT that she's ready."

With barely a nod, Dr. Briggs marches from the room. Brittany and the gaggle of white coats follows. But Erik remains at the foot of the bed.

"I'm just gonna do a quick post-op check," he explains, his tense expression relaxing into that to-die-for smile.

Danielle springs up and announces in an absurdly cheery voice, "And I'm going to go make a couple of phone calls!"

She gives me a wink before scurrying out the door. But over Erik's shoulder, I see her poke her head back inside the room. Now she's mouthing, *Doctor Kent is better* to me.

With a playful raise of her eyebrows, she slips out again, leaving Erik and me alone.

"The nurses said you did alright overnight. Are you still feeling okay?" Erik asks while he examines my left toes, which are sticking out of a bulky cast.

"Uh-huh." I reach back to make sure that my blue-and-white checkered hospital gown is at least tied shut. They really should design these things with zipper closures.

Erik seems to study my face. "That was a pretty bad fall you took, from the sound of it. Like Doctor Briggs said, it was good that your ankle got reduced right away. Could've been a lot worse."

I swipe strands of hair from my eyes. "Well, I guess if you're going to fall off of a cliff, it's best to do it when there is a group of emergency medicine doctors around."

He seems amused. "Especially Kent, I'm sure."

"Yes. Especially Doctor Kent," I reply, not mirroring his humorous tone. "Doctor Kent is the one who reduced my ankle."

Erik pauses, and then he changes the subject. "So you must be about to apply for residency, right?"

"Yes." I adjust how I'm sitting and try to appear at ease. But I know it's basically impossible to appear attractive in a hospital gown. "Application season starts soon."

He resumes his exam. "What specialty were you going into again?"

"Pediatrics, I think."

Wait a second. Did I just say, *I think*? As if I'm not sure? What's going on? I have been planning on going into pediatrics since the first day of medical school! Since the first day of college! Since forever!

I must still be concussed.

"Well, at least there are still some people out there who want to do pediatrics." Erik finishes his exam and casually leans against the wall.

I gesture to his ID badge. "Just like there are still some people who want train with trauma surgeons who haven't smiled in about thirty years?"

He chuckles. "Doctor Briggs is notorious for being that way."

"That scary, you mean."

He pulls a face that is oddly similar to hers, and we both break into laughter. Only then do I realize that someone else is standing in the doorway.

"Hello, Savannah," Doctor Kent says when I notice him.

I feel a weird rush in my chest. "Hi, Doctor Kent."

He steps into the room. I can't help noticing that his shirt is wrinkled and he hasn't shaved. Frankly, he appears tired. But despite his ragged appearance, Doctor Kent's eyes flicker with warmth as he greets me. He then shifts his attention to Erik, and his demeanor gets serious.

"Good morning, Doctor Prescott."

Erik breathes in stiffly. "Good morning, Doctor Kent."

"I trust you're taking good care of this patient?" Doctor Kent continues tracking him.

"Of course I am." Erik fidgets. "I mean, we are."

"Good." Doctor Kent keeps his attention trained on Erik for an extra second before turning again to me. The hard lines on his face relax. "Sorry I interrupted. I just wanted to see how you were feeling."

I smile. There is something very reassuring about having Doctor Kent here. "Thanks. I'm doing alright."

"Well, it's nice to finally see you really awake." Doctor Kent is now smiling, too. "And lucid."

I moan. "I can only imagine what I might have said in my delirium."

His grin broadens. "It wasn't too incriminating. Don't worry."

I shake my head. Doctor Kent chuckles.

I gesture to Erik. "The best news is that Erik, er, Doctor Prescott thinks I'll be discharged today."

Doctor Kent is back to being serious. "Then I should let you two continue."

Before I can say anything else, Doctor Kent leaves the room. I stare at the empty doorway, listening to his footsteps fade.

Erik's pager goes off.

"I have to go too," Erik announces, clasping the pager to his scrubs. "I'll talk to you soon, though, okay?"

My eyes remain on the doorway. "Okay."

Erik slips out. The room becomes strangely quiet. I drop my aching head and shut my eyes. I'm not sure if it's due to post-concussive syndrome or whatever pain medication they have me drugged with, but I can't make sense of the last few minutes.

"So that was your man, huh?"

I whip my head up and see Danielle waltzing into the room with her cell phone in hand. "Shh!" I bark at her. "The entire hospital wing can probably hear you!"

But she makes an exaggerated curtsey and goes on just as loudly, "I'm *so* honored that I finally got to behold Erik the Great!"

Ignoring her sarcasm, I slide farther under the covers. "I'm glad you finally got to see what I've been talking about. He's amazing, isn't he?"

Danielle drops into the chair and shrugs. "I guess."

"You *guess*? You saw him. He's perfect."

She twists her lips thoughtfully. "Hmm. Maybe that's exactly what's wrong with him. He's too perfect."

"Too perfect is a problem?"

"Yeah." She sits up as though she's had an epiphany. "And I think that's exactly why you've convinced yourself that you're attracted to him."

I snort. "Okay, I may be the one who's concussed, but you're the one not making any sense."

"I'm making total sense. Being attracted to Erik is safe and non-threatening because no relationship with him would ever actually materialize—"

"Gee, thanks," I interject.

"Sav, you know what I mean." Danielle rolls her eyes. "You've singled Erik out because he's one of those guys you can safely drool over from a distance. It's no different than crushing on a movie star or something. The truth is, though, you'd never really want to date Erik. He's just someone to distract yourself with so you can avoid thinking about the man you're really attracted to."

I point at her. "Danielle, you are officially crazy."

"I don't think so. Tell me honestly: if the opportunity to be in a romantic relationship with smug, cocky Erik presented itself, would you pursue it?"

I hesitate. "What kind of a question is that?"

"Precisely. You wouldn't want to be in a relationship with that guy. As I said, he's too perfect."

"Perfect?" another person remarks. "Are you talking about me again?"

We both face the door. Joel is standing there with a balloon and some flowers in his hand.

Danielle lights up when she sees him. "We're discussing Savannah's super-safe crush."

"Uh oh, more girl talk, huh?" He sets the flowers and balloon on a table. "Sav, I'm glad to see you doing well."

"Thanks, Joel," I tell him warmly.

He takes a chair beside Danielle. "So when are they going to let you get out of this joint?"

"Today, I think." I pull my hair back. "Speaking of today, what day is this, anyway? How long have I been here?"

Danielle's eyes get big. "You really don't remember?"

I shake my head.

She slides to the edge of her chair. "Please tell me that you remember Doctor Kent rescuing you, at least."

I fiddle with the corner of the blanket. "I remember some of it."

"Good." Danielle sighs dramatically. "Because it was extremely romantic."

I cast a pleading look at Joel, who only throws up his hands. I then say to Danielle:

"Again, you're overreacting. I remember most of what happened, and there wasn't anything romantic about it."

Danielle clasps her hands. "Are you kidding me? Everything about it was romantic, especially when Doctor Kent rowed you to the cabin. We were waiting there for you guys to arrive. You tried getting out of the canoe by yourself and fainted. Doctor Kent caught you and carried you inside. We called 911. When the ambulance arrived, he rode with you to the hospital. Austin and I collected your stuff, and we followed in the car." She sighs again. "Really, Doctor Kent was extremely worried about you."

"Well, he is a doctor," I point out dryly. "Worrying about patients is what he does for a living."

"True," Joel agrees.

Danielle gives him a look and then goes on insistently. "No, this was different. Doctor Kent wasn't just worried about you as a patient, Sav. He was worried about *you*. I could see it in his eyes."

She finally lowers her voice. "I don't even think that Doctor Kent has gone home since you've been here."

"Danielle, you're really . . ." I break off once her words sink in. "Wait. What!"

She nods earnestly. "You got here late on Friday night, and Doctor Kent stayed close by the whole time you were getting worked up in the ED. And after you got admitted, he made sure that you were getting good care from the trauma service." She stops only to catch her breath before rushing on. "And yesterday, both before and after your ankle surgery, he came by regularly to see how you were doing. He was still wearing the same clothes that he had on the day prior. I think he's been here the whole time. My guess is that he's been sleeping in his office."

I don't reply. The thought of Doctor Kent making sure that I was alright when I was unable to care for myself is . . .

No. This is not what Danielle is making it out to be. Doctor Kent is the attending who is in charge of the rotation, and he's responsible for us. He would have done the same for any student who got hurt.

Diverting the discussion, I motion to a bag in the corner, which I see is crammed full of Danielle's belongings. "You've been here too, haven't you?"

"Of course." She seems almost offended. "Where else do you think I'd be while you were in the hospital?"

A few tears prick my eyes. "Thanks."

Danielle smiles. She then gestures to her phone. "I've been keeping your parents informed. They're really concerned and about to fly out here. You should probably call when you feel up to—"

There is a brisk knock on the doorframe.

"Excuse me, I'm looking for Savannah Drake. Am I in the right place?"

The question came from a short, balding man who is dressed in a crisp suit and already welcoming himself into the room.

"I'm Savannah," I say, glancing in bewilderment at Danielle, who is staring at the man with her mouth dropped open.

"Do you have a moment?" the man asks me, although I get the sense that he'd stay even if I told him I was busy.

I pull the blanket closer around me. "Sure. I guess."

He steps right up to the bed, and that's when I notice that the man is being followed by a wiry woman who is dressed in a red blouse and tweed jacket with matching pencil skirt. Her thin auburn hair is cinched tightly into a bun. She has glasses perched on the end of her nose, and she's actually taking notes on a pad of paper.

"You must forgive the unannounced visit," the man goes on to me with exaggerated graciousness. "I hope that I'm not interrupting."

"No, you're not interrupting," Joel interjects flatly. "We're only her closest friends who came to spend time with her in the hospital."

Danielle gives Joel a hard nudge in the side.

The man flashes a patronizing smile. "Allow me to introduce myself. I am Rick Gatz."

The man reaches out to shake my hand. With feigned apology, I lift up my splinted arm so he can see it.

"Sprained," I tell him. "Sorry."

Over Mr. Gatz's shoulder, I see Joel trying not to laugh.

"Ah." Mr. Gatz awkwardly puts his hand back at his side. "Well, Savannah, I understand that you are currently receiving top-notch care here, which our surgical department is famous for providing."

I peer at him warily. "Yeah. Top-notch."

Joel turns to Danielle and says loudly, "Hey, aren't there hippo or hippie laws that prevent patients' medical information from being leaked to people who aren't involved in their care?"

Danielle drops her head in her hands. "I think you mean HIPAA."

"Yeah." Joel studies the guy suspiciously. "That."

Mr. Gatz's eyes narrow briefly. "I certainly appreciate your concern. Allow me to alleviate your distress. We are authorized to access privileged patient information."

Joel crosses his arms. "Who's we?"

Mr. Gatz throws his head back importantly. "The hospital administration."

Joel does not seem impressed.

Mr. Gatz gives up on Joel and faces me again. "I also understand that you are currently a medical student, Savannah?"

"Yeah."

Though I am saying little, my mind is racing. This guy is a hospital administrator? Why is he here?

Mr. Gatz continues, "When we heard about your accident, we thought it was quite an incredible story. In fact, we're hoping that you'd be willing to share your tale with others who would also be interested."

I rub my forehead. "I don't think I understand."

Mr. Gatz's smile widens. "In a few weeks, this hospital will be holding a small reception on behalf of the surgery department. During the reception, we hope to have a few former patients talk about the amazing care that they received from various surgical teams here at Lakewood Medical Center. Savannah, when we heard your story, we immediately wanted one of those speakers to be you. A future health care provider receiving care herself! What a great story!"

He stops for emphasis. I glance at the others. Danielle is wide-eyed and Joel maintains his look of disdain. After a protracted moment, I focus again on Rick Gatz. He tips his head as if satisfied and then turns to the woman, who begins scribbling furiously in her notebook.

"Wait a second." I hold up my good hand. "I never said that I would do it."

The woman whips her head up as though someone has just told her that her hair is on fire.

Mr. Gatz eyes me, appearing unsure of how to react. "I'm sorry?"

"You have to excuse her, Mr. Gatz," Danielle suddenly cuts in. "Savannah is still recovering from surgery. And a concussion. And she's on pain medication. And she needs a nap. And maybe she's developing delayed frostbite. And—"

"Of course." Mr. Gatz's tone regains its smoothness. "We realize that you have been through a lot, Savannah. We'll give you some time to make up your mind. In a few days, we'll contact you to get your official decision."

Mr. Gatz gives the woman another glance, and then, in unison, they spin away and stride from the room.

"What was that?" Joel demands as soon as they're gone.

"Ridiculous, is what it was," I mutter while smoothing the blankets on my bed. "I can't believe that guy thought I'd help him out."

Danielle makes a funny sound. "Wait a sec, you're not going to refuse the invitation to speak, are you?"

"Of course I'm gonna refuse," I reply. "That guy is one of the hospital administrators, which means that he's one of the people who decided not to fund an ED remodel. There are little old ladies being treated in the ED walkways because of suits like him."

Danielle shakes her head. "But, Sav, that was Rick Gatz! He's the vice president of the hospital! He's Mark Prescott's right-hand man!"

"He is?" I glance at the doorway. "He works with Erik's dad?"

"Wh-what?" Danielle sputters. "Erik Prescott is Mark Prescott's son?"

I face her again. "Yep. And grandson of Prescott Tower himself."

"Wow." Danielle breathes out slowly. "I can't believe that I missed that information while doing my pre-rotation research."

"Ah, so perhaps Erik isn't quite so undesirable, after all, eh?" I quip.

Danielle tosses her hair. "No, it's not that. Erik's still not your type, Sav. But this is . . ." She goes quiet, as if not quite sure what she is trying to say. I rest my aching head on the pillow. "Well, it doesn't matter who that guy is or what the little reception is for. I'm not about to help out the hospital's administration while they're refusing to help the ED."

Danielle drums her fingers on the arm of her chair. "Don't get me wrong, your opinion is noble and all. But this speaking engagement would look really good on your residency application."

I slowly raise my head. Danielle is right. A speaking gig— even a small one like Mr. Gatz described—would be a great way to make my residency application stand out from the countless others. Most medical students would do anything for an opportunity like this.

But I can't do it. I cannot help the same administration that is neglecting the ED and its patients. I just can't.

Yet if anyone needs a boost to her residency application, it's me. I have probably blown my grade for this rotation ten times over. This speaking gig might be my only way to remain competitive with other applicants.

"I can't do it. I'd be a sell out," I eventually declare.

"You wouldn't be a sell out," Danielle counters. "All you have to do is talk for a couple of minutes at some little reception about the good medical care you received here. And you did receive good care, so it's not lying."

"But it's like helping the enemy," I insist, though I can feel my conviction fading.

"No, it's not. You getting good care from the surgical service has nothing to do with the ED funding issue."

"But what would—"

"What would Doctor Kent think?" Danielle softly finishes for me. "You're worried about that?"

"Of course I am. He's the head of this rotation, which I still need to salvage a passing grade on."

Danielle shrugs. "No one will care about your grade if you have something as impressive as a speaking engagement on your resume. Besides, you can always explain a low grade away by your accident."

I throw the blanket over my face. I cannot think about this right now.

"Uh, Savannah?"

It takes me a moment to realize that the voice does not belong to Danielle or Joel. I pull the blanket down, messing up my hair even more. Erik is reentering the room. I would pretty much kill for some mascara right now.

"I talked to the folks from PT and asked them to see you first," Erik explains, fingering his stethoscope. "They should be coming in soon. Then you'll be able to get out of here. I've already got your discharge summary written up."

"Thanks," I tell him. "That's great."

"You're welcome." He shoves his hands into the pockets of his white coat. "Hey, is it okay if I . . . if we call you after you get home to see how you're doing?"

Danielle promptly sits up, scrutinizing him. And she doesn't seem particularly happy.

"Sure," I say, hoping that I don't sound too eager. "Oh, wait. Actually, you can't call me. My cell phone is busted—most of the time, anyway—so you should probably email my hospital account instead."

"Right." Erik scratches his head and pauses, and then he heads for the door. "Anyway, I'll be in touch. See you later."

After Erik is gone, Danielle says to Joel, "That's the guy Sav has been raving about."

"Oh, that's Doctor Incredible, eh?" Joel also seems unenthused. "I can certainly see why he couldn't spare more than two minutes to talk with the patient he's about to discharge from the hospital. After all, he's probably got to rush off and bench press another thirty reps before lunch."

Even I can't help snickering. "You're not jealous, are you, Joel?"

Joel jokingly flexes his lean arms. "Are you kidding? Get a load of these guns."

"I love you exactly as you are." Danielle leans over and kisses his cheek.

While the two of them adore each other, I yawn wearily and slide down under my blankets. Danielle notices and gets to her feet, motioning for Joel to do the same.

"We'll head out so you can rest before the PT folks get here," she tells me.

"Thanks," I mumble. "I'm really, really glad you guys are here."

Danielle comes over and gives my hand a squeeze. "We'll be in the lounge waiting to take you home."

My eyes are starting to droop. "Sounds good."

They slip out. I soon feel myself drifting off to sleep. Erik, Rick Gatz, speeches, Doctor Kent . . .

What am I going to do?

Chapter Seven

Whoever invented crutches should be imprisoned.

I toss the torture devices to my feet, shake out my arms, and lean against the bathroom wall so I'm balanced enough to pull my hair into a low ponytail.

"How are you doing?" Danielle comes out of her bedroom and appears behind me in the mirror.

I observe my reflection. "I think my ponytail is crooked."

"For crying out loud, who cares, Sav? You got out of the hospital, like, thirty-six hours ago. The fact that you're already going back to work is so heroic that you'd be fine even if your scrubs were on upside-down."

I quickly glance at myself in the mirror again, just in case.

"But I still don't get why you're going back to the ED so soon," she goes on. "It's insane."

"Insane, perhaps, but better than missing so many days that I have to make up the rotation at the end of the year and wreck my ability to apply on time for residen—"

"Doctor Kent told you not to worry about missing extra days. The message that he left for you on my voicemail specifically stated that you shouldn't return to work until you are completely better, remember?"

I say nothing.

"But you obviously know this, considering that I played the voicemail for you about three hundred times." Danielle now has an annoying sparkle in her eye, "So maybe there's another reason that you want to get back to the ED so soon?"

"Stop, Danielle." I bend down to reclaim my crutches. "I can guess what's going through your warped little head, and you're wrong."

She giggles. "I'm sure Doctor Kent will be thrilled to see you, too."

"It's not about seeing Doctor Kent." I face her squarely. "I've got my grade on this rotation to rescue. Plus, I . . ."

I don't finish, though I know what else is bothering me. Guilt. As much as I loathe Rick Gatz and the rest of the hospital administration, I still haven't written off the idea of speaking at that little reception for the surgery department. It would be an amazing boost to my residency application. Yet the fact that I'm even considering doing it makes me feel like such a traitor that I've been anxious to get back to the ED. Maybe going back will somehow prove to everyone where my true loyalties lie—or at least quiet my own conscience.

"By the way, did you ever hear from Mr. Gatz about speaking at that thing?" Danielle inquires, apparently reading my thoughts.

I shrug nonchalantly. "Nope. Maybe he forgot all about me, which is probably for the best."

Danielle is about to respond when her phone chimes. She checks her new text message. "Joel's here," she announces. She slings her bag over her shoulder and studies me worriedly. "Are you positive that you're up for this?"

"Yep."

"Really? You're sure? You're one hundred percent sure?"

"I'm sure."

She does not seem to buy it, though she puts on a supportive smile. "Okay. Let's go."

Following Danielle, I maneuver my way out of our apartment and down the two flights of stairs to the street level—which, between crutches and having one arm in a splint, is no easy feat.

"You're actually going in today, huh?" Joel reaches over to grab my crutches as I slip into the backseat of his car.

I nod. "Thanks for picking us up."

"No worries. It's easy when you work from home," he replies with a smile. "Anyway, you're pretty dedicated to be heading back to work so soon."

"She's not dedicated, she's crazy." Danielle buckles her seatbelt. "I mean, Sav just—"

Her phone starts ringing.

"Hello?" Danielle answers, and then a huge, evil grin appears on her face. "Why yes, she's right here, *Doctor Kent*. Let me get her for you." She holds her phone out to me with obnoxious sweetness. "It's for you."

I don't move. My mouth is suddenly dry, and my mind has become a black hole. Danielle pushes the phone closer to me. I recoil and start shaking my head, but she shoves the phone right in my face. I reluctantly take the phone and put it to my ear.

"Hello?"

"Savannah? It's Wes."

"Hi, Doctor Kent." My voice is about eighteen octaves higher than usual. "How are you?"

"Me? I'm doing fine, thanks."

Why does it sound like he's smiling?

"The bigger question, though, is how are *you*?" Doctor Kent goes on. "I would've tried your phone, but my guess is that you probably haven't gotten around to getting that thing replaced yet."

I realize that I'm smiling myself. "Nope. I've been too busy hanging out in the hospital and getting attacked by an army of trauma surgeons."

"Sounds horrible."

"Yeah, I . . ." I fade out when I notice how giddily Danielle is listening to the exchange.

"So you're doing alright?" Doctor Kent asks after a moment.

"Yeah. I'm sorry that I'm running late. I'll be there in just a few minutes."

Silence.

"You'll be where in just a few minutes?" Doctor Kent eventually asks.

"Um, at the ED. For our shift."

Another pause.

"Savannah, you're not coming to work today, are you?"

"Yeah. I am." I sink down in my seat as the words come out of my mouth. I sound like an idiot.

"I left a message with Danielle about this. You shouldn't come until you're well."

What am I supposed to say? That I might be selling my soul to the hospital administrators and speaking on behalf of the surgery department, and so I want to work in the ED as penance? That I actually kind of miss working in the ED? That I miss—

"Savannah?" he presses.

I clear my throat. "I'm feeling better. I want to come in."

"Okay," Doctor Kent remarks slowly. "Then I'll see you soon."

He hangs up.

Danielle squeals as soon as the call is over. "He is *so* the right guy for you!"

"Stop it, Danielle! For the last time, stop!" I blurt out. "He's my attending! That's all! Okay?"

Danielle seems as surprised by my outburst as I am. Joel examines me through the rear-view mirror but says nothing. I drop my head and make myself busy tightening my wrist splint. I don't know why I feel so rattled. I've only been on this rotation for a week or so, yet it seems like my whole life has gotten tossed on its head because of it.

Other than a few short exchanges between Joel and Danielle, no one says anything during the drive. As Joel pulls up in front of the emergency department, I open the car door and begin the arduous process of getting out. Danielle gives Joel a quick kiss and then comes to my side do help.

"Sav," she starts to softly say, "I wasn't trying to be—"

I give her a quick hug. "Sorry I lost my temper. It's no excuse, but this has just been a really strange past several days."

She nods understandingly and takes my bag so I don't have to carry it. I'm struck with a wave of gratitude for my best friend. Danielle doesn't need to say anything else, and neither do I. All is forgiven.

When Danielle and I enter the ED, I spot Doctor Kent. He's standing near the charge nurse's desk, almost as if he was waiting for us. He's dressed in dark green scrubs, his facial scruff is gone, and his affect is as unemotional as always. When he sees the two of us, he starts walking our way. Then I notice that Dr. Godfrey is behind him.

"So how's our mountain climber doing this morning?" Dr. Godfrey asks me.

I attempt a joking salute. "Reporting for duty."

Dr. Godfrey laughs appreciatively, but Doctor Kent does not.

"I asked Ned if we could swap shift locations for today," Doctor Kent explains to Danielle and me. "I thought it would be better for Savannah if she and I covered low acuity patients in Fast Track. Danielle, is working in the main ED today with Doctor Godfrey alright with you?"

"Of course," Danielle answers with over-the-top professionalism. "Whatever you think is best, Doctor Kent."

"Great!" Dr. Godfrey enthusiastically gestures toward the ambulance entrance. "We've got someone from a high-speed MVC coming in soon, so let's go and get ready."

Danielle waves before following Dr. Godfrey into the resuscitation bay. Doctor Kent watches them go, and then he peers down at me.

"I hope you realize that you're going to be sicker than most of the patients you'll be treating today."

I shift the crutches under my arms. I hadn't thought of this. "You're probably right."

"You should be at home."

"I'd rather be here."

Doctor Kent doesn't respond and starts down the hallway toward Fast Track, going slowly enough for me to keep up. As we get closer, I begin hearing music. Harmonica music.

"Hmm. This could be interesting," Doctor Kent remarks.

We enter Fast Track as Hadi wheels a stretcher into Room Three. The stretcher is piled high with blankets, and the sound of bluesy harmonica music seems to be moving along with it.

"New arrival," Hadi announces to us with a grin.

Doctor Kent strolls into Room Three to investigate the situation. Before long, he steps back out and grabs a chair from the nursing station, which he places beside the blanket-filled stretcher. "Alright, Savannah, come and meet your first patient for the day."

I crutch curiously into Room Three. With a grandiose gesture, Hadi pulls the huge mound of blankets off the stretcher, revealing a disheveled-appearing man who is sitting cross-legged upon it and playing the harmonica. The patient breaks off from his playing and grouchily snatches for the blankets, clearly wanting them back on top of him, but Hadi keeps them out of the man's reach. With an indignant snort, the patient shuts his eyes and resumes playing his song.

I hobble closer. The harmonica man appears is probably in his fifties, though he looks older than that. His hair is dirty and matted, his clothes are soiled, and there are cigarette burns covering his hands. Yet he smells—very strongly—like mint.

"I'm going to be over at the desk," Doctor Kent tells me, straight-faced. "Remember, any time you need a break, you say so."

Doctor Kent exits the room. Still holding the blankets in one hand, Hadi starts snapping in time to the music with his other. I guess this is where I'm supposed to get involved. I sit down in the chair that Doctor Kent placed beside the stretcher and begin:

"Hello, sir. My name is Savannah Drake, and I . . ."

The patient is paying me zero attention and still playing the harmonica.

"Sir?" I call above the music. "I'm Sa-van-nah! What brings you in today?"

The man finally stops and opens one eye to peer my way. He flashes a nearly-toothless grin and makes a happy, growling noise. Another rush of mint floods my nose. Then the man shuts his eye again and resumes playing.

I hear a chuckle behind me. Glancing over my shoulder, I see Doctor Kent seated at the attending's desk, observing the scene.

"You're finding this funny, aren't you?" I ask, grinning myself.

"Maybe a little." He gets to his feet. "Unfortunately, though, I need to go check on another patient. Don't have too much fun without me."

With another chuckle, Doctor Kent strides away.

I giggle and then address Hadi. "So do you know anything about this guy?"

"He was brought in by ambulance." Hadi is still snapping along to the tune. "Sounds like he's pretty well known to the EMS crew. Heavy drinker. Gets picked up all the time. Today, he was found in the local GoodMart drinking the mouthwash."

"The mouthwash?" I repeat, confused.

"Yeah. That stuff's loaded with ethanol. It's a cheap way to get drunk. This guy was sitting in the back of GoodMart, surrounded by empty mouthwash bottles. No one has any idea how long he was enjoying his makeshift bar before a GoodMart employee found him."

Wide-eyed, I resume watching the patient. He's drunk out of his mind. But he sure smells nice. For a few measures, I wonder what to do with him. Finally, I decide that I should examine the guy as I would any other patient, and so I get up to proceed. However, between trying not to aggravate sore ribs, balancing on crutches, and attempting to auscultate cardiac sounds over harmonica music, it's not the easiest exam I've ever performed. While

I carefully maneuver to evaluate the patient's abdomen, a new noise causes me to check beyond the partly-open curtain. Other patients are coming out of their rooms to enjoy the concert.

Just then, Doctor Kent returns. He steps in and shuts the curtain behind him. I hear the other patients grumble with disappointment and start shuffling back to where they belong.

"So what do you think?" Doctor Kent asks me.

I scratch my head. "Considering he's not the best historian, I would start with a normal tox workup: lytes, ECG, aspirin and acetaminophen levels, and a utox. And screen for various alcohol ingestions."

"Spot on. Nice job."

I pause. Did Doctor Kent really give me a little bit of praise? For one moment, I actually felt like a real doctor. As if I kind of knew what I was doing. I think.

"I'll get the stuff to draw labs," Hadi offers, sliding out to the beat of the music.

"And I'm going to discharge my other patient, Mr. Alberts. He's in a hurry because he's trying to make a flight," Doctor Kent remarks. "He's got otitis media, and—"

"Doctor Kent?" The same female nurse, Cassie, who worked in Fast Track the last time I was here pokes her head around the curtain. "I've got the mother of a patient who was discharged overnight on the phone. Do you mind speaking with her?"

"I can take the discharge paperwork to Mr. Alberts while you answer the call, if you want," I offer.

"That'd be great." Doctor Kent goes to the attending's desk, picks up a prescription and discharge paperwork, and hands them over to me. "Thanks."

While Doctor Kent sits down to answer the phone, I scan the patient tracking board. I spot the initials "H.A." listed in Room Nine. The chief complaint is "Head Pain." Discharge papers in hand, I go that direction.

"Mr. Alberts?" I ask, sliding the curtain of Room Nine aside.

The young man who is waiting inside looks up. "Yes? Are you the nurse?"

"No, I'm the medical student who is working with Doctor Kent. I understand that you've been seen by Doctor Kent and diagnosed with an ear infection, and you're waiting for your discharge instructions?"

"Yes," the young man answers. "That's right."

I hold out the paperwork. "Here you go. This is your paperwork and a prescription for an antibiotic to treat that ear infection."

"Great." He politely takes the papers. "Thank you very much."

"You're welcome. Have a safe flight, and I hope that you feel better soon."

"I will. Thanks again."

The patient slides past me and walks out. I follow him from the room and make my way back to the desk. Doctor Kent is just hanging up the phone. Out of the corner of my eye, I see someone from registration put a new patient chart in the bin. I promptly change directions and go pick it up.

"I'm going to see this new patient in Room Fourteen, Doctor Kent," I announce.

He is watching me. "Or you could rest. Remember, you're recovering from a concussion and several other serious injuries. Not to mention, surgery."

"I'm fine. Really." I try not to react when there's another spasm of pain in my ribs.

He hesitates, and so I spin away and charge toward Room Fourteen before he can tell me to sit down. I pull the curtain aside. Inside the room, there's a young couple seated beside the stretcher, which has a tiny infant lying upon it. I feel a rush of delight. Finally, a pediatric patient.

"Hi, my name is Savannah Drake," I tell them warmly. "What brings you in today?"

"I think he might have a fever," answers the mother, who I'm guessing is several years younger than I am.

I move closer. "How old is your son?"

"Three weeks."

I sit gently on the edge of the stretcher and peer down at the baby. He's lying quietly. Way too quietly. With a surge of alarm, I bend down to get a better look at him. His skin is dusky, and he is working hard to breathe. My throat gets tight. This baby does not belong in Fast Track. This baby is really sick.

I stand up so fast that a burst of pain in my ribs nearly causes me to lose my balance. "Excuse me for a moment," I say breathlessly. "I'll be right back."

The father, who is about as young as the mother, now seems concerned. "He's going to be alright, isn't he?"

"We're going to do everything we can to make sure of that." I crutch from the room and call out, "Doctor Kent?"

Doctor Kent is at the computer. He jerks his head up when he hears my voice. Immediately, his expression tenses and he stands up.

I move toward him while gesturing to Room Fourteen. "That baby is sick."

Doctor Kent starts coming my way.

I spot Hadi exiting another room and flag him down. "We're going to need your help in Room Fourteen. IV, labs, blood culture, straight cath, and an LP."

Hadi picks up his pace. "You got it."

"I'll go put orders in the computer," I tell Doctor Kent, who nods and keeps going for the baby's room.

I hurry to the computer, my hands shaking as I put in orders. That infant is septic. There's a bad infection brewing somewhere in that tiny body. It could be in his blood or his urine. Maybe in his lungs. Or it might be meningitis. We have to figure it out, and every second matters.

I finish entering the orders and crutch back to the room. I find Doctor Kent examining the baby. The mother is crying, and the father is trying to console her. Hadi has already put the infant on oxygen and the cardiac monitor, and he is working on placing an

IV in the baby's little arm. The infant barely lets out a cry when the needle pierces through his skin.

I take in the scene in a second. I drop my crutches, sit in a chair beside the stretcher, and start setting up to perform a lumbar puncture.

Doctor Kent reads my thoughts. "You ready to go?"

"Yes."

Doctor Kent addresses the parents. "We're going to do the spinal tap that I was explaining to you."

"Okay." The mother wipes tears from her face.

"First IV is in," Hadi announces.

"I've already put in fluid and antibiotic orders," I inform him while putting on a pair of sterile gloves.

"Great. I'll go get everything." Hadi moves to exit the room. "You guys good in here for a moment?"

Doctor Kent glances my way. "We're good."

I slide right up to the bedside. My heart continues to pound, yet I also feel oddly calm and focused. Somehow, though my mind is racing, my thoughts are clear. It's like there is nothing else in the department except for this infant and me.

With Doctor Kent positioning the limp baby on his side, I palpate the bones in the infant's back, finding my landmarks. I clean the skin and put in the spinal needle. Cerebral spinal fluid soon starts dripping out, which I collect in the tubes that I have positioned to catch it in. But the liquid isn't clear like it should be. It's cloudy. I peer over at Doctor Kent, who returns my worried gaze. He then speaks to the parents.

"From the way that this fluid appears, it suggests that there is an infection surrounding your son's spinal cord and brain." Doctor Kent's tone is kind, measured, and firm. "We'll be starting antibiotics, and we need to admit your son to the pediatric intensive care unit. I know a lot is happening fast, but time is essential. The faster we move, the better chance your son has."

The mother rests her head against the young man's chest and continues to sob softly.

"I'll get these sent off to the lab," I tell Doctor Kent, gathering up the tubes with the collected fluid inside.

"And please have the secretary notify the pediatric intensivist," Doctor Kent asks me.

Hadi arrives with the antibiotics before I have even left the room. As I step out, a tech takes the tubes from my hands and scurries off to deliver them to the lab. I go as fast as I'm able to the secretary's desk.

"Room Fourteen needs the pediatric ICU," I tell her. "Could you please get the pediatric intensivist on the phone?"

As the secretary starts dialing, I sit down at the attending's desk to wait. Seconds seem to take hours before the secretary's phone rings. She answers, and I hear her talking quickly to someone on the other end. After she hangs up, she says to me:

"The pediatric intensivist is on the way. They're getting a bed ready in the PICU."

"Thanks."

I get to my feet. The movement causes another awful pain in my ribs, worse than the last, but I ignore it and beeline for Room Fourteen. As I approach, the curtain is pushed away. Doctor Kent and Hadi already have the baby on the portable monitor, ready to transport.

"They're working on the PICU bed," I report. "And the intensivist is on the way."

Hadi motions over my shoulder. "She's already here."

Following where he points, I spot a short, kind-appearing woman heading for us. She's got light-colored hair, and she's wearing scrubs and a long white coat. Accompanying her are two people who, based on the teddy bear and space ship patterns on their scrubs, I am guessing are PICU nurses.

"Hi, Wes," the intensivist says, already focused on the infant on the stretcher.

Doctor Kent pushes the stretcher from the room. "Hi, Caroline. Three-week-old male. Born at thirty-seven weeks. Uneventful pregnancy and delivery. Fever since last night. Two lines are in. IV fluid is running. Labs, including culture, and urine are sent. Cloudy CSF. Antibiotics going."

"You already got the LP? Nice work."

Doctor Kent motions my way. "Thank Savannah, our medical student. It was all her."

The intensivist gives me an appreciative smile. Then she gestures to the PICU nurses, who take control of the stretcher and drive it away, while she steps over to the parents and speaks with them. Soon, the intensivist and the parents start to follow the baby's stretcher down the hall.

"Thank you," the mother whispers to me before hurrying away.

The group turns a corner and disappears from view. A moment passes. Then, like a fog lifting, I again become aware of everything else around me. I hear noise. I see the other patients. And I am acutely aware of how badly my head, ribs, and ankle are hurting.

I make my way to the attending's desk and drop into a chair. The fog continues fading, and I am hit by a flood of intense emotion. That was a baby. A tiny, innocent baby. Will he make it? Did we do everything that we could for him? How will his young parents cope?

I realize that someone has sat down beside me.

"Do you know what you just did?" I hear Doctor Kent ask.

I look at him, and my entire body goes cold. I must have screwed up somehow. That baby might die because of me. I may—

"You ran that resuscitation as well as, or better than, any resident in this hospital would have." Doctor Kent says. "Most physicians—even experienced ones—would have understandably panicked around a sick newborn. You didn't."

I take some deep breaths, and my eyes drift over to Room Fourteen. "This sounds stupid, but I was so focused that I almost didn't realize what I was doing while it was happening. It was like I had an invisible shield around me, blocking out distraction and not letting my emotions affect me. Only after the baby was gone did I start feeling it all."

When Doctor Kent does not reply, I blush and sheepishly turn to him again.

His expression has not changed. "Welcome to emergency medicine," he tells me.

I gaze at him. Somehow I think that I understand it all a little better now.

"Doctor Kent?" Cassie comes toward the desk, causing us to both look up. "There's a new patient who needs a post-op eval, so I've paged the on-call trauma surgery resident. Also, Mr. Alberts is wondering when he'll be discharged. He's still hoping to catch his flight."

"Mr. Alberts?" Doctor Kent glances at me inquisitively.

Puzzled, I reply, "I discharged Mr. Alberts a while ago."

Doctor Kent scans the patient tracking board. "So how come he's still listed as being in Room One?"

"Room One?" I echo faintly. "Mr. Alberts was in Room One?"

Doctor Kent pauses. "Yes. Gregory Alberts. Room One."

"Not . . . not Room Nine?"

He replies with deliberateness. "Mr. Gregory Alberts. Sixty-three-years-old. African-American male. Room One."

"Whoops," I say before I can stop myself.

Doctor Kent raises an eyebrow. "Whoops?"

"I discharged a young Caucasian male from Room Nine."

Doctor Kent surveys the board again. "I wasn't even aware that we had a patient in Room Nine."

"I was wondering what happened to him!" Cassie chimes in. "Henry Anders. Really weird guy. When he arrived, he refused to tell me what his visit was for, other than it was something about his head. A few minutes later, I saw him walking out, and I figured that he had decided to leave."

Doctor Kent ruffles his hair. "Let me get this straight, Savannah. You walked into Room Nine, addressed a patient by the wrong name, discussed a diagnosis that he didn't have, and gave him a prescription for antibiotics he didn't need?"

I gulp. "Pretty much."

"And he willingly accepted the discharge instructions and left without bothering to ask why he hadn't been examined or why he was being treated for an ear infection?"

"I even wished him a good flight," I add miserably, hanging my head. I shouldn't have come today. What was I thinking? I'm not well enough to be doing this. Doctor Kent might get sued because of me!

"That has got to be one of the best stories I've ever heard," I hear Doctor Kent say.

I raise my eyes. Doctor Kent is laughing silently.

"I'll go let the real Mr. Alberts get out of here," he adds. "Cassie, would mind calling Henry Anders?"

"You got it," she replies brightly and heads off toward a phone.

Doctor Kent smiles again before he steps away. After a few seconds, I realize that I'm smiling too.

Harmonica music reaches my ears. Mouthwash Man is still going strong, which reminds me that his lab results might be available. So I reach over to Doctor Kent's computer and grab the mouse. The screensaver clears, revealing an email that Doctor Kent left open. It's from someone named Monica.

I'm sorry to have ended our phone call like that. I understand how you feel, but I think we need to talk about this in person. I am going to—

"Alright, Savannah, the real Mr. Alberts is now out the door and on the way to the airport."

The sound of Doctor Kent's voice nearly causes me to fall off my chair. I lunge for the computer mouse, trying to minimize the email before he can see that I'm reading it. He gets to my side just as I click the email off the screen. He stops. I freeze. I don't know if he saw what I was reading or not.

"I was gonna review the labs for the mouthwash guy," I practically whisper, opening up the information. "It, um, looks like he can be discharged. I'll go do that right now."

I leap up to get away, but a shock of pain bursts from my ribs, which is followed by crippling nausea. I drop my crutches and reach out to the desk to support myself. I start seeing stars. I can't breathe.

Doctor Kent is at my side, bracing me. "Okay, you're done for the day."

"No. I just need a second," I pant. "I'll be alright."

"I said you're done," he orders unemotionally. "You're not going to wear yourself out on my watch."

I don't reply. I can't. He actually appears angry.

"Everything alright?" someone interrupts.

I raise my head and see Erik coming our way.

"I came down to consult on a post-op patient." Erik focuses on me. "Hey, Savannah. Sorry I never contacted you to see how you were doing after discharge."

Doctor Kent frowns.

"No worries." I attempt to stand up straight. "I know you're busy."

"Savannah, sit down. I'll discharge your patient." Doctor Kent guides me into a chair, takes the discharge paperwork, and walks off.

Erik lowers his voice. "So Kent twisted your arm into working already, huh? What a jerk."

"No. He told me to stay home. I came on my own."

"You came when you didn't have to?" Erik scoffs. "Why'd you do that?"

"Because I . . ." I let myself fall quiet, not sure what I mean to say.

Erik suddenly seems to remember something. "By the way, I heard about the invitation that Rick Gatz extended to you to speak in a couple of weeks. Congratulations."

"You heard about that?" I glance around to make sure that Doctor Kent isn't within earshot. "How'd you find out?"

Erik appears surprised. "They announced the schedule for the event at our morning didactics yesterday."

I stare up at him, totally bewildered. "They did?"

His pager goes off.

"Guess I've gotta go," Erik remarks after reading his message. He moves to leave but stops again. "Hey, a bunch of us are going out on Friday. Do you want to come? You can invite other friends, if you'd like."

I nod. "I'd like that."

"Alright. I'll shoot you an email with the details." Erik gives me a slight wave and then heads away.

Before I have a chance to process what just happened, the curtain of Room Three is pulled aside and Doctor Kent emerges. Behind him, I can see our social worker talking to Mouthwash Guy. I keep my eyes trained on the desk as Doctor Kent makes his way to my side.

"I appreciate you coming today, Savannah, but it was too much too soon," he states. "You're not allowed to work anymore this week."

My mouth drops open.

"Room Eleven is vacant," he continues in monotone. "I want you to rest in there until Danielle is done with her shift and can help you home."

I get to my feet. Doctor Kent puts a hand on my arm. Too worn out to protest, I let him guide me to the Room Eleven, where I crawl onto the stretcher and set my head down on the pillow. And I realize that I am utterly exhausted.

"I'll be back in a few minutes to see how you're doing," Doctor Kent informs me before stepping out and closing the curtain behind him.

Chapter Eight

"How do I look?"

Danielle somberly studies me before breaking into a grin. "You look exactly the same as you did when you asked me ten minutes ago."

I laugh. "Sorry. I suppose I was hoping that you'd say these stupid crutches had become invisible or something."

"Are you kidding me? The crutches aren't going to matter, Sav. You look even more gorgeous than usual." After a moment, her smile falls. "But I wish your loveliness wasn't going to be wasted on Erik Prescott. Too bad Doctor Kent can't see you tonight. He'd lose his mind."

Ignoring her, I check my reflection again in the side mirror of a car that is parked along the curb. After wearing scrubs almost every day for the past year, getting dressed up feels kind of foreign to me now. Lately, I've been considering it an accomplishment if I style my hair into anything more than a ponytail; it's a bonus if I remember makeup.

But this evening is different. This evening, I'm kind of meeting up with Erik for a kind of date. Well, it's more like a group thing, but still. So after much deliberation, digging through my closet, and consulting Danielle, I chose to wear a fitted red top and black pants. I styled my hair in loose curls. And in addition to mascara, I even applied eyeliner, eye shadow, and lip gloss.

Unfortunately, I think the crutches are killing the whole look.

"So do you ever plan on actually going inside the restaurant, Sav?" Joel inquires playfully. "Personally, I'd rather stay out here all night and stare through the windows, trying to freak out Doctor Bench Press Prescott."

Danielle snickers, and I blush. For several minutes now, the three of us have been congregated on the sidewalk outside of The Blue Room, one of the most popular restaurants in town, while I've been trying to get brave enough to enter the building.

Admittedly, I didn't think tonight was actually going to happen. After Erik spoke to me in Fast Track about going out, I never got an email from him. I figured that he had forgotten. I attempted explaining to Danielle that Erik's oversight was understandable—he is a busy intern, after all—but she wouldn't let him off the hook. And this morning, when Danielle caught me checking my email for the one millionth time, she finally went on a tirade about how you can't trust orthopedists and Doctor Kent never would have forgotten to contact me. She concluded by declaring that we were going to have a girls' night in, bingeing on ice cream and watching rom-coms.

But about two hours ago, Erik actually sent me an email about where he and other residents were going for dinner. Danielle practically hurled herself in front of my computer and demanded that I tell Erik I had other plans. But I calmly pointed out how hypocritical it was for her to insist that I refuse Erik's invite when she is always accusing me of avoiding romance. She had no rebuttal and finally agreed to accompany me.

I adjust my crutches one more time. "Sorry, you guys. I'm ready."

Joel lets out a feigned groan of disappointment before opening the restaurant door. I trail Danielle inside. I've only been here once before, and it's even cooler than I remember. The decor is very modern and minimalist with dim, white-and-blue lighting. I hear jazz music playing, and the song's smooth beat is mixing with the sounds of conversations and softly clanking glasses.

"I see Erik," Danielle whispers unenthusiastically.

My immediate impulse is to run from the building, but I remind myself that I am on crutches and should probably stay put.

"Over there," Danielle adds with a discreet tip of her head.

I peek toward the far side of the restaurant. Seated with his back to us, Erik is at a table with several people whom I recognize as other surgery residents.

Joel leans toward me. "Yikes, Sav, who's the girl giving you the death glare?"

My eyes shift farther down the table. Brittany is beside Erik and staring directly at me. And she doesn't exactly radiate happiness.

"Let me guess, that's the super model you were talking about?" Danielle inquires under her breath.

I pretend to read a message on my busted cell phone. "Yep. Brittany. General surgery intern."

"Got it." Danielle stands up at straight. "Let's go."

Danielle confidently starts toward the group. Joel follows close behind. I put my phone into my purse and go after them, weaving awkwardly on my crutches around the tables and chairs that are in the way. Brittany's glare evolves into a smirk as she observes my clumsiness. Erik turns around and also watches me approach. He gives me an approving once-over, chuckling politely when I stumble yet again.

"Hey, Savannah," he says once I get to his side. "Glad you could make it."

"Hi," I tell him. I try to position my crutches as inconspicuously as possible and motion to the others. "Everyone, this is my best friend, Danielle, who will be applying to OBGYN. And this is her boyfriend, Joel, who—"

"Hates the sight of blood and works with computers," Joel finishes for me.

There is a spattering of laughter from the group.

"So you're Savannah?" a guy at the table calls out. "I heard Gatz invited you to speak next month. Congratulations."

I peer at him in surprise. Why on earth does a random surgery resident know that Rick Gatz invited me to speak at some little reception?

"Yeah, congrats," another resident chimes in. "That's pretty cool."

Now I'm totally bewildered. "Gee, thanks."

Erik observes me admiringly again before suggesting to the group, "Well, since we've done introductions, how about ordering dinner?"

As everyone voices their agreement, Erik motions to the empty chair on the other side of him. My stomach does a little dance of excitement as I maneuver into the seat and stash my crutches away. I take a deep breath, soaking in the moment. I am now officially seated beside Erik Prescott. At a restaurant. On an almost date.

Joel and Danielle go to the other side of the table and take the chairs opposite Erik and me. I give them an excited look. Danielle curls her lip slightly, which means she's not impressed with Erik in the slightest. Meanwhile, Joel makes a few tiny movements with his arm like he's doing a bicep curl. Even I have to drop my head so no one sees me stifling a laugh.

"So what are you going to get to eat?" Erik leans toward me.

Wow. I think I could sit here and smell his cologne all ni—

A sharp kick against my leg underneath the table snaps me to attention. It's Danielle. She gestures subtly to the menu.

"Oh!" I start scanning the list of entrees in front of me. "I don't know. Let me see."

As I read the descriptions of the overpriced dinner options, my stomach growls. I'm starving. A hamburger sounds delicious. And maybe a—

"Hey, Savannah?" Brittany unexpectedly pipes up in a sing-song way. "I want to ask you something."

I shift so I can see her better, every ounce of me on high alert. But she gives me a charming smile, and I can't help wondering if I've possibly misjudged her.

"How is your speech coming along?" Brittany's question drips with sweetness.

"My speech?"

"Yes, your speech. For the event next month," Brittany articulates slowly.

The other conversations at the table die away as the rest of the group starts listening in.

I take a sip of my water. "Oh, my *speech*. I haven't quite got it prepared yet."

"You haven't? Why not?" Brittany raises her voice, ensuring that the whole table—and probably the entire restaurant—can hear her. "You *are* going to speak, aren't you?"

Every eye is on me.

"Of course Savannah is going to speak," Erik answers on my behalf, as though it's the dumbest question he has ever heard. "It's like a med student golden ticket to be a keynote speaker at something like that." He gives me a little nudge. "Right?"

I play with the straw in my water glass. "Right. Golden ticket."

"Hmm. That's odd." Brittany tips her head innocently. "This morning, I happened to notice that the surgery coordinator still has you listed as unconfirmed to participate."

Brittany pauses so her words take full effect. Erik fixes a quizzical look upon me. Danielle starts chewing her lip the way that she always does when she's distressed.

"You're not going to do it?" Erik's tone has a hint of disapproval.

I glance around, my mind working fast. "I just haven't heard from Mr. Gatz yet. He was going to call after I got out of the hospital so we could discuss it further. That's all."

Erik nods, appearing convinced. I breathe out in relief. Bullet dodged.

I attempt to change the subject. "So, Erik, how about that patient you saw—"

He cuts me off, "Hey, I'll see Gatz on Monday morning. I'll tell him that you're planning to do it."

I hesitate. I can't admit to Erik that I'm actually undecided about speaking. Part of me has been hoping that Mr. Gatz really did forget, since it would make the choice for me. But if I'm still desired as a speaker, should I accept the invitation? I definitely don't want to participate, but I would be an idiot to pass on this chance to enhance my residency application. Refusing would be insane. But with old ladies being treated in the ED walkways, how can I not refuse?

I need more time to sort this out.

"Thanks," I tell Erik. "Don't worry, though. I'll reach out to Mr. Gatz myself."

"But Erik will see Gatz first thing on Monday." Brittany narrows her eyes. "Why not have him get you on the speaking schedule?"

"Yeah, I can take care of it," Erik insists.

Everyone is waiting for me to answer.

I give Erik a forced smile. "Alright. If you're sure that you don't mind, it'd be great if you told Mr. Gatz for me. Thanks."

"No problem." Erik proudly takes my hand.

There is a distinct pause before everyone at the table resumes what they were doing. I glance down at Erik's hand resting lightly upon mine. I know I should be ecstatic right now, but I feel sick. I agreed to support the hospital administration even though I totally oppose what they're doing. I'm a sellout. A traitor. What am I going to tell Doctor—

"Hey, check out who's here tonight," an intern pipes up, motioning behind me. "It's Doctor Kent from the ER."

I freeze, and my heart seems to leap into my throat.

Danielle's eyes are getting wide as she stares over my shoulder. She makes a slight-but-insistent gesture with her hand. Very slowly, I turn around.

Doctor Kent is entering through the main doors on the opposite side of the restaurant. He's dressed in a dark sports coat, a button up shirt, and slacks. His hair is combed, and his facial scruff is gone. And he is wearing a pair of rimless glasses.

I. Can't. Move.

Suddenly, Doctor Kent looks over, and he does a double take when our eyes meet. My body jolts in alarm, and I whip around so I'm facing away from him again.

"Maybe we should ask Kent to join us," Erik suggests to the group with over-the-top sarcasm.

Everyone at the table except for Joel, Danielle, and myself begin laughing. Erik lets go of my hand. I had forgotten that he was holding it.

As the laughter dies away, Danielle peers at the others in confusion. "Why don't you guys like Doctor Kent?"

"You mean, why don't we like the attending who makes us waste time trying to resuscitate a dead patient?" Brittany replies.

"Or who demands a STAT consultation for a pediatric patient because she had a ruptured appendix?" an intern adds.

Joel interjects casually, "I'm obviously no doctor, but isn't a ruptured appendix dangerous? I think I'd want my kid taken to the OR as fast as possible for something like that."

The intern has no chance to reply before another resident—a gal with a sleek bob cut— chimes in.

"Well, I don't care what the rest of you think, I wouldn't mind if Doctor Kent joined us. He's *gorgeous*. I've had a crush on him since I was an intern." She takes another big sip of her drink. "Is being attracted to an attending bad?"

I feel an unexplainable surge of alarm.

A resident sitting farther down the table answers excitedly. "Yeah. There's even a written hospital policy about it. We looked it up one time when we were bored while on-call. An attending could even get fired for becoming involved with a student or a resident. It's completely taboo."

The girl with the bob cut finishes her drink off. "Well, I've only got two years of residency left. I'm sure Doctor Kent will wait for me."

"I hate to burst your bubble," another intern tells the girl with the bob cut, "but it doesn't look like Doctor Kent is waiting for anyone."

Once more Danielle glances past me. Her eyes narrow, and she jerks her head, telling me to take another look. Though I'm growing leery, I obey.

Doctor Kent is still on the far side of the restaurant, and now he's talking with someone who is standing quite close to him—someone who happens to be a slim, tan woman with perfect curls in her bleached hair. She's wearing a short black dress and strappy shoes. And she is gazing up at Doctor Kent while wrapping her arm around his. It takes me about one split-second to recognize her: the woman from the photo on Doctor Kent's desk.

Doctor Kent is out on a date with his perfect D.C. girlfriend.

I face forward again, avoiding Danielle's questioning gaze and trying to squelch the troublesome ache that is rising inside of me. After all, I knew that Doctor Kent had a girlfriend. And it's not like I care, anyway. He's just my attending.

"Whoa, Doctor Kent's date is hot," a guy at our table remarks.

"That should be me." The gal with the bob cut emphatically starts downing a new drink.

The conversation is interrupted when the waiter approaches and begins taking orders. When it's my turn, I can't bring myself to order anything. My appetite is gone.

Erik nudges me. "So where are you planning on applying for residency? You said that you're probably going into pediatrics, right?"

"What do you mean, *probably*?" Danielle cuts in, apparently not worried about revealing that she's eavesdropping. "Sav has always been planning on going into pediatrics. Right, Sav?"

I squirm. "I think so."

Danielle's mouth falls open slightly.

"You haven't decided what specialty you want to go into?" Brittany doesn't hide the patronizing edge to her voice. "You're in your fourth year of medical school, and you're still not sure?"

Danielle glances between Brittany and me, and then she quickly stands up. "Sav, I'm going to the restroom. Wanna come?"

"Sure," I reply gratefully.

Using my good arm, I push away from the table and reach for my crutches. Danielle comes over and helps me get to my feet. Then we dash for the bathroom like we're racing for the safety of an embassy or something, dodging the maze of waiters, chairs, and tables that are in the way. Once we're inside the bathroom and the door swings shut behind us, Danielle spins around and stares at me.

"Okay, Sav, fess up. What's going on with you?"

"Well, my ankle is aching, Erik wears great cologne, I—"

"Stop it. I mean about the whole pediatrics thing."

"There's nothing going on."

She puts her hands on her hips. "You aren't sure about doing peds anymore, are you?"

"I'm sure. I think."

She allows a moment to pass. "I've always thought that you'd be great at emergency medicine. Have you ever considered that?"

I make myself busy examining my makeup in the mirror. The truth is, maybe I have started to think about what it would be like to go into emergency medicine. This admission stuns me. A couple of weeks ago, the idea would have seemed ludicrous. But now? Not so much.

Danielle waits a while before changing the topic. "By the way, I think Brittany is about to explode with jealousy because Erik's hitting on you."

I pull my focus from the mirror. "Do you think Erik likes me?"

"Well, he's definitely hitting on you tonight."

"He even held my hand."

"Yeah, and it was right when Doctor Kent was looking at you," she growls. "Now Doctor Kent is going to think that—"

"Danielle, it doesn't matter what Doctor Kent saw or what he thinks!" I interrupt, unable to keep my emotions at bay any longer. I take a deep breath and look away from her. What in the world am I getting so upset over?

Danielle's tone softens. "You knew about his girlfriend, didn't you?"

I nod. "When I was in his office, I saw a picture in a frame on his desk. And I accidentally broke it."

"What? You broke a frame that was holding a picture of his girlfriend?"

"Yeah."

"Ha!" Danielle exclaims triumphantly. "That's, like, a sign or something! Doctor Kent is supposed to be with you, not with that woman he's out there with right now!"

I'm about to reply when a toilet flushes, which is followed by a stall door being opened. Doctor Kent's girlfriend steps out.

This is bad. This is extremely bad.

The girlfriend's perfectly done-up eyes track between Danielle and me. Then she walks toward the sink, the clicking of her shoes on the tile floor echoing like gunfire through the silence. Danielle promptly charges for cover inside another stall, slamming the door shut behind her. Before I can do the same, the girlfriend reaches the sink and starts washing her hands, blocking my path and studying me in the mirror.

"Um, Danielle?" I call out, my mouth extremely dry, "I'll meet you at the table."

Without waiting for a reply, I hobble for the exit. As I burst out of the bathroom, I run into a guy who's standing near the door. I lose hold of my crutches and tumble forward. The guy reaches out and grabs me by the arm so I don't fall, but he drops the glass that he was holding, which shatters loudly on the floor. A woman at a nearby table shrieks in surprise. The restaurant goes silent as everyone looks over.

"Thanks," I mumble, keeping my eyes on the mess of broken glass at my feet. "Sorry about your drink. I'll buy you another one."

"Don't worry. It wasn't for me, anyway."

I know that voice.

With a stuttering breath, I lift my head and meet Doctor Kent's gaze. There's a pause before he lets go of my arm, bends over, and picks up my crutches.

"Are these the latest fashion accessory?" He grins while holding the crutches out to me. "They go well with your outfit."

I take the crutches from him but don't smile back.

Doctor Kent's grin fades. "It's nice to see that you're feeling better."

"Thanks."

A restaurant employee has begun scurrying around us, sweeping up the broken glass. Doctor Kent steps closer to me, giving the employee room to work, and adds:

"Between picture frames and drinking glasses, Savannah, I've decided that I should keep all fragile objects out of your reach."

I realize that I'm breaking into the tiniest of smiles.

"Wes?" asks a woman behind me.

I stiffen as Doctor Kent's girlfriend saunters up to his side with her long, tan legs shining in the ambient light.

She views me without betraying a hint of recognition. "Who's this?"

Doctor Kent motions from his girlfriend to me. "Monica, this is Savannah Drake. She's a fourth-year medical student who is currently doing her emergency medicine rotation with us. Savannah, this is Monica Winthrop."

Monica holds out a manicured hand and flashes dazzlingly white teeth. "It's nice to meet you, Savannah."

I shift on my crutches, freeing up my good hand to shake hers in return. She barely touches my fingers.

"Nice to meet you too," I tell her, my voice cracking.

Monica faces Doctor Kent again and gives him a pouty face. "I thought you were getting me a drink. What happened?"

"I ran into Savannah," Doctor Kent replies, dead-pan.

I seize the opportunity to make my escape. "Yes, and I'll let you two carry on. Have a nice night."

Doctor Kent steps aside to make room for me to pass, and his dark eyes scan the route back to Erik's table. "Monica, excuse me for a moment. I'll help Savannah through this obstacle course and then rejoin you."

She strokes his arm. "Alright. Don't take long."

Monica sashays toward the bar. Doctor Kent goes the other way, walking toward Erik's table while moving chairs and politely asking people to slide aside. I head after him, maneuvering easily, despite my crutches, thanks to the path that Doctor Kent has created. Up ahead, I see Erik and the other residents going quiet one-by-one as they notice us approaching. Doctor Kent reaches the table, pulls out my chair, and waits. I give him a thankful glance as I sit down.

"Good evening, everyone." Doctor Kent takes my crutches and places them under the table.

There is a round of half-hearted greetings. The resident with the bob cut opens her mouth to say something, but an intern nudges her in the side.

In my peripheral vision, I see Danielle hurrying over from the bathroom. Her eyes are about to spring out of her head. Thankfully, she manages to compose herself before reaching the table.

"Well, hello, Doctor Kent." She takes her seat beside Joel. "It is *extremely* nice to see you tonight."

"And it's nice to see you." Doctor Kent then surveys the rest of the table, pausing for an extra moment on Erik. "Have a good evening, everyone."

Doctor Kent gives me another casual smile and then starts to walk away. But Brittany clears her throat and calls after him:

"Doctor Kent, congratulations. You must be proud of Savannah."

He stops and faces her, his expression revealing nothing. "I am. She's doing well on the rotation."

"I was referring to her upcoming speaking engagement," Brittany clarifies. "As her attending, you must be proud."

Doctor Kent's eyebrows rise with surprise, and my stomach drops through the floor.

"Oh, hey!" Danielle points exuberantly at the approaching waiter, clearly attempting to create a distraction. "Here comes our food!"

But Doctor Kent doesn't get sidetracked. "I didn't hear about her speaking engagement, actually," he tells Brittany. He shifts his attention my way, appearing genuinely curious. "Whatever it is, Savannah, congrats."

"She didn't tell you about it?" Brittany exaggerates her surprise. "You didn't hear that Savannah has agreed to speak at—"

"Wes? Our food is going to get cold."

Monica has come to Doctor Kent's side. She puts her arm securely around his waist, and studies everyone at the table. She stops when she spots Danielle, who drops her head and acts like she is scraping something off her dinner fork.

Doctor Kent glances at Monica, and then he says to all of us, "Have a good night, everyone."

I lower my eyes, unable to bring myself to watch Doctor Kent leading Monica away. As I swirl the straw in my water glass, I hear the resident with the bob cut sigh loudly and say:

"Doctor Kent is *so* hot."

Chapter Nine

It's eleven o'clock at night, but no one would be able to tell. The emergency department is as brightly lit and chaotic as it is during the daytime. Maybe even more so.

The week has finally passed, which means that I'm no longer banned by Doctor Kent from coming to work. So I've just arrived for my first overnight shift of the rotation. To be honest, I'm harboring a weird mixture of anticipation and nerves about it. If the rumors are true, patients with the strangest problems (and stories) always show up to the ED in the middle of the night. As I step farther inside the department, though, my uncertainty evolves into a comforting, familiar excitement mixed with contentment. Somehow, the havoc in here makes me calm.

"Hey, Sav! You're on overnights now?"

I spin around and see Hadi giving me a salute.

"Yep!" I smile while pulling my hair up into a tight bun. "You?"

"Uh-huh." He glances around. "Have you seen Wes yet?"

I clear my throat. "No."

"That's weird. He's never late for a shift."

"Mm-hmm."

I start setting my things on the desk where Doctor Kent and I will be stationed, trying to focus on the work at hand. Soon, though, I hear Hadi chuckle and say:

"Ah, there he is. I think we have our reason for the delay."

In spite of myself, I quickly raise my head. Doctor Kent is coming into the ED, dressed in scrubs and carrying his bag over one shoulder. And tonight he has an extra accessory: Monica. She is walking beside him with a determined gleam in her eye and deliberateness in her steps. Even though it's practically the middle of the night, she has her hair curled, and she's wearing a stylish top, jacket, and skinny jeans. Oh, and super cute boots.

I'm suddenly aware that I only took about ten minutes to get ready for this shift.

"Hi, guys," Doctor Kent greets us as he and Monica reach the desk.

Hadi smiles. "Hey, Wes."

"Hi," I chime in quietly.

Doctor Kent sets his bag under the desk. "Monica, this is Hadi, one of our best nurses."

"Hello, Hadi," Monica says charmingly.

Hadi reaches out and shakes her hand. "Nice to finally meet you."

"Likewise," she replies.

Doctor Kent motions from Monica to me. "And I'm sure you remember meeting Savannah. She was at the restaurant last Friday night."

Monica turns. "Yes. I remember."

"Good to see you again," I manage to tell her.

She doesn't reply.

"So, Wes," Hadi pipes up jokingly, "you dragged poor Monica to the ED tonight, eh? What kind of a boyfriend are you, anyway?"

Monica lets out a polite laugh. "Actually, I asked to come."

"Really?" Hadi faces her again. "Are you in the medical profession?"

Monica scoffs. "Me? Absolutely not. I wouldn't have the tolerance for this. I mean, some of these patients! How do you put up with them?" She tosses her hair, which somehow lands perfectly atop her shoulders once more. "I work in D.C. as a business advisor."

Hadi nods. "That's cool."

"But I've always wanted to see what Wes actually does around here," Monica adds. She sits down on the chair where I just hung my white coat and eyes me. "Oh, I'm sorry, was this where you were going to sit?"

"No worries." I peel my coat off the back of the chair. "I can work somewhere else. You stay by Doctor Kent."

Balancing on my crutches, I re-gather my things. Hadi steps in to help and then walks alongside me to an empty workstation on the other side of the department.

"Whenever you're ready, a new patient has arrived." Hadi sets my belongings down on the desk. He lowers his voice. "Forty-nine-year-old woman who got beat up by her jerk of a husband."

I throw on my short white coat and put my stethoscope around my neck. "Show me where," I tell him, ready to get to work.

Hadi hands me the new patient's chart and gestures toward the exam room where the patient is waiting. I head to the room, announce that I'm outside, and then step around the curtain. As my eyes fall on the patient, I barely stop myself from gasping aloud. I was not ready for this.

The woman who is seated on the stretcher has injuries everywhere. Her face is swollen and bruised. There is blood oozing from her nose. Her lower lip is gashed, and dried blood is pooled at the corners of her mouth. Contusions and what I am guessing are choke marks color her neck. She is hunched forward, cradling her right wrist. Abrasions, burn marks, and shallow lacerations cover her legs.

"Hi." I struggle to keep my voice steady and take a chair. "My name is Savannah Drake. I'm the fourth-year medical student who will be caring for you tonight."

"Hi, Savannah." She is obviously holding back tears as she attempts to smile. "I'm Amy Nichols. Apparently, you and I are in a race for who's the most injured, huh?"

I laugh gently and set my crutches on the floor. "What happened, Amy?"

"My husband got angry again." Her voice trembles as her expression grows distant.

I wait for her to go on.

"Today is our anniversary," she continues after a while. "Pathetic, isn't it?"

"He's pathetic, yes."

She drops her head. "This happens every year. Last time, he locked me up in the house for three days. He said he'd never do it again, and today things seemed fine. I thought we were going to have a good day. But this evening, he smashed my phone. He said that he would kill me if I tried to get out or scream for help. That's when the beating started."

An icy, sickening sensation is growing in the pit of my stomach. I hand her a tissue from the box that's on the counter beside me. "You're safe here, Amy."

She wipes her nose. "Thanks."

"May I ask how you got help?"

She sits up and actually laughs a little. "He got too drunk to keep going. So when I had my chance, I crawled out the kitchen door and went to our neighbors' house. They called 911. The ambulance brought me here."

I let a few moments pass. "Do you have any family or close friends who can come be with you?"

"I have a son who's in college. He's on his way over tonight to stay with me."

"Will you be safe in your home? Where's your husband?"

Tears start falling down her cheeks. "The police arrested him. They said he wouldn't be getting out any time soon."

"I'm glad you'll be safe." I stand up and put a hand on her shoulder. "Amy, I'd like to do an exam. It already appears as though we're going to have to get some imaging. Once we figure out the extent of what we're dealing with, we'll take care of your injuries, let you talk with our social worker, and hopefully get you home tonight, okay?"

"Okay. Thank you."

I move to the bedside and begin my exam. Although I somehow manage not to show it, I am becoming more and more horrified by every scratch, burn, cut, and bruise that I find on her body.

"Alright, Amy," I say once I finish. My throat is dry, and my is skin crawling. "I'll go put in the orders and ask our social worker, Dwayne, to come chat with you. Are you going to be alright for a few minutes while I get your workup started?"

"I will. Thank you."

I push the curtain out of my way and leave the room without betraying my emotions. But as soon as the curtain closes behind me, I collapse with my crutches against the wall and shut my eyes. I shudder from the chill that rolls down my spine.

"Savannah, are you okay? Savannah, look at me."

Startled, I open my eyes. Doctor Kent is coming my way, and he looks concerned. I see a movement in his arm like he's about to reach out to me.

"I'm alright." I quickly stand up straight and take a deep breath. I motion toward Amy's room. "Sorry. I know it shouldn't bother me, but I haven't treated someone who . . . who has been abused before."

He halts. "Do you think that seeing a patient like her shouldn't bother you?"

I wasn't expecting that. "Well, I'm training to become a doctor. I can't let that kind of stuff rattle me."

"Yes, you're training to become a doctor, but you're also a human being, Savannah." He glances at Amy's room. "Seeing something like that—whether for the first time or the thousandth time—*should* bother you. If the day ever comes when taking care of patients who are hurt, sick, or otherwise in pain doesn't affect me anymore, that's the day I'll find a new line of work."

I meet his gaze, and there is a moment of quiet between us.

"Wes!"

We both turn and see Monica heading our way.

"Wes, have you seen that drunk guy in the walkway?" As she looks between us, a playful smile arises on her lips, but it does not reach her eyes.

Doctor Kent steps back from me and scratches his head. "Which drunk walkway patient would you be referring to?"

Monica's giggle is forced. "The *super* drunk one. You would not *be-lieve* some of the things he's saying."

"You'd be surprised. I've heard quite a lot in my time," Doctor Kent points out humorously.

"Maybe, but this is over the top! Come on! Come and listen to him!" She takes Doctor Kent by the hand and tugs him away.

I watch them go, doing my best to ignore the ache that is growing in my chest. I then move to my desk and start putting orders into the computer for Amy Nichols. Above the ambient noise, I'm pretty sure that I can still hear Monica laughing. It's like nails on a chalkboard.

"Code Blue, ETA five minutes," comes an overhead announcement. "Code Blue, ETA five minutes."

My pulse spikes. EMS is bringing in a patient in cardiac arrest. I spring up from my chair and crutch toward the resuscitation bay as fast as I can, all other emotions left behind as adrenaline starts coursing through me. Up ahead, I see that Doctor Kent is already waiting. When he spots me, he continues inside. I follow. While everyone begins setting up, the charge nurse comes in to give the report.

"Eighty-six-year-old male found unresponsive. Last seen three hours ago when he went to bed. Asystolic in the field. Resuscitation has been ongoing for thirty minutes. Patient is intubated. Two large-bore IVs are in place."

From where he's standing at the head of the stretcher, Doctor Kent asks me, "Do you want to run this one?"

My eyes get huge. "Me?"

"Yes, you, Savannah Drake."

143

I should remind him that I'm only a med student. I should plead not to be given such a frightening amount of responsibility. But that sense of focused calmness is now settling over me, and so I nod.

Doctor Kent goes on, "Alright, so what are you going to have the team do when the patient arrives?"

"Continue chest compressions," I say. "Confirm airway. Get him on the monitor. Confirm rhythm. Epinephrine. IV fluid. Bedside ultrasound. Labs—"

"Do you actually think you'll save this guy's life?" Doctor Kent interrupts.

I stop, taken aback.

"Based on what you've heard," he goes on in the same tone, "do you think there's a chance of saving this guy's life?"

I observe the team setting up around us. "Eighty-six-years-old. Asystole for at least thirty minutes. Actual time of arrest unknown." I breathe out heavily. "I would guess not."

"I would guess not, too," Doctor Kent agrees. "We may have a lot of gadgets and medications, but sometimes we can't fight Mother Nature." He, too, scans the resuscitation bay. "And that's probably a good thing. I think that if I were eighty-six, dying in my sleep wouldn't be a bad way to go."

His words strike me. I peer up at him. "So what do we do?"

"We do exactly what you said. That's our job. We confirm airway and that we're truly dealing with an asystolic patient. We evaluate for any reversible causes. We run the code as indicated. But barring any surprises, this code will likely be a short one."

"Barring any surprises, like he's cold, you mean," I say.

He tips his head. "What?"

"Unless he's cold. He's not dead until he's warm and dead. Right?"

There is a glint in his eyes. "Exactly."

A noise from the doorway causes us both to look over. Erik is entering the resuscitation bay with a sleepy medical student trailing behind him. Before the door closes again, Monica also slips inside, gives Doctor Kent a wave, and goes to a corner to watch.

"What's the story?" Erik inquires, stifling a yawn.

Doctor Kent gestures to me. "Please go ahead with report, Savannah."

Erik appears amused as he flashes me a smile.

"Eighty-six-year-old male," I say, not letting Erik's smile fluster me. "Last seen three hours ago. Asystolic. Thirty-plus minutes of resuscitation so far. Airway in place."

"So no trauma," Erik clarifies.

"None that has been reported."

"Well, you don't need me." Erik puts a hand on my shoulder and adds in a whisper, "With Kent around, you'll probably spend your whole shift doing chest compressions. Have fun with that."

Erik and his medical student exit the trauma bay without looking back. Moments later, the door is slammed open again and the EMS crew flies inside with the patient on their stretcher. CPR is in progress. The ED team lifts the patient over onto our stretcher, and one of our techs takes over chest compressions. As the lead paramedic prepares to give report, I move to the foot of the bed, ready to run the code. But then another motion in the doorway catches my eye. I see an elderly woman being led into the resuscitation bay by the charge nurse.

A lump forms in my throat. It's the patient's wife.

I look again at the body on the stretcher. There is no question that the man has been dead for quite a while. We are not going to revive him. I peer once more at the wife, who is staring while everyone works on her husband's motionless body.

I should run the code. I need to show Doctor Kent that I can do this.

But that woman shouldn't be by herself.

"Hey, Savannah! What meds do you want?" a nurse calls out.

I look at the nurse. I look at the body on the stretcher. I look at the patient's wife.

"You're running this, right?" The nurse already has a syringe in her hand, just waiting for the okay to inject medication. "What meds?"

I turn to Doctor Kent. His dark eyes shift from me to the patient's wife.

"Slight change of plans," he announces. "I'll be running the code."

As Doctor Kent steps to the foot of the stretcher, I slide out of the way and approach the patient's wife.

"Hello, ma'am, are you . . . ?"

"I'm Vernice Barnes," she says in a warbling voice. "Sammy's wife."

Sammy. She calls him Sammy.

I inch nearer. "Do you understand what's going on, Mrs. Barnes?"

"Sammy has gone home to God."

I blink hard. "Yes."

Vernice wraps her wrinkled hand around my arm and looks toward the stretcher. "We've been married for sixty years."

I follow her gaze, but my tears are making it hard for me to see.

"Don't worry, sweetheart." Vernice pats my hand. "We all must go home to God some time. Tonight was Sammy's turn. And Sammy will be waiting for me when I go. I'll see him again."

A few tears fall down my cheek. I lower my head. Aren't I supposed to be the one who's comforting her?

"Sammy loved to ballroom dance." Vernice holds me a little tighter. "He was a very good dancer. He took me dancing on our first date and on every anniversary after that."

I grip her hand.

"He told me that he loved me every evening," Vernice says, her voice not quite as strong. "It was the last thing that he said before he went to sleep tonight."

In silence we hold each other as the code continues. It's not long before I sense someone watching me. Almost reluctantly, I look to the foot of the stretcher. Doctor Kent has his eyes on mine. My throat gets thick as I feel another swell of emotion. I know what he is trying to tell me. It's time.

"Vernice," I whisper, "would you like to go over there and say goodbye?"

She looks at me earnestly. "Would you come with me?"

I catch my breath, praying for the strength to do this.

Supporting one another, we move across the resuscitation bay—Vernice with her slow, shuffling gait and me hobbling on crutches. Doctor Kent motions for the tech to stop doing CPR and step away. The nurses also back off to give room. Everything becomes very still. When we get to the stretcher, Vernice lets go of my arm. She leans down over her husband and gently cradles his head in her hands.

"Goodbye, Sammy. I love you. Thank you for being the light of my life these past sixty years." She gives him a kiss on the forehead.

"Time of death: twelve thirty-four a.m.," Doctor Kent pronounces in a low voice.

The team falls into a respectful silence. That's it. It's all over.

"Vernice, would you like to stay for a while?" I ask softly.

She shakes her head. "No need. Sammy's not here anymore."

After a last, gentle brush of her husband's forehead, Vernice takes my arm again and, as if buoyed up by the strength of angels, leads me toward the door.

Dwayne, our social worker, steps into the resuscitation bay. "Hello, Mrs. Barnes. If you want to come with me, I can help you make phone calls or any other arrangements that you might need."

"Thank you," Vernice replies to him. She then gives me a pat on the cheek. "And thank you, dear, so much."

"You're welcome," I whisper.

Overcome, I watch Dwayne lead her from the resuscitation bay. I will never forget Vernice.

"Savannah, are you alright?" someone asks.

I check behind me and see Monica coming my way.

"Don't feel badly," she goes on as I brush tears away. "Not everyone can handle working in the ER. In fact, I'd bet that most people are like you and get too bothered by this kind of thing." She proudly motions to the far side of the room. "I think that's why Wes is so great at this job. I've never once heard him say to me that an ED patient has made him emotional. He doesn't get affected by what he sees here."

I use my sleeve to wipe my cheek. "I'm sure you're right. Now, please excuse me. I need to go see my other patient."

Without glancing back, I slip out of the resuscitation bay. Instantly, I'm again surrounded by the whirlwind of noise, people, and activity.

Hadi, who is working at a computer nearby, catches my attention. "How did it go in there?"

I sniff and grab a tissue. "About this good."

"I'm sorry," he replies genuinely.

"Thanks. How is Amy Nichols doing?"

"She's doing alright. I let Dwayne know about her. And I think most of her results are back."

"Cool. Thanks."

I crutch to my computer and scan Amy Nichols's imaging reports: an ulnar fracture, a nasal fracture, and a cracked rib. And the sickest part of all is that she's lucky. Had her abusive husband not gotten so drunk, he would have continued to beat her. She could have been tortured for days. She might have wound up with a head bleed, internal abdominal injuries, or worse. I wince as the possibilities roll through my mind.

I page the trauma team before going to the orthopedics cart to gather what I need to splint her arm. Crutching ungracefully with the supplies in my hand, I return to Amy's room. When I enter, I find a young man seated at her side.

"How are you doing, Amy?" I ask.

"I'm okay. Hadi told me about my injuries." She lets out a sigh. Then her face brightens as she motions to the young man. "Savannah, this is my son, Ryan."

"Hi, Ryan. I'm glad you were able to come."

"Hi," he greets me nervously. I think he's been crying.

I go on, "Amy, I'm going to splint your wrist fracture. And the trauma resident will come down to meet with you before you go home. We'll give you thorough discharge instructions, including the information that you need to arrange follow-up with the trauma service, orthopedics, and ENT."

"Maybe we'll be at the same ortho appointment," Amy jokes, gesturing to my busted leg.

I laugh with her. "Maybe."

"So how'd you get your injury, anyway?" she asks curiously.

"Doubt you'd believe the story."

"Try me."

"I was hiking a trail at night, and I sort of fell off a cliff."

"Are you serious?"

"Serious."

Amy giggles. "Sorry. I shouldn't laugh."

"Laugh away. It was pretty stupid."

We settle into a comfortable quiet as I put on her splint and place her arm in a sling. When I'm done, I address both Amy and her son:

"Are you sure that you feel okay about going home tonight?"

"Definitely," Amy assures me. "Frank's in jail, which is probably the one good thing that has come from this. He can't hurt me anymore."

"Mrs. Nichols?" Erik steps in the room, interrupting the conversation. He glances my way before continuing. "My name is Doctor Prescott. I'm from the trauma service. I'm here to do a brief exam, and then I'll let you get out of here."

I move for the curtain. "In the meantime, I'll go print off the referral information."

"Savannah?" Amy calls after me.

I stop and look at her.

"Promise me that you'll only date good men, okay?" she pleads. "Don't waste your time with anyone who doesn't treat you well and doesn't deserve you. Promise me."

More emotion charges through my heart. "I promise, Amy."

"Thank you for your help tonight."

"You're welcome. I'm glad you're safe."

I leave the room and head for the computer to get the discharge paperwork started. New tears are stinging my eyes, but I ignore them. I can't focus on my feelings right now—if I do, I'll fall apart. So I numbly finish the discharge paperwork, which I hand to Hadi to take to Amy Nichols. Then, without pausing even to update Doctor Kent, I snatch up the chart of the next waiting patient and scan the triage note:

Fifty-one-year-old male endorsing chest pain.

Relief fills me. Finally, a straight-forward case. Something that is not going to suck out every remaining ounce of energy from my exhausted soul. Almost robotically, I head to the exam room, announce that I'm there, push away the curtain, and walk inside. I find a short man with glasses sitting on the bed. He's smiling—actually, he's smirking. He definitely does not appear to be in pain.

"Hello, I'm Savannah." I skim the triage note again. "I'm a fourth-year medical student. I understand you're having chest pain?"

He casually positions himself as if lounging on a beach chair. "Nah. I'd like to get out of here, if you don't mind."

"Of course, you can choose to leave," I reply, puzzled. "However, chest pain is a pretty serious thing. I recommend allowing us to do some testing first, at least to make sure your heart is okay."

He seems extremely amused. "Honey, it's cute you're concerned. But I never had any pain. I'd like to leave now, alright?"

"Of course." I check the chart again to find his name. "Mr. Nichols. Like I said, you are welcome to go, but you would be . . ."

I lose my voice as I read the rest of the triage note:

51-year-old male brought in by police for evaluation of reported chest pain.

He was being booked into jail when his symptom began.

I raise my eyes again to the man lying so comfortably on the stretcher. He still has that smirk on his face, as if he's gotten away with something. I then notice scratch marks on his arms and the stench of alcohol on his breath. My body goes cold.

It's Frank. Amy Nichols's alcoholic, abusive husband. Wasn't he arrested? Where are the cops? Why isn't he in handcuffs?

"Did you hear what I said?" he snaps with sudden impatience.

"Yes. You want to go home." I instinctively back away. "But do you mind waiting for a moment? My attending should see you before you go."

"Fine. But make it fast."

I escape the room, breathing hard.

Hadi notices me as he strolls past. "Hey, Sav, you alright?"

"Hadi, how did that man get here?" I whisper, pointing to Mr. Nichols's room.

He shakes his head. "Not sure. He's not mine. Let me go get the charge nurse."

Hadi jogs off. I remain where I am, trying to steady my breathing. Soon, Hadi reappears, and now he's accompanied by an older woman. She's the same nurse who gave us report on Sammy Barnes.

"Hi, dear," the woman greets me. "I'm Laura. What can I do for you?"

"The patient in Room Nineteen came from jail, right? Where are the cops?"

"The cops are gone." She sighs. "That guy is just another one who lied about having a medical emergency."

My eyebrows shoot up. "What?"

"It happens all the time," Laura explains with a hint of disgust. "If someone in police custody claims to be having a medical emergency, the police are obligated to bring that person in for evaluation—even if it's obvious that the person is lying."

"Okay." I rub my forehead. "But where are the police now?"

Laura is observing me sympathetically. "If the police took the time to wait for everyone who faked a complaint, they'd never get anything else done."

"Do you mean that Frank Nichols is no longer in police custody?"

"Unfortunately, that's exactly what I mean. Scumbags like him know that if they pretend to have a medical emergency, there's a good chance the police will let them go and move on to the next person who's breaking the law."

"Then what are we going to do?" I demand. "We can't let him leave! I discharged his wife, and she thinks she's safe! But he could go to their house to hurt her even more!"

Laura only shrugs.

I anxiously pick up a phone. "I'll call Amy and warn her that—"

"You can't do that," Laura interrupts.

I stop with the phone halfway to my ear. "What?"

"You can't disclose to his wife that he's in the ED. That would be divulging his private medical information without his permission."

"But he's violent! He's dangerous!"

Laura tips her head. "Did he say anything to you that suggests he's at risk of harming himself or others right now?"

"Well, no. Not to me. But he was just at home beating up his wife and—"

"If he didn't say anything about currently wanting to hurt himself or others, then you can't call his wife or anyone else without his permission. That's the way the law is interpreted in this state, I'm afraid. You can go discuss it with Dwayne if you want, but he already knows the patient was brought in here, and I'm sure he'll tell you the same thing."

I'm speechless.

Hadi leans past me. "Sav, I hate to say this, but I think he's gone."

I spin around and see that the curtain for Room Nineteen is open wide. The room is empty, the wrinkled sheets on the abandoned stretcher the only evidence of Mr. Nichols's visit.

"I'm sorry that I can't help more," I hear Laura remark.

My mind is working fast as I turn back to her. "I understand."

After patting me on the shoulder, Laura walks away. Hadi gives me an apologetic smile before heading to another patient's room. Clutching the chart, I go over to my workstation and sit down. As quickly as I can, I log into the computer and open Amy Nichols's chart. Thankfully, her cell phone number is listed. I pick up the phone at my desk and dial.

"Hello?" answers a familiar voice.

"Amy? This is Savannah Drake from the emergency department."

"Hi, Savannah. It's nice of you to—"

"Amy, you should leave your house."

There's a stunned silence.

"I can't say anything else," I tell her. "But go to your son's place right away. Better yet, go to a hotel."

"Okay." Amy sounds as though she has started walking fast.

"I'm sorry that—"

"Savannah," she cuts me off. "Thank you."

She hangs up. I put the phone down and drop my head in my hand. Soon, I hear footsteps coming my direction, and I look behind me. Doctor Kent is approaching with Monica practically glued to his side.

"I heard that you saw another patient," Doctor Kent explains in his usual steady tone. "Hadi told me about Frank Nichols. I'm sorry—"

"I called her," I blurt out.

He halts. "What?"

"I called Frank's wife."

Doctor Kent takes in a slow breath. "You called Amy Nichols?"

"Yes." I sense the color draining from my face. "I told her to leave her house."

Monica tosses her hair. "Isn't it illegal to call someone like that, Wes?"

"What's illegal?" Laura is stepping out of a nearby room. "Everything okay over there?"

"Savannah called a patient's wife without his permission," Monica explains.

With an incredulous look, Laura starts to head our way. Clinging to the back of my chair, I become genuinely terrified. I may have broken the law. *The law.* I could get kicked off of this rotation. Or booted out of medical school. Or fined. Or arrested.

But how could I have stayed silent?

"So what happened, exactly?" Laura inquires.

Doctor Kent hasn't taken his eyes off of me.

I am barely able to answer. "I called Amy Nichols and told her to leave her house."

Doctor Kent sits on the corner of the desk. "You did the right thing." His eyes go between Monica and Laura, as if daring them to challenge him. "She shared no medical information. She broke no law."

Laura tips her head, mulling it over. "Agreed. I'll go give Dwayne the update, so he can follow up with Amy."

Laura walks off. Monica scrutinizes me in silence, and then she gives Doctor Kent a smile and saunters off to the attending's desk while checking her cell phone. Doctor Kent gazes after her. As I watch him, it's like the floodgates inside my heart finally burst open. Exhausted, aching, and overwhelmed, all of the emotions that I've been trying to suppress tonight come raging to the surface.

"Doctor Kent, I'm going home," I tell him, not caring how my voice shakes.

Doctor Kent spins around. Surprise is written all over his face. He opens his mouth but closes it again. With what little dignity I have left, I collect my things, put my crutches under my arms, and leave the emergency department without looking back. Beyond feeling and drained to empty, I reach the lobby and call Danielle. I keep her number with me now. After leaving her a message, I sit down to wait for my ride. And I begin to sob.

Chapter Ten

"Savannah, dear, how are you doing?"

I manage to give Lynn a smile as I hand her my completed assignment. "Better every day. Thank you."

"That's wonderful," she says kindly. "I've been worried about you. Doctor Kent told me that you went home early from your shift the other night."

"I appreciated him understanding."

She pats me on the shoulder. "Well, you keep your chin up. You're going to be better in no time."

"I will. And thanks again."

I snatch up my crutches and head toward the exit of the Discovery Conference Room, following after Danielle and the rest of the med students. Another Wednesday is in the books, and I'm glad. Another Wednesday down means that this rotation is closer to being over, which also means that I won't have to interact with Doctor Kent or think about the ED for much longer. Soon, life will be back to normal.

As I leave the room, I nearly trip over Rachel. She's seated on the ground just outside in the hallway, still writing furiously on her assignment.

"What are you doing?" Danielle asks her.

Rachel keeps scribbling on her paper. "I came out here so I could concentrate."

"I'm sure you've written enough, Rachel," Austin remarks dryly. "Doctor Fox wanted a two-sentence response to her lecture, not a manifesto."

Rachel flips her paper over and continues writing on the other side. "But I want to make sure that I include *everything* so she knows I was paying attention."

Austin shakes his head.

Tyler looks around the group with interest. "Hey, were any of you working last night? I heard about the building fire downtown and that several victims were brought to the ED. Sounds like it would have been an awesome shift."

Please no one answer, I think. *Please no one know that I was supposed—*

"That was Savannah's shift," Rachel replies, without even glancing up. "She was scheduled to work with Doctor Kent in the main ED last night."

Everyone turns my way.

"Yes, it was supposed to be my shift." I avert my gaze. "But I was at home. I wasn't feeling well."

Which is sort of true. I guess. No, not really.

The truth is, after bailing out early on him two nights ago, Doctor Kent forbade me from going back to work last night. He called Danielle to convey his instructions. He didn't even ask to speak with me, but he obviously didn't want me around. And, frankly, I can't blame him. After one bad day, I had a meltdown and left the ED early. As if no one else has ever had to tough out a horrible shift.

How could I have been stupid enough to ever consider pursuing a career in emergency medicine?

Anyway, since I wasn't wanted at work, I stayed home yesterday. I slept for over thirteen hours—my concussed brain and battered, fatigued body finally getting the rest that they had been screaming for. When this morning rolled around, I was feeling better than I have in a long time. Nonetheless, I had no desire to come to didactics today; I didn't want to see Doctor Kent. So

Danielle practically had to drag me out of the apartment door to get me here. Thankfully, everything wound up working out—Doctor Kent wasn't even here today. Lynn explained to us that he has been in meetings all morning.

"I'm gonna head down to the cafeteria to grab some lunch, if anyone wants to join me," Tyler announces, bringing me from my thoughts.

"I want to go! I just need a few more minutes!" Rachel writes even faster.

Austin shakes his head again.

"Savannah Drake?" someone says.

I turn to look down the hall, as does everyone else. For a brief moment, I contemplate faking a syncopal episode: Rick Gatz and that frizzy-haired woman with the notebook are coming toward me. And they're accompanied by a taller man who is decked out in a suit that's even crisper than the one Mr. Gatz is wearing.

Rachel makes a strange sound and scrambles to her feet.

"Rachel, do you know who they are?" I whisper, keeping my eyes on the approaching trio.

She nods stiffly.

"Who's the taller one?"

"Mark Prescott! The president of the hospital!" Rachel nearly chokes. "Why are they after you? What did you do?"

I gulp. Only something huge would cause both Mark Prescott and Rick Gatz to hunt down a lowly medical student. Am I being kicked out of the hospital for leaving my rotation the other night? Am I in trouble for calling Amy Nichols?

Other than Danielle, the rest of the students have started stepping back, placing a distance between themselves and me. All I can do is wait nervously while the trio keeps advancing. Then, as if on cue, both Mr. Gatz and Mr. Prescott put on a smile.

"Hello, Savannah," Mr. Gatz greets me insincerely.

I dare to breathe. Insincere or not, he doesn't sound like he's ready to drag me away to jail. At least, not yet.

"Savannah, we haven't had the pleasure of meeting yet. I'm Mark Prescott," the taller man states with the air of someone who is well-practiced with conversation.

"Hi." I analyze Mr. Prescott's face. He's somewhere in his fifties, and I can definitely see the resemblance to his son. I can't help wondering if he knows that Erik and I sort of went out to dinner together the other

Rachel leaps forward. "Mr. Prescott and Mr. Gatz, it is a pleasure to meet you both. My name is . . . is . . ." She freezes with her mouth half-open. She has forgotten her own name.

"Rachel Nelson," Austin fills in for her.

"Hello, Rachel," Mr. Prescott says. "It's a pleasure."

Rachel steps back, practically glowing with delight.

Mr. Prescott faces me again. "Savannah, we understand that you have agreed to speak at our upcoming reception for the surgery department. We're thrilled."

I see the other med students exchanging surprised looks, and I sigh. The reception. That stupid little reception for the surgery department. That's all this is about. Erik must have followed through on his promise to tell Mr. Gatz—and his own father, apparently—that I agreed to speak. Unfortunately, now everyone here is about to find out that I'm a traitor to the emergency department. I peek over my shoulder. Luckily, the doors to the conference room are closed, so at least Lynn, who remains inside, can't hear what is going on.

Setting my eyes back on Mr. Prescott, I reply, "Only if you really want me to."

Mr. Gatz laughs oddly. Perspiration is appearing on his forehead. "You're the speaker we're most excited about."

"Yes, and when we got out of our meeting just now, we wanted to tell you in person how thrilled we are that you'll be speaking," Mr. Prescott adds in a measured, polite kind of way.

My eyes jump between them. Something doesn't add up. The hospital's president, his right-hand man, and his note-taker (or whoever she is) all took time out of their busy schedules to track me down? Just to thank me for agreeing to say a few words at some little reception? I think it's time that I get a little more information.

"Well, I'm actually glad you're here," I say. "Because I've actually been wondering what this reception is about, exactly, and what you want me to say."

Mr. Prescott's eyes widen with obvious surprise. He turns to Mr. Gatz. "Rick, haven't you briefed her about—"

Behind me, I hear the conference room doors get pushed open.

"My goodness!" comes Lynn's voice. "What are all of you still doing here? This is your afternoon off!"

I cringe and look over my shoulder once more. Lynn is backing out of the conference room with her arms full of papers. When she faces forward and sees the trio, she halts.

"Hello," Lynn greets them, her smile faltering. "I take it that your meeting has concluded?"

"We heard everything that we needed," Mr. Prescott answers in a manner that is neither cold nor friendly.

Lynn purses her lips. "Then is there something that I can help you with?"

Okay, now I really am done for. Mr. Prescott is about to reveal to Lynn what they came to talk to me about. Lynn will then inform Doctor Kent that I'm a sell-out and—

"No, no," Mr. Gatz interjects, sounding strangely anxious. "Nothing at all."

I face the trio again in surprise. Mr. Gatz is shifting restlessly. The woman jots down some more notes. Mr. Prescott maintains his calm, professional smile.

"Very well. Then I need to get going." Lynn passes by us, her smile reappearing. "Have a good rest of the day off, everyone!" she calls out before walking off toward the attendings' offices.

Mr. Gatz hurriedly checks his watch. "Unfortunately, we need to be going, too."

"Excuse me," I pipe up. "When am I going to get information about the reception?"

Mr. Gatz glances uncomfortably at Mr. Prescott before motioning to the frizzy-haired woman. "Myrle will contact you soon."

Mr. Prescott looks between Rick Gatz and Myrle before tipping his head toward me. "Is that arrangement alright with you, Savannah?"

"Sure," I reply, not sure what else to say.

The two men display more smiles, and then the trio marches away. As if the elevator knew who was approaching it, the doors promptly slide open with an attentive pinging sound. Still moving in near-unison, the three of them step into the elevator. The doors close. Finally, they're gone.

Rachel has begun examining me like I'm Deity. "You're going to speak at a reception for the hospital? Mark Prescott extended a personal invitation to you?"

"It's a small thing," I insist. "Really small."

"Are you kidding? That is a major honor!" Rachel's voice is getting higher. "How did you get selected to do that?"

I tap my leg with my crutch. "I fell off of a cliff."

Rachel stares at me.

"No, Rachel, it would not be a good idea for you to hurl yourself off a cliff in the hopes of receiving a speaking invitation, too," Austin pipes up.

"What?" Rachel makes a weird sound. "I wasn't thinking about doing that."

"Okay, team, I'm officially starving," Tyler declares. "Time to hit the cafeteria."

There's a round of agreement from the group. Grateful for the change of subject, I head with Danielle and the others toward the elevator. Tyler steps ahead of us and hits the elevator call button. After a few seconds, the elevator doors swoosh open. Instead of stepping inside, though, Tyler steps back, making way for someone to get off.

It's Monica.

Monica begins weaving past us, but when she sees me, she stops abruptly. I duck my head and hurry to get in the elevator with the rest of the group.

"Savannah?" Monica calls out. "Can I talk to you?"

I come to a halt only inches before reaching the sanctuary of the elevator. "Alright."

"Should we wait for you, Savannah?" Austin is inside with the others, holding the door open.

"No. Go ahead," Monica tells him for me. "She'll be down in a minute."

Austin lets go of the door. From where she's trapped near the back of the elevator, Danielle can only look at me with panicked, big eyes as the doors slide shut. Then Monica and I are alone.

"Savannah, I am so glad that I caught you." Monica is as self-collected as ever. "I was hoping to see you again before I left."

"You're leaving?"

She frowns. "Unfortunately, yes. Work in D.C. is calling. Vacations are never as long as we want them to be, are they?"

"I guess not."

There's a pause.

"Savannah," she resumes in a gentle cadence, "I just want you to know that, no matter what your grade on this rotation winds up being, and no matter what Wes says about you, *I* still think that you'll be a good doctor one day."

"What?" I stare at her.

Monica's eyes fill with sympathy. "Emergency medicine may not be your thing, but don't lose hope. It takes a very special person to do well in there."

"I have no idea what you're talking about," I tell her.

She appears to deliberate before she leans in and whispers, "Wes would be upset if I told you. I know that grades aren't supposed to be discussed until the rotation is over."

My heart lurches. Grades? What does she know about grades?

She makes sure that no one is around us before going on. "But I like you, so I'm going to tell you anyway, okay?"

I hesitate. How do I know that she's telling the truth? Then again, why would Monica try to dupe me?

I lower my voice to match hers. "Okay."

Monica speaks intently. "All I know is that your performance during your overnight shift may have, well, solidified Wes's opinion about you."

My breathing is starting to feel strained. "I see."

"It's not like one bad shift would have been a total deal-breaker, of course, but it sounds like Wes already had some concerns about you."

If Monica is still talking, I'm not hearing her anymore. Concerns. Doctor Kent has had concerns. As the words soak in, an avalanche of humiliating recollections plummets down my mind: announcing in the elevator that I wasn't interested in emergency medicine, insulting the way Doctor Kent ran the ED, not telling him the correct size for an endotracheal tube, submitting my assignment late, sending the wrong patient home with a prescription he didn't need, choosing to talk to Vernice instead of running a code, coming back to work against Doctor Kent's advice, calling Amy Nichols, leaving the night shift early . . .

Was there ever a shift when I didn't screw up? Was there ever a time while working with Doctor Kent when I didn't make a fool out of myself?

With painful clarity, I realize that the answer is no.

"Savannah, you're going to be fine," I hear Monica insisting. "I'm sure that you have talents in other areas of medicine. You're going to get into a residency program, regardless of the evaluation that you get from this rotation. I'm sure of it."

I don't reply. All I can think about is how Doctor Kent told me to stay home from last night's shift. He doesn't want me in the ED anymore.

Monica watches me with concern. "I'm sorry to drop this on you, but I thought it would be better to tell you now, rather than having it come as a shock when you received your grade."

I finally manage to speak. "I appreciate it."

She gives me a little side-hug. "Hang in there, okay? You promise?"

"I promise."

She gestures toward the hallway that leads to the attendings' offices. "I'd better go now. I think Wes is waiting for me."

"He's here?" I blurt out before I can stop myself.

"He had some meetings in his office this morning. The poor guy didn't even get to come home after his overnight shift. He's going to take me to the airport."

For a moment, my mind clears. Rick Gatz and Mark Prescott said they were in a meeting. Were they talking with Doctor Kent? Were they talking about the ED remodel? Was—

No, I need to stop worrying about it. I can't care about this anymore.

"Goodbye, Savannah." Monica walks off.

I stagger backward and hit the elevator call button. "Bye."

The elevator pings, and the doors slide open. I nearly fall inside, somehow managing to keep on a brave face until the elevator doors shut. Then everything hits me again. Doctor Kent has had concerns about me this whole time. The embarrassment and disappointment are more than I can take.

I drop my head, letting tears tumble down my cheeks. I should have focused on achieving a good grade on this rotation—a good grade that I so desperately needed—instead of getting caught up in something that wasn't even real. And what was that imagined something, exactly? A romance? A political crusade? A discovery of a love of emergency medicine? I don't even know. All I do know is that Doctor Kent is my attending, he has a girlfriend, and he thinks that I'm a mediocre medical student.

How could I have gotten everything so wrong?

There's another ping as the elevator bumps slightly and comes to a stop on the ground level. The elevator doors open. I raise my tear-stained face and find myself looking right at Doctor Kent. He's waiting to get inside, and he's got a cup of coffee in each hand. Of course he does. Perfect Doctor Kent is bringing perfect coffee to his perfect girlfriend.

Doctor Kent's expression becomes one of alarm when he sees me. "What's wrong?"

"Nothing," I snap.

I crutch out of the elevator and try to pass him, but Doctor Kent steps back so he's blocking my path.

His dark eyes flash. "Something is obviously wrong. Are you okay?"

I refuse to be fooled by the worry in his voice. "Why did you want me to stay home from last night's shift?"

He acts surprised. "Because you had that terrible shift on Monday night. And you're still recovering from your fall. And—"

"And you thought I couldn't cut it? You thought I would get in your way?"

"Of course not," he answers sharply. "I thought—"

"Don't worry, I am very aware of what you think. I definitely understand what you think of me."

Doctor Kent's jaw twitches. He sets the coffee cups down on the window ledge beside him and focuses again on me. "I think there's something you're not telling me."

I stare at him. Could he possibly be more condescending?

"Savannah," he repeats slowly, "what is wrong?"

"I said that nothing's wrong, so don't worry about me. You keep being the attending, and I'll keep playing the role of the inept med student until this rotation is over, okay?"

I stop, shocked by the words that came out of my own mouth. But I refuse to regret it. I won't be afraid to defend myself or say what I think simply because Doctor Kent is an attending. I won't apologize.

He hasn't moved. He hasn't said a word.

"Excuse me," I say.

Jerking my crutches up under my arms, I move to pass him, but one crutch catches on the edge of the tiled floor. I stumble slightly, and it's enough to cause my phone to fall from my purse and hit the ground. But I don't even blush as it starts playing another messed-up ringtone.

Doctor Kent bends down, picks up my broken phone, and holds it out to me. He isn't even close to cracking a smile. I take the phone from him with my good hand and jam it back into my purse.

"And in case you've forgotten," I add, "tomorrow and Friday are my follow up appointments with trauma and ortho, so I won't be at work. But I suppose that's what you'd prefer, anyway."

Without waiting for him to reply, I begin making my way across the lobby for the cafeteria. Behind me, I hear the elevator doors open. After a moment or two, they close again. Only then do I dare to check over my shoulder. Doctor Kent is gone.

Chapter Eleven

"Today's x-rays demonstrate that your ankle continues to heal excellently, Savannah."

I'm really trying to listen to Dr. Briggs, but it's hard not to be distracted by her impenetrably stony affect. How is it possible that someone can be this intimidating all the time? What about on Christmas Day? Or when she's eating a donut? Surely her face must relax at some point—at least, for the sake of those residents on the trauma service, I hope it does.

"So if there are no other questions or concerns, we will plan on seeing you at your next appointment," Dr. Briggs continues. "I'll send someone in to schedule it with you."

"Sounds good."

Dr. Briggs starts for the door but stops once more. "Also, I understand that you'll be speaking on August second. My congratulations for being invited to participate in something so prestigious."

Now I want to vomit. I am so sick of hearing about the reception. Why does everyone know about it? And why does anyone care? And why haven't I been contacted by Mr. Gatz or Myrle-And-Her-Notebook with the details yet?

I realize that Dr. Briggs is waiting for me to reply.

"Thanks," I remark, trying to sound enthused.

Dr. Briggs strides out of the room, letting the door shut behind her. Alone in the quiet, I let my eyes drift around absentmindedly. I'm not in any particular rush, and in spite of everything, I actually feel pretty relaxed. The last forty-eight hours have been liberating. Since I already had these days off to attend my appointments, I've spent the rest of the time catching up on sleep, doing laundry, and stocking up on groceries—anything but thinking about Doctor Kent, my grade, or the emergency department. Because I'm done worrying about all of that. I'm moving on. As Danielle said, a bad grade on this one rotation isn't going to matter much, since I'll have the speaking engagement listed on my resume. Plus, regardless of what Doctor Kent says about me on my evaluation, no one is going put much stock into it—after all, I wound up being admitted to the hospital and undergoing surgery this month.

There's a knock on the exam room door, and someone opens it before I can say anything. To my surprise, it's Erik who pokes his head inside.

"Hey. I saw on the list that you were coming in today."

"Hi."

He steps into the room. "Mind if I come in?"

"Nope."

He almost seems nervous as he runs a hand through his hair. "So how've you been?"

"Well, thanks. Doctor Briggs said that my x-rays looked good."

He's quiet for a moment, and I observe him thoughtfully. How do I really feel about Erik, anyway? It should be an easy question to answer—I mean, he's Hollywood gorgeous, launching his career as a hot-shot surgeon, and Mr. Popular. Now that I'm moving on with my life, I'm sure that I could develop real feelings for Erik . . . couldn't I?

"Cool," he says. "Hey, I was wondering if—"

There's another knock on the door. Erik's expression falls.

"Come in," I call out, keeping a curious watch on Erik out of the corner of my eye.

The door opens. In steps the girl from the receptionist desk, holding a writing tablet.

"I'm here to schedule your next appointment," she explains, taping on the tablet to open the scheduling calendar. "Doctor Briggs wants to see you some time the first week of August. Is there a particular date that works well for you?"

I shrug. "I'm pretty wide open. My emergency medicine rotation will be over by then, and my next rotation won't have started yet."

"Great." She checks the calendar. "We have a three o'clock slot during our weekend clinic on August second, and there are also availabilities on August fourth at nine or two, August fifth at noon, and August seventh at one or four."

"I think the August second option is out," Erik chimes in, winking at me.

I peer blankly back at him. "Why?"

He laughs. Only after a few seconds does he notice that I am still watching him quizzically. His laughter promptly dies away. "August second, Savannah."

Now the date is making little bells go off in my head, though I'm not sure why.

Erik's eyebrows go up. "August second? The day of the hospital celebration? The day you're going to be speaking?"

Oh yeah. Now I remember. August second is the date of that huge PR event that's being put on by the hospital administration—the event Doctor Kent told me about when I was in his office the other evening. August second is the day when Mark Prescott and Rick Gatz will formally announce to the public their plan to renovate the elective surgery center. I can't believe that I forgot, considering that there have been non-stop newspaper and radio ads about it, and signs plastered all around the city. From what I can tell, it's going to be quite the affair: media coverage, important politicians and donors in attendance, speakers, ribbon cuttings, food and games, blah, blah, blah . . .

The rest of Erik's words finally trickle into my brain, and I feel the color leave my face.

That's the 'little reception' I'm scheduled to speak at?! The gigantic, important, well-attended, publicized event, which is taking place here at the hospital on August second?!

No, I must be mistaken. There's no way that a lowly medical student would be recruited by the president of the hospital to speak at the kick-off celebration for the expensive remodel of the elective surgery center. It makes absolutely no sense.

Yet as I frantically think it over, it *does* make sense. Terrible, nauseating, nerve-wracking sense. No *wonder* everyone acted so impressed when they learned that I had been invited to speak. I'm slated to be a keynote speaker at one of the biggest events in Lakewood Medical Center's history.

"August second," I finally repeat, my eyes jumping between Erik and the scheduler, still hoping that there has been some sort of misunderstanding.

But Erik only nods proudly, and my stomach sinks the rest of the way to the floor. It's really true. I agreed to speak on August second. I'll be showing support of the hospital administration's decision to remodel the elective surgery center rather than the ED. I might as well be waving the flag of the very cause that I oppose. This changes everything. Speaking at a small reception about the care I received while in the hospital is one thing, but actively promoting a plan that will leave patients on stretchers in the walkways is entirely another. I can't do it. I won't do it.

The gal with the tablet clears her throat.

"August third at six o'clock is fine," I say distractedly.

"There is no appointment on August third." She purses her lips. "Again, the dates are—"

"August fourth, I mean."

She is now tapping the clipboard with her pen. "What time?"

"Eleven?"

She shakes her head.

"Twelve?" I venture. "One?"

She lets out a sigh. "Two o'clock?"

"Sounds good."

The girl scribbles the information down on a little card and hands it over. Then, after giving Erik a glance, she spins on her heels and exits the room.

I shove the card into the pocket of my jeans, trying to understand where things went so wrong. Residency application or not, I never would have agreed to participate had I known what event it was that I was being recruited to speak at. How did I get into this mess?

Erik clears his throat. "Hey, I was wondering if you already have plans for after the celebration."

I'm yanked from my thoughts. Plans? Is he talking about a date? Who can think about dating at a time like this?

"No," I hear myself respond.

He smiles. "Would you like to go out? With me?"

I'm still not sure that I am hearing him correctly. "What?"

"Would you like to go out after you speak at the celebration?" he repeats, and now there is a mixture of ego and timidity behind his eyes.

"Sure. That'd be nice."

Only then do I register the words that stumbled out of my mouth. I am going on a date with Erik Prescott. A real date. Yet I don't even care. Things are getting more surreal by the moment.

"Awesome." Erik motions for the door. "I've got to head to clinic, but I'll be in touch, alright?"

"Alright."

As soon as the door shuts behind him, I sigh aloud and stare up at a water stain on the ceiling. After a while, I slide off the exam table, throw my purse over my shoulder, grab my crutches, and make my way to the lobby. I spot Danielle waiting on a couch and reading a newspaper. The moment she sees me, she springs up and hurries over with the newspaper in her hand.

"Are you doing okay?" She sounds panicked.

"Not really. Wait until I tell you about the huge mess—"

"Did you hear about August second?"

I wince. "Yeah. I really screwed up. I never realized what event I was agreeing to speak at. What am I . . . wait a second, how did *you* find out?"

She bites her lip.

"Oh no," I whisper. "What is it?"

Danielle quickly checks over her shoulders, as if we're being followed or something, and then she drags me toward the doors. We burst out of the building, and she hurries me over to where Joel is parked.

"Hey," Joel begins as we pile into his car. "How did the—"

"Joel, I love you, but this is no time for small talk," Danielle cuts in. She holds up the newspaper. "Sav, have you seen this?"

I shake my head. "Do I want to?"

Without replying, she hands the paper over to me. It's a copy of the city's biggest newspaper, *The Chronicle*. Danielle has it open to page three. I glance at the headline:

Lakewood Medical Center to Celebrate Start of Major Remodel

Underneath the headline are two pictures. On the left is a current photo of the elective surgery center. On the right is an artist's rendition of the to-be-remodeled facility. I have to admit, the remodeled building will be even more gorgeous than the current one. I wouldn't have thought that possible.

"I know. The media promotion is absurd." I make a disgusted face. "I can't believe they're attempting to justify spending that kind of money on the elective surgery center while the ED is in such desperate shape."

I hold the paper out, but Danielle doesn't take the paper back.

"Keep reading," she says.

I swallow and lower my eyes to the paper once more.

Lakewood Medical Center continues preparations for remodeling its elective surgery center, with the commencement to be celebrated on August second.

Old news. I skip to the next paragraph.

We're extremely excited about the start of this remodel," said Richard Gatz, the hospital's vice president. *"We spent long hours deciding where the patient need was greatest.*

I snort. "What a joke. The remodel has nothing to do with patient need. It's all about what brings in the most money for the hospital."

"Go to the fourth paragraph," Danielle blurts out, as if she can't wait any longer.

With a pulse of alarm, I obey.

The keynote speaker at the celebration will be Savannah Drake, a twenty-six-year-old medical student who is currently completing her ER rotation at Lakewood Medical Center.

"I'm mentioned in this?" I screech. "Who gave them the right to mention me?"

"Keep going. It gets worse," Danielle warns.

Worse? How can it possibly get worse? Panicked, I resume scanning the article.

"Miss Drake has been a particularly avid supporter of the remodel," Gatz explained. *"Not only is she a future health care provider, she was also a recipient of the excellent care that our surgery department is famous for providing. After her wonderful experience as a patient, Miss Drake requested to speak at the ceremony to show her support for the remodel. With such interest from a future doctor, how could we refuse?"*

"He's lying! He's totally lying!" I barely stop myself from chucking the newspaper out the car window. "I never asked to participate in this; they hunted me down! But Gatz is making it sound like I begged to participate!"

Danielle moans. "I know. I'm so sorry. This is my fault."

"Your fault?" I echo. "What are you talking about?"

She drops her head. "I kept encouraging you to accept the invitation to speak. I told you what a great addition to your resume it would be. I didn't know that—"

"This is not your fault. I was the one who was stupid enough to agree to do it." I toss the paper to my feet. "I knew what I was getting into."

"Did you?" Joel inquires thoughtfully.

I look at him. He's drumming his fingers on the steering wheel.

"Well, obviously, yeah. I told them I'd do it, didn't I?" I grumble.

He tips his head. "You agreed to participate, but did you understand exactly what you were getting into?"

"Huh?"

"On that day when he came into your hospital room, I don't remember our friend Mr. Gatz disclosing to you any specifics about what event you were being recruited for. Do you?"

Joel has a point, I realize. When Mr. Gatz spoke with me in my hospital room, all he said was something about a 'little reception.' He certainly didn't give me any details then or when he and Mr. Prescott found me in the hallway. Not to mention, Mr. Gatz still hasn't contacted me in follow up, even though he said that he would.

"Joel, you're right," I declare. "I didn't know what I was getting into because I was never told."

Joel continues, "And would you have agreed to speak, had you understood what event it was that they were recruiting you for?"

"No way." I shake my head fiercely. "Not even for the residency application boost."

Danielle shifts to face Joel. "So what are you getting at? That they deliberately avoided telling her?"

"I'm not sure, but I have to wonder," he admits. "Sav, is there any chance that the administration knew about your bias for the emergency department? Would they have known that you'd refuse to speak, had you been made aware of exactly what the invitation was for?"

"I don't think so," I reply. "It's not like I ever chatted with anyone but you guys and Doctor Kent about my opinions regarding the remodel . . ." I trail off, and my heart speeds up. "I take that back. I *did* talk to someone. I talked to Erik. When he came to Fast Track to see a patient with a splenic laceration, I told him that I respected Doctor Kent for trying to get funding for an ED remodel. I even mouthed off about the hospital administration."

"You mouthed off about the hospital administration to Erik? Erik, as in Mark Prescott's son? Erik, as in my bench pressing hero?" Joel mockingly flexes his arm.

I chuckle, in spite of myself. "Yep. But you're not suggesting that—"

"That Erik was some sort of informant?" Danielle sounds as excited as she does when discussing her favorite television drama. "That he went and told his dad what Sav said? That they realized Sav wouldn't agree to speak unless they hid the truth from her?"

Joel scratches his chin. "Again, I can't say for sure. But if I were a hospital administrator and inviting someone to speak at my facility's biggest event in years—an event that would be attended by the media and potential future donors—I'd make sure that my speaker was well-informed. At the very least, I'd give that speaker the details he or she needed to prepare appropriately."

"Maybe they tried calling me but couldn't get through because of my busted phone," I suggest.

Joel looks out the window. "Possibly. But there's this brand new technology out there called email, which they might have used as an alternative."

The three of us fall into silence.

"I can't buy into a conspiracy theory," I finally decide. "There are tons of other people whom they could have invited to speak if I declined—people far more relevant to the event than I am, frankly. There's no motive for why the administrators would trick me into participating, let alone want me to speak in the first place."

Danielle flops against her seat. "Bummer. I thought we were on to something."

Joel stays quiet as he puts his keys in the ignition and starts the car. As we pull out, I glare down at the newspaper at my feet. I can't resist. I lean forward, pick it up, and start to read the rest.

In a strange twist, Savannah Drake is also the medical student who is currently being mentored during her emergency medicine rotation by none other than Dr. Wesley Kent, M.D.

I'm hit with a pang of sadness. I was a jerk to Doctor Kent the other day. I can't believe some of the biting things that I said to him. I shouldn't have—

No, I need to stop feeling guilty. Doctor Kent has a girlfriend, he's my attending, and he is planning on giving me a low grade on this rotation. That's all.

But what's this "strange twist" that the article is referring to? I continue reading the page.

Dr. Kent has spent over two years campaigning to raise awareness of what he claims to be the hospital's "drastically undersized and out-dated" ER. Kent also attempted to convince the hospital administration to allocate the forty-three million dollars toward renovating the ER rather than the elective surgery center.

I flip to the next page and stop abruptly. I'm staring at a black-and-white picture of Doctor Kent. He's wearing a shirt and tie, standing behind a podium, and speaking to a large crowd.

Dr. Kent spoke at several town meetings to discuss what he refers to as the "abysmal circumstances in which we must care for our patients." In his most recent appeal, Kent reported that sixty-one percent of patients are treated in ER walkways, due to lack of available exam rooms.

"There's no excuse for this," Kent stated. "The hospital obviously has the funds to remodel the emergency department but is choosing not to."

I drop the paper onto my lap, that sense of injustice brewing inside of me again. It's that feeling that makes me burn to fight Rick Gatz, Mark Prescott, and the other hospital administrators. I don't want the feeling to be there—I know I wouldn't make a difference, anyway—but it's coming on stronger by the second. I keep reading.

Dr. Kent's arguments have generated substantial buzz around the community. Many people have begun to question why the hospital is not renovating the ER. Some donors even retracted their promised monetary donations, and others are threatening to do the same if the ER's troubles are not addressed.

My mouth drops. Doctor Kent has caused a far bigger headache for the hospital administration than I appreciated. Funding has been lost because of the concerns he raised, and the hospital stands at risk of losing even more money. Intrigued, I pull the paper closer.

In response, Rick Gatz said: "The statistics provided by Wes Kent are simply inaccurate. For him to suggest that over sixty percent of our ER patients are not treated in exam rooms is nonsense. We run frequent evaluations, which repeatedly demonstrate that eighty percent of our ER patients are seen in exam rooms. The few patients who are in walkways are awaiting an inpatient bed. Our numbers are consistent with, or better than, ERs all around the country with similar censuses."

There's a small picture of Rick Gatz alongside the column. I mash my thumb into that part of the page, causing it to wrinkle. I actually feel a little bit better.

Gatz went on: "Not to mention, even Wes Kent's own medical student, Savannah Drake, has taken our side on this issue. Miss Drake works in the ER, and so she obviously knows what's really going on in there. If a problem existed, someone as bright and proactive as Miss Drake would speak out about it. But as it is, she's voicing support for the elective surgery center remodel. Unlike her attending, Miss Drake is focused on patients rather than self-promoting politics. Wes Kent's allegations are false. "

I scan the words again in shock. "This is bad, you guys. This is really, really, really bad."

Joel glances at me. "What is?"

"I've figured out why the administration wanted to recruit me as a speaker so badly."

Joel immediately pulls the car over to the side of the road and kills the engine. "Keep talking."

I hold up the paper. "I may be a no-name med student, but the administration definitely wanted me—specifically me—to speak at the upcoming ceremony. Not because they thought I'd be an amazing addition to the program, but because they wanted to use me to discredit Doctor Kent. I'm being used as a pawn in their PR game."

"What?" Danielle's eyes bulge.

I gesture to the article. "Doctor Kent has been openly critical of the administration's failure to address the outdated ED, and in doing so, he's managed to generate some pretty bad press about the hospital. So bad, in fact, that donors have started pulling their support."

Danielle grips her seat. "Okay. And what does that have to do with you?"

"I'm the med student who's working with Doctor Kent, right? So I'm being lauded by Mr. Gatz as a credible witness from the ED frontlines. Gatz is spinning my participation in the ceremony as proof that I disagree with Doctor Kent's assessment of the ED's needs."

"It's like having Doctor Kent's wingman publically denounce him," Joel declares.

"And suggesting that he's making all this fuss for his own political gain." I sink down in my seat, feeling sick.

"Convenient timing," Joel remarks snidely. "A story slandering Doctor Kent gets released right when the hospital needs to lock in donors for a forty-three million dollar remodel. No wonder they had to go to such lengths to discredit their biggest critic."

"This is awful," Danielle whispers.

I say nothing as thoughts race furiously through my head. Doctor Kent has probably read this article by now. What must he be thinking? That I intentionally conspired with hospital administrators behind his back? That I wanted sabotage him because he plans on giving me a lousy grade? After the terrible, irrational things I said to him the other day, that's probably exactly what he thinks.

"You know, Sav, you don't have to speak at the celebration," I hear Danielle tell me.

I look at her. Could it really be that simple?

"True," Joel agrees. "You can't be forced to do anything. Just tell them that you've changed your mind."

I feel a gigantic weight lifting off of me. "You're right. What can they do if I refuse? Nothing."

"But what about Doctor Kent?" Danielle chews on her lip. "Don't you think that you should . . . well, given how badly this article came across . . . I mean, would it be a good thing if you tried to explain?"

I sigh loudly. As much as I don't want to admit it, I know that she's right. I need to clear things up with Doctor Kent. Regardless of everything else, I still want him to understand the truth.

Danielle holds her phone out. "I kept his number in my phone log."

I attempt to calm the manic butterflies that are now slamming around in my abdomen. It's only a phone call. I can do this. I am a professional. I will explain the misunderstanding, clear my reputation, and then this nightmare will be over.

I take the phone from Danielle, who gives me an encouraging smile. Only then do I notice that she already pushed the *TALK* button. And it's ringing. I clear my throat and put the phone to my ear.

"This is Wes Kent."

I freeze. What on earth am I doing? I can't talk to him. Not after what happened the other day.

"Hello? This is Wes."

"Talk to him!" Danielle barks in what is definitely not a whisper.

I cradle the phone in my sweaty palm. "Doctor Kent, this is Savannah Drake. How are you?"

"Well, I'm reading the newspaper right now," he says dryly. "So I'm doing about as well as can be expected."

I cough. "Yes. That's why I'm calling. I want to explain that there's been a huge misunderstanding."

"You don't need to explain, Savannah. You're entitled to your opinions."

Stung by his words, I don't reply. I've done nothing wrong. If there is anyone who should be apologizing or explaining, it's him. He's the one who planned to blindside me with a bad grade. He's the one who made me think that—

"I'm not calling to apologize," I snap.

I see Danielle clap a hand over her mouth, horrified. Even Joel gives me a surprised look.

Doctor Kent's tone is unchanged. "I see. So what can I do for you?"

I grit my teeth. "Nothing. Nothing at all."

I hang up before he can say anything more.

"Savannah!" Danielle is aghast. "What happened? Why didn't you tell him?"

"He doesn't need to hear it." I toss the phone to her. "He can believe whatever he wants to believe. I don't care."

But the frustrating thing is that I think I do care. I care a lot.

Chapter Twelve

This is going to be awkward.

I'm staring at the doors that lead into the emergency department. My shift with Doctor Kent starts in three minutes, which means that I am supposed to go in there.

I don't move.

Okay, I need to get a grip. I will stay busy taking care of patients, and the shift will fly by. I'll remain professional, courteous, and efficient. No drama. No acting as though anything is wrong. I am determined to prove to Doctor Kent that I am a good medical student. I'm going to make him see that the low grade he has decided to give me is unfair. And I won't reveal how I feel about—

There is a loud clank, and the monstrous doors start to swing open. I crutch backward in surprise, nearly colliding with someone behind me. It's Doctor Kent, still holding his ID badge against the card scanner.

"Good afternoon." Doctor Kent shows no emotion as he clips his badge to his scrubs pocket.

I stand up as straight as I can and try to mirror his aloofness. "Hello."

He motions for me to enter first. I cross into the emergency department and, without waiting for him, head straight for the attending's desk and start laying out my things. I glance eagerly at the tracking board to see how many patients are waiting to be seen.

This can't be right.

The tracking board indicates that every patient has already been seen by one of the other doctors; it also shows that a few of the walkway stretchers are actually vacant. In other words, although every exam room is occupied, the ED is not ridiculously overcrowded this morning. I cannot believe my bad luck. Of all the days when a fluke in the universe makes it get slow in here, why did it have to be today? Is there a major sporting event that I don't know about? ED visits always drop off significantly during a World Series game or the Super Bowl. Or maybe it's the weather—clear skies and eighty degrees never fail to help people decide that their life-threatening emergencies can wait until they're done water skiing. Anyway, whatever the cause of the atypical lull today, it sure doesn't help me.

"How've you been, Savannah?" Doctor Kent has reached the desk, and he's setting his bag down beside it.

His totally unaffected demeanor aggravates me, but I remain calm. I have nothing to feel guilty about. Unbeknownst to Doctor Kent, I have already emailed both Myrle and Rick Gatz, and I also left a voicemail on Mr. Gatz's office line, explaining that I would not speak on August second. I did everything that I could to fix the situation.

"I'm fine," I tell him, empowered by the way I'm keeping it together. "Great, in fact."

"So your injuries are healing alright?" He observes me. "Your follow up appointments went well?"

I give in and meet his gaze. "Yes, thanks," I reply, my tone softening. "Things went well."

"Glad to hear it." He pauses and then motions to the tracking board. "Looks like they just put a new patient in Walkway Twenty-One."

He strolls away and returns with the chart in his hand. "Sounds like this is one of those strange days where Fast Track is busier than the main ED, and so they're shuttling some lower-acuity stuff up here."

He hands me the chart. Without even reading the triage note, I hurriedly move away from Doctor Kent to go find where the patient is located. I take a deep breath. Alright, this shift may not have started off how I would have liked, but I from here on out, I will be professional, efficient Savannah.

I see on the chart that the patient is in Walkway Twenty-One, which proves to be a small area of corridor space designated by a piece of paper that's taped to the wall with *"21"* written upon it. Seated on a chair underneath the paper sign is a man who appears profoundly nervous.

"Hello, Sir." I lower my voice, trying to give him a shred of privacy from the patients who are seated on either side of him. "My name is Savannah Drake. I'm a medical student, and I'll be taking care of you today."

"Hi," he mumbles.

"Sir, please tell me why you came to the emergency department."

"I've caught a disease from my girlfriend."

I groan inwardly. *This* is the guy whom the triage folks put in a walkway space? I know Fast Track is overflowing with patients, and every room in the main ED is occupied, but there really wasn't anywhere else in this entire department where this man could have gone?

"I see," I whisper to him in my most understanding tone. "Please tell me what symptoms you're having."

Without warning, he stands up and uses one hand to yank his tightly fitting t-shirt up to the top of his chest. With his other hand, he squeezes his belly fat, which is rolling out over the waistband of his shorts.

"This! You see this?" he shouts, shaking his fat. "I caught this! I caught this disease!"

The nearby walkway patients start sliding their chairs away from him with looks of alarm. One lady even pulls a facemask from her purse and slips it on.

"Sir, please take a seat," I order him, glancing around.

The man releases his fat and tremulously wipes the sweat from his brow. He remains standing while mumbling to himself. I decide it's good enough, and so I resume speaking to him quietly:

"Now, sir, just to be clear, you're referring to the . . . the extra adipose tissue around your abdomen?"

"The what?" His voice booms while he uses his finger to poke repeatedly at his stomach. "I'm talking about all of this blubber! Look at this! Look! At! This!"

"Okay, okay!" I shout over him. "I understand! You can stop that now!"

The guy gives his tummy one last poke, grumbles with disgust, and then peers at me. "What's the cure? There is a cure, isn't there? I need the cure!"

"The cure?"

"Yes, the cure!"

"Sir, I—"

"There's got to be a cure! I never had this blubber until I started dating my girlfriend seven months ago! Now see what's happened to me?" He uses both hands to smack his abdomen for emphasis. "Look at what I caught from her! She never told me that she was carrying a disease!" The man drops into the chair and hangs his head in his hands.

I somehow manage to keep my tone steady. "Sir, fat isn't contagious."

"Oh yeah?" He lifts his head and whacks his abdomen once more. "Then how do you explain this?"

He stands back up, this time so fast that his chair topples over with a clatter. With everyone in the walkway gawking at him, the man begins shimmying side-to-side so his fat sloshes around.

I step closer to him, clenching my teeth. "Sir, sit down. Right now. *Right. Now.*"

He stops and observes me. Seeming to decide that I'm serious, he picks up his chair and takes a seat.

I straighten my white coat. "As I was saying, fat isn't contagious like an infectious disease."

He seems skeptical. "You're sure about that?"

"Yes." I adopt the most solemn, doctor-ish tone that I can. "I am sure."

He exhales. "Well, that's a relief!"

"Decreased exercise and increased caloric intake are the two most common causes of developing . . . blubber." I adjust the chart in my hands. "Is it possible that your routine has changed since you started dating your girlfriend?"

He appears to be thinking really hard. "Well, we go to restaurants a lot. And she likes to watch movies and eat ice cream."

"Ah, it's possible that those actions might be contributing to your current condition," I state insightfully.

He has begun tapping his finger on his cheek. "And she gives me rides to work. I used to walk."

"Mm-hmm," I remark in a wise way.

He stands up again, his shirt still gathered up around his chest. "I need to go tell her the good news!"

I put out my hand. "Could you wait until my attending has a chance—"

"You're good to go, sir. Have a nice afternoon."

I spin around. Doctor Kent is not far behind me.

The patient glares suspiciously at Doctor Kent. "Who are you?"

"My name is Doctor Kent and—"

"I've already seen a doctor." The guy gestures toward me. "So mind your own business, buddy."

Keeping a wary eye on Doctor Kent, the guy backs away and heads for the exit. After he's gone, the other walkway patients begin sliding their chairs back into place.

Straight-faced, I look up at Doctor Kent. "He was concerned about weight gain, which he thought that he had contracted from his girlfriend."

"Yes. I gathered as much when he was doing his belly dance." The corners of Doctor Kent's mouth twitch.

I break into a laugh. Doctor Kent's eyes flash humorously. He's about to say something else when a nurse interrupts:

"Doctor Kent, we've got a new patient. A woman with abdominal pain. She comes in all the time for this, and she's demanding narcotics, of course." The nurse rolls her eyes. "She's in a walkway stretcher for the moment, but we'll get her to Room Five as soon as the patient who's currently in there is taken upstairs."

"Great. We'll be right there. Thanks," Doctor Kent replies.

Another nurse hurries over. "Doctor Kent, an admitted patient who's boarding in Room Eleven is complaining of chest pain. We're getting an ECG right now."

"We're on the way." Doctor Kent takes a step toward Room Eleven but pauses. "Actually, Savannah, how about we divide and conquer. You go see the belly pain, and I'll go see the chest pain."

"Sure," I reply.

Doctor Kent heads to Room Eleven, and I go the opposite direction. I can hear the abdominal pain patient long before I spot her. She's letting out high-pitched, dramatic shrieks that make my eardrums burn. I round a corner and finally see her. She's lying on a stretcher in the walkway between the social worker's office and the drinking fountain. The patient is morbidly obese, and I'm guessing she is in her early thirties. She's still in her street clothes, and she has her enormous purse on her lap. The nurse tending to her is attempting to place an IV, but the patient keeps yanking her arm away. For a moment, the patient becomes calm. But when she sees me, she grimaces and lets out another piercing shriek.

"You need to hold still!" the nurse exclaims with frustration as he has to stop working on the IV yet again.

"I'm trying!" the woman barks at him.

I step up to the stretcher. "Hello. My name is Savannah Drake. I'm a—"

"I don't care who you are!" the woman yells. "Go get me some pain meds!"

I stay where I am. "I need to ask you some questions first, so I can determine the best way to help you. Can you please tell me what's going on?"

"I've told a million people already!"

"I understand. But it would help for me to hear the information directly from you."

The woman snorts with exasperation. "Fine. I was alright until three hours ago when I began having belly pain. I have a high pain tolerance, so I wouldn't be here if my pain wasn't really bad. I need Dilaudid—it's the only thing that works for my pain."

As if for emphasis, she lets out another obnoxious scream.

"And where is your pain, exactly?" I nearly have to shout over her.

She immediately stops screaming and motions to her entire abdomen. "All over."

"Any other symptoms?"

"No! When do I get Dilaudid?"

"You won't be able to get anything until I get the IV in," the nurse interjects testily. "Please hold your arm still."

The woman makes an annoyed noise and holds her left arm out for the nurse to try again.

"Have you ever had this type of pain before?" I resume.

The woman eyes me. "Maybe."

"Any urinary symptoms?"

"No."

"Any nausea?"

"No. Any other useless questions?"

The nurse cuts in, "So this pain is not like last four times that you've come here for non-specific abdominal pain?" He motions to the patient's chart, which is on the tray beside him.

The woman glares at him and does not reply.

"Have you noticed anything that makes your pain better or worse?" I attempt.

"No! It just comes and goes on its own, alright? And you're making me suffer! I need Dilaudid!"

I take a deep breath, determined to finish taking her history. "Any vaginal discharge or spotting?"

"Do you always ask such personal questions in public?" The woman gestures at the patients around us who are unashamedly watching the show.

I blush. "We're getting a room ready for you as quickly as we can."

She squeezes her eyes shut and lets out another horrible cry. The nurse takes the opportunity to mouth to me, *"Drug seeker."*

I resume observing the woman, who is still crying out. I'm definitely not used to seeing this kind of behavior, but as ridiculously as she is behaving, she also appears to be legitimately uncomfortable. I reach out and push on her abdomen, but she is too obese to distinguish anything at all.

"Do you mind sending off basic labs?" I ask the nurse. "And we'll need a UA, too."

"Sure. Whatever you say." The nurse smiles, clearly trying to humor me. He begins drawing tubes of blood from the IV that he managed to place. Then he walks away to take the blood samples to the lab.

"It's getting worse!" the woman bawls. "Get me pain medicine!"

I peek over my shoulder. Already, this place has gotten busier. Room Five is still occupied, as are all the others exam rooms. Even the resuscitation bays now have trauma patients in them. There is nowhere else for this patient to go, which means that I'm going to have to do the best that I can under the circumstances. With a sigh, I turn back to her. As I do, I have one distinct, disturbing thought.

No. There's no way.

But I have to ask.

"Ma'am, I'm sorry to ask you this in public, but is there any chance that you could be pregnant?"

The woman is practically panting as she jerks her head up from the pillow. "I think I would know if I were . . . arg!" She lets out another agonized roar.

"Ma'am, when was your last period?" At this point, I don't care if others can hear me.

She is now staring at me like I'm insane. "Months ago, but my periods are never regular!"

She yells again, reaches out, and digs her fingernails into my arm until the pain subsides.

I look her in the eye. "I need you to take your pants off."

"What?"

"Now." I snatch the folded blanket from off the end of the stretcher and toss it over her lap to keep her covered. "Right now."

The nurse rounds the corner and starts strolling back toward us. He stops, his mouth falling open, when he sees what is going on.

"I would like a mask, eye protection, and some gloves, please," I tell him. "Oh, and a clean towel. And the baby warmer. And one of those suction bulb things, if we have them."

"You got it!" The nurse rushes off.

I spin around and point at an intoxicated guy who is seated beside the social worker's office. "You. Bring that chair here . . . please."

"Sure. No problem, little lady," he grins, getting unsteadily to his feet.

The intoxicated man staggers over with the chair, brushes the sandwich crumbs off of it, and hands it to me. I drop the chair at the foot of the woman's stretcher, toss down my crutches, and sit so I am at her feet and facing her.

"This is crazy," the woman mutters as she finishes peeling off her sweatpants, keeping her lower half concealed under the blanket. "I'm going to sue you for privacy violation and . . . I can't take this!"

With another scream, she collapses back on the bed and grips both rails of the stretcher.

The nurse returns with the supplies. "Here you go!"

"Thanks." I hastily don the gown, gloves, and mask. "Do you have any idea where Doctor Kent is?"

"He's busy with an active MI," the nurse informs me. "The other nurses are with a septic patient. I think it's just you and me for now."

I face the woman. It's been over six months since my OBGYN rotation—and they only let me deliver two babies (and one placenta, which barely counts). But I can't just sit here and wait for the on-call OBGYN to get to the ED. For now, at least, this woman is my patient. As the realization hits me, my anxiousness somehow morphs into clarity. I get the patient into position and then discreetly lift the blanket to see her pelvic area.

She is practically crowning.

"Something is coming out!" the woman shouts.

"Ask the secretary to call OBGYN and peds," I say to the nurse, scooting my chair as close as I can to the stretcher. I then eye the woman squarely. "Ma'am, I need you to listen to me. You're about to deliver a baby."

"What? You're crazy!"

"That's certainly possible, but I'm also staring at the top of your baby's head." I position my gloved hands around the perineum in the way I remember being taught.

"There is no way that . . . the pain is coming again!" the woman hollers.

The nurse runs back from the secretary's desk and grabs the patient's hand. "Here! Squeeze as hard as you need!"

"Arrrggghhh!"

The woman's tortured cry fills the department. Patients from other areas of the ED are wandering over to see what's going on.

"Is that woman is having a baby?" I hear one patient ask excitedly.

Another patient shouts in reply, "She sure is!"

"I bet it's a boy!" proclaims the intoxicated guy.

"It'll be a girl!"

The woman screams yet again. Suddenly, the baby's squished, slimy head slides out. I snatch up the suction bulb and clear the infant's nose and mouth. There is a moment of anxious hush. Then the baby begins to cry.

"Oh my! Oh my! Oh my!" the woman repeats as the sound reaches her ears. "Oh my! Oh my!"

Cradling the infant, I guide the rest of the body out and hold on tight. The nurse hands me a towel, and I rub the baby down.

I'm holding a newborn child.

I raise my head to the woman. She is staring at me in shock while beads of sweat drift down her forehead.

"Would you like to hold your son?" I smile at her, holding the baby up for his mother to see.

"Ha ha! A boy! I knew it!" The intoxicated guy pumps his arms in triumph.

The woman's eyes fall upon her infant, and an amazed, wonderful smile comes to her face. "My baby," she whispers, her voice catching. "They told my husband and me that I wouldn't be able to have a baby."

I hand the infant to the nurse, who places him gently on the woman's chest.

"Hello, baby." The woman speaks softly, nestling her face close to the infant. "I love you. I love you so much." She starts to laugh and says to me, "I suppose I should call my husband, shouldn't I?"

I grin. "Probably a good idea. But be sure to tell him to sit down before you give him the news."

There are footsteps behind me. I peer over my shoulder. I am guessing that the gal who is wearing a teddy bear clip on her stethoscope is the pediatrics resident. The two folks who are wearing scrub caps and surgical booties must be from OBGYN.

I take my gloves off. "It's a boy. The placenta isn't out yet."

The three of them descend upon the stretcher faster than I can get out of the way. I grab my crutches and dart aside to give them room. Only then do I notice that the gown I'm wearing is covered in blood.

"Savannah Drake, what have you been doing over here?"

I lift my eyes. Doctor Kent is approaching fast, taking in the scene. Meanwhile, from behind me, the baby's healthy cry continues filling the walkway.

"Oh, hey." I motion behind me. "It's a boy."

Doctor Kent's gaze moves from me to the woman and back to me.

"Hon, I'm guessing that you'd like to get some new scrubs and clean up a bit?" one of the other nurses inquires warmly.

I pull my eyes from Doctor Kent and reply to her, "Yes, please."

"The nursing locker room is right around the corner." She points. "Code to get in is 2436."

"Thanks." I start moving away.

"Savannah?"

I check over my shoulder.

"Nice job," Doctor Kent says.

I shrug. "Just another day on the job, right?"

He cracks a grin, which makes my heart skip a beat. So I grab my bag from the desk and hurry toward the locker room, reminding myself that I'm supposed to be mad at him. As the locker room door shuts behind me, I become enveloped in quiet. Now alone with my thoughts, I peel off the soiled gown and change into a new pair of scrubs. Then I look in the mirror and practice my "I'm-a-professional-medical-student-who-isn't-ruffled-by-her-attending" face. Once I feel resolved, I head back out into the ED. I see that the woman and her baby are gone—no doubt they have been taken upstairs to the postpartum floor. She never did make it into an exam room. I sure hope she still doesn't want to sue me about that.

"Delivering a baby on crutches. In the hallway. That's got to be a first, even for this place."

I hear his voice and look his way. Doctor Kent is picking up another chart, and he still has a smile on his face. I'm about to reply when I spot a terrifying sight over his shoulder: Rick Gatz storming into the ED.

"Excuse me, Doctor Kent." I gulp and hastily begin retreating from him. "I need to slip away for a sec."

Doctor Kent's smile fades. I bolt. Mr. Gatz hasn't spotted me yet, but he is blocking my escape route back to the locker room. So I change directions, rush out the back of the ED and into the hallway, slip into a vacant bathroom, and lock the door. I collapse against the wall, exhaling with relief. That was close.

A knock on the door causes me to jump.

"I'll be right out!" I lie.

There's another knock on the door, more impatient this time. I lunge for the toilet and flush it.

"Almost done!" I shout moronically.

I go to the sink and let the water run for a while. When there is yet another knock on the door, I start feeling guilty. Someone really needs to get in here. Surely Mr. Gatz can't still be around. Or maybe he and Doctor Kent ran into each other and had a huge fight! I chuckle at the thought of Doctor Kent slamming Mr. Gatz down onto a stretcher like he did to that drunk guy on my first day. I can see it now: Mr. Gatz in his fancy suit, strapped down to a walkway stretcher. Actually, that might not be a bad way to let him see how busy this ED really—

The person outside pounds on the door.

"Okay! I'll be right there!" I call.

As I reach to shut off the sink, my bag slides down my arm and hits the faucet, causing my cell phone inside to start playing another mutated song. I dig through my bag, yank out my phone, and start hitting buttons until the song stops.

The person outside rattles the door handle. I jam my phone into the pocket of my scrubs top, fix my crutches, and open the bathroom door.

"Sorry about that. Things go a little slower when you're on crutches and . . ."

I don't finish. It's Myrle. And she has her notebook.

"Mr. Gatz would like to speak with you," she states in a nasally voice. She pulls a walkie-talkie from her jacket pocket, which chirps before she speaks into it. "I've found her. Hallway bathroom."

The walkie-talkie chirps again.

"I'm on my way."

Seconds later, I hear footsteps. Then Rick Gatz marches around the corner.

"Savannah," he growls.

I give him a look. "Hi, Mr. Gatz."

He stomps closer. "I received your voicemail."

I keep my cool and stay silent, telling myself that I had every right to refuse to speak.

Mr. Gatz, however, does not appear to be making the same effort to remain composed. "Savannah, your attempt to discard your obligation—with only four days to go—ranks as some of the most irresponsible and unprofessional behavior that I have ever witnessed from a medical student."

Yikes. This man is furious. But it doesn't matter. He can try to intimidate me all he wants. I made the right choice.

"I'm sorry you feel that way, Mr. Gatz," I reply. "But the fact is, you never informed me what event I would be speaking at. Nor did you give me the details when I asked for them. I find that irresponsible and unprofessional, too."

He appears absolutely livid. Scary, even. "Savannah, we have gone to a lot of effort to secure you as a speaker for this event."

"That may be, however I can't participate," I explain with exaggerated patience. I'm actually enjoying watching him squirm.

He takes another step, getting so close that I can see the pulse bounding in his temples. "Very well. But when Wes Kent loses his job and can't get hired anywhere else, be sure to tell him that it was your fault."

My body goes ice-cold. What is he talking about?

Mr. Gatz seems to sense that he has hit a weak spot. "I can ensure that no respectable hospital will ever hire Wes Kent. A few words of concern from me—perhaps suspicions of stealing medication or poor patient management—will guarantee that he'll never work again."

"But you'd be lying," I declare, horrified. "You'd be slandering him."

Mr. Gatz is clearly amused. "Who could prove it? More importantly, who would want to take the risk of hiring someone whose previous employer had such significant concerns?"

This cannot be happening. I cannot be standing here listening to Rick Gatz threaten to end Doctor Kent's career.

"We want August second to be the day we put the past two years of fighting with Wes Kent behind us." Mr. Gatz's nostrils flare. "We want the ceremony to be a success, the renovation to begin, and Wes to go quietly back to D.C. where he belongs."

I cling to my crutches.

"Wes has caused our investors to get nervous," Mr. Gatz continues. His eyes narrow into slits. "Relationships with them have been tenuous, to say the least. It took a great deal of effort to convince them to still fund our remodel."

I remain quiet, trying to come up with some sort of plan.

"If you refuse to speak, we're going to have a lot of investors wondering why you backed out." Mr. Gatz's expression darkens even more. "Significant questions would resurface. Questions that might make more investors pull out of the project. Questions I don't want to answer, since it was difficult generating false statistics about the ER census in the first place."

"You faked your numbers?" I gasp. "You lied to the investors? Did you lie to Mark Prescott, too?"

He observes me with a condescending air. "It was a means to an end, Savannah. A little number adjustment now will lead to massive revenue for our hospital in the future." He displays a terrible smile. "Welcome to the business world."

"So the numbers that Doctor Kent cited about the ED overcrowding were accurate? Over sixty percent of the patients don't even get into an exam room?"

He waves his hand dismissively. "Those patients are still getting treated, and most of them are getting treated for free. Patients should be grateful that the hospital is covering the cost of their care, not demanding more of us. We're a business not a charity."

I'm so stunned that I can't reply. What do I do? *What do I do*? Should I tell Mark Prescott? No, Mr. Prescott isn't going to believe a medical student over the word of Rick Gatz. Especially not when the accusation is something this unfathomable. I doubt anyone would believe that this conversation ever took place.

Except, maybe, Doctor Kent.

If I tell Doctor Kent, he'll fight back. He'll talk to the press about the rigged statistics and alert investors. But then what? Who would believe Doctor Kent's accusations without proof, especially given his history of being at-odds with Mr. Gatz? In the end, Doctor Kent would be accused of lying about his superiors. It would lead to a career implosion. If I tell Doctor Kent, he'll wind up worse off than if I don't.

Mr. Gatz adjusts his suit jacket. "I'm going to be generous here. If you speak at one o' clock on August second as planned, I won't convince Mark Prescott that Wes Kent should be fired immediately. Do we have a deal?"

Things are going too fast for me to think. "Deal. It's a deal."

Our conversation is interrupted when my cell phone makes a strange noise. I snatch the phone from the pocket of my scrubs top and shove it into my bag. Then I peer angrily at Mr. Gatz and add:

"Anything else? I have patients to care for." The irony of my remark is not lost on me.

"No, there's nothing else. In fact, we'll accompany you back to the ER," Mr. Gatz says more as a threat than an offer.

So I find myself crutching into the ED with Mr. Gatz and Myrle on my heels. As we enter the department, Mr. Gatz suddenly addresses me in a raised voice:

"It was a great pleasure speaking with you today, Savannah. I'm so glad that I happened to run into you. We are excited to hear your remarks at the ceremony. Thank you for volunteering to support us."

I glare at him. With a mocking bow, he walks off. Myrle follows, still writing in her notebook. Only after they are gone do I notice Doctor Kent coming out of a nearby exam room. What did he hear? It's impossible to tell. For a second, we look at each other. Then he picks up a new chart and heads toward yet another exam room. He didn't even wait for me.

Chapter Thirteen

Non-invasive positive pressure ventilation is a key component to managing CHF exacerbations. Options that you have from the emergency department include . . .

Keeping my head down, I read the test question for the fifth time. It's the last Wednesday of the rotation, so instead of didactics, we're taking our final exam, which covers all the textbook material that we were supposed to study during the month. I completed the test a while ago, but I've remained in my chair, pretending as though I'm still working on it.

After another minute or two, I check over my shoulder yet again. Doctor Kent is still near the doorway, speaking in hushed tones to Lynn. I cannot submit my exam to Lynn while he's standing right beside her. That would mean I would have to interact with him. And I can't do that—it would just be too awkward. I need to keep stalling until Doctor Kent goes away.

One-by-one, the other students are getting up from their desks, handing in their exams to Lynn, and exiting the conference room. Doctor Kent continues to remain by the door. I shift in frustration. Doesn't he have something else that he could be doing right now?

A motion catches my eye. I see that Danielle has finished her test. She gives me an encouraging smile and mouths, *"I'll wait outside for you,"* before heading away.

I scan questions eleven and twelve for about the one thousandth time, and then I peek at the clock. It's noon. Our exam time is up. Except for me, Rachel is the only student still working on the test. From what I can tell, she's in the middle of writing a novella on the back of the last page.

"How are you doing, ladies?" Lynn comes toward us. "Almost wrapped up?"

"Yes!" Rachel squeezes a few final words into the very bottom right corner of the paper.

"And what about you, dear?" Lynn glances at the test on my desk. "It looks like you're all done?"

"I was just reviewing my answers." I hand the paper over.

"Congratulations on approaching the completion of another rotation," she tells me. "And good luck to you, if I don't see you again."

"Thanks, Lynn," I say appreciatively. "Thanks for everything."

"You're welcome, Savannah. You did a great job this month."

I barely stop myself from letting out a dry laugh. Scooping up my things, I steal another look at the door. Doctor Kent is still there, but he has his head down while he's texting on his cell phone. If I go fast, I'll be able to slip out without having to acknowledge him. Snatching my crutches from the floor, I charge for the exit. I am just crossing into the hallway when I hear him say:

"Savannah, do you have a moment?"

I stop to breathe before turning around to face him. "Sure."

"Rachel, whenever you're done, this involves you, too," Doctor Kent adds.

Rachel? What does Rachel have to do with any of this?

"I'll be right there." Rachel respectfully places her test in Lynn's hands and then scuttles over to join us. "What can I do for you?"

"We've run into a scheduling problem," Doctor Kent explains. "Doctor Fox's daughter has to undergo surgery. So she has asked if I could work her Saturday shift. She'd work my Friday shift as a trade."

Rachel is "mm-hmm-ing" with every word that Doctor Kent is saying. But I remain quiet. If the attendings trade, I would do my last shift on Friday with Doctor Fox rather than Doctor Kent. I might not have to interact with him again, after all.

Doctor Kent goes on, "Ideally, since Doctor Fox is Rachel's mentor, Rachel would also swap from Saturday to Friday so they could work their last shift together. Similarly, Savannah would change from Friday to Saturday to work her final shift with me."

My throat gets tight. Saturday. Saturday is August second. The day I'm supposed to speak at the ceremony.

Doctor Kent addresses me. "By racking up one last shift together, it will also keep the medical school satisfied that you've completed enough shifts with your mentor for the rotation." He shakes his head. "Even though you underwent surgery, the credentialing folks remained pretty strict about the number of shifts they expected you to finish with me to get credit for the month."

"The swap would be absolutely fine with me, Doctor Kent," Rachel declares, and I swear that she nearly salutes him. "I can work on Friday with Doctor Fox. Is there anything else that I can do for you?"

Doctor Kent turns to her, and the corners of his mouth twitch so slightly that I doubt Rachel notices. "No, Rachel. I believe that's everything. Thanks." He observes me again. "What about you, Savannah? Would the swap work okay?"

"Saturday?" I say carefully. "This Saturday?"

"This Saturday."

"Saturday, August second?"

"August second."

I study his face. Is he making the connection, or has he forgotten? No, there's no way that Doctor Kent forgot what's happening on August second. He's spent over two years embroiled in the politics that led up to the event. I also doubt that he forgot what I'm already scheduled to do on that day. He knows that I'm slated to speak at that ceremony. So why would he agree to make the swap with Doctor Fox? Is he testing me? Is he trying to figure out whose side I'm really on?

Maybe he's trying to prevent me from speaking. I grow indig nant at the thought. While I certainly don't want to participate, it's beyond insulting to think that Doctor Kent would be presumptuous enough to attempt to swoop in and stop me. As if he thinks that he can control what I do. As if . . .

Or maybe he's trying to give me an out. Perhaps he's trying to give me an excuse so I don't have to speak, if I don't want to. The thought makes me want to laugh and cry at the same time. I would give anything to get out of my commitment, but I can't. If I fail to speak, Rick Gatz will make sure that Doctor Kent's career is ruined.

I feel my heart sink as the impossibility of the situation becomes clear. I have to speak on Saturday to save Doctor Kent's career, and so I can't swap shifts to work in the ED with him that day. And since I won't work one last shift with him, the medical school won't give me credit for completing this rotation. I'll have to delay graduating. I'll miss the window to apply for residency this year.

But then another thought strikes me:

"What time would our shift be on Saturday?"

Doctor Kent's expression changes barely. "Nine in the morning."

A flicker of hope lights within me. I actually might be able to make this work. I could get to the Saturday shift at nine. Then a little before one, I'll pretend that my ankle is hurting. I'll slip away to the ceremony and say a few words, and then return to the ED before Doctor Kent has a chance to wonder what's up.

"The nine o'clock shift on Saturday morning sounds fine, Doctor Kent." I'm unable to hide the relief in my voice.

He takes a second before replying. "Great. I'll tell Doctor Fox. Thanks, ladies, for being flexible. I know she'll appreciate it."

After a last glance at me, Doctor Kent heads off down the hall. I stare after him, until I hear Rachel gasp in horror.

I spin toward her, alarmed. "What's wrong?"

"I forgot to include something in one of my answers!" She rushes back into the room to find Lynn.

With a shake of my head that even Austin would approve of, I step out into the hallway. I find Danielle waiting for me with a curious gleam in her eye. She charges to my side.

"Soooo, what did you and Doctor Kent talk about?" Danielle can barely contain her enthusiasm as we start toward the elevator. "Did you guys clear up your misunderstanding? Did he ask you out?"

I give her a side glance. "We were discussing a schedule swap."

"A schedule swap?" Her face falls. "That's all?"

I push the elevator call button. "That's all."

Danielle purses her lips thoughtfully. "Maybe he was talking in code about something else, like going out on a date."

"Doubt it."

The elevator doors open, and I find myself staring at Rick Gatz and Mark Prescott.

"Savannah!" Mr. Gatz lets out an uneasy laugh. He steps off the elevator. "Our little star of the show!"

"Hi," I mutter.

Mr. Gatz starts moving past me. "Sorry we can't stay and chat, but we have a meeting."

However, Mr. Prescott doesn't seem to be in the same kind of rush. He smiles. "Nice to see you again, Savannah. How are your injuries healing up?"

"They're doing well. Thanks for asking."

I glance between the two of them. It's staggering to realize that Mr. Prescott doesn't know that his own vice president has been lying to investors and generating false statistics about the ED. Mr. Prescott has no idea what's going on behind his back, and I do. But if I try to tell him, he will never believe me.

"So are you prepared for Saturday?" Mr. Prescott goes on pleasantly.

"No, actually, she's not," Danielle cuts in before I can answer. "She hasn't received any information about what she's supposed to be doing." Danielle finishes by looking at me proudly, as if she's just done me a huge favor.

Mr. Prescott peers at Mr. Gatz and says, "Savannah still hasn't been given the information about this Saturday?"

Mr. Gatz, who had already started escaping down the hallway, slinks back to join us. "We met yesterday, actually." He shoots a threatening look my way. "We discussed quite a few things, didn't we, Savannah?"

I glare right back at him. "Yeah. Our meeting was quite *insightful.*"

"You met yesterday?" Danielle asks me, clearly bewildered. "But last night you were telling me that you didn't even know how long you were supposed to speak for."

Now Mr. Prescott is the one who seems puzzled. His eyes shift between Danielle and me, and then he places his attention on Mr. Gatz once more. "Is this true?"

Mr. Gatz wipes his brow. "Savannah and I have discussed everything, but I suppose that we can chat about the details *again.* You can never be too prepared for these types of things, after all."

"No, you can't," Mr. Prescott remarks in an odd tone.

Mr. Gatz fakes another smile and starts to speak fast. "Savannah, the program will take place on the large lawn in front of the hospital. You should be there no later than twelve-fifteen. Then you—"

"Twelve-fifteen?" I cut in.

Mr. Gatz narrows his eyes. "Twelve-fifteen."

My stomach knots up. Twelve-fifteen. I'll have to slip out of the ED earlier than I was planning. So I'm going to have to come up with a really good excuse to explain to Doctor Kent why I'm gone from work for so long. Will he buy it?

Mr. Gatz goes on, "You'll begin your speech shortly after one. We've blocked out thirty minutes for you to discuss—"

"Thirty minutes?" I screech before I can stop myself.

"Were you really not informed about any of this, Savannah?" Mr. Prescott actually sounds a little upset.

I see Mr. Gatz clench his jaw as he watches me. I get the hint.

"Maybe I'm just getting stage fright." I force a laugh. "It's probably affecting my memory."

Mr. Prescott nods understandingly. "We don't want you to be nervous. This should be a fun experience—one that you remember as a highlight of your medical school career. Right, Rick?"

"Absolutely," Mr. Gatz pretends to agree.

I hate Rick Gatz.

"Do you have any other questions?" Mr. Prescott asks me in a kind way. "We want to make sure that you feel completely prepared."

I unclench my fists and kick the carpet with my good toe. "Um, yeah. Could you please *remind* me what you actually want me to talk about?"

I think Mr. Prescott is truly alarmed now.

Mr. Gatz hastily pipes up, "*As we already discussed,* Savannah, you should introduce yourself and talk about your career plans. Then describe your accident and discuss the magnificent care that you received from the trauma and orthopedic surgery services. That will be a nice lead-in for you to discuss your support of the decision to remodel the elective surgery center. Alright?"

"Fine. I can do that."

"Wonderful!" Mr. Gatz again begins moving away. "Well, we must run. Please excuse us."

Mr. Prescott casts another curious look at me before the two suits stride off down the hall.

"Geez, what was Gatz so wound up about?" Danielle wonders.

"Hmm?" I fake surprise. "Wound up? Did he seem wound up to you?"

"Definitely. He was nervous or something. Really jittery."

204

I am suddenly very interested in examining my fingernails. "I guess I didn't notice."

"And I still don't get it, Sav, why did you change your mind and decide to speak at the ceremony?"

I shrug. "I didn't want to flake out on something that I had agreed to do."

Danielle is not buying it. "But we talked about this. You never would have agreed to speak if they had been upfront with you. They misled you on purpose! So you're under no obligation to help them out!"

"I know. But at the same time—"

"At the same time you're agreeing to support them, and you shouldn't. Look, I get that there was a lot of confusion, and I didn't help matters any, but you shouldn't cave to their demands. That's letting them bully you."

"Danielle, I—"

"Besides," she sounds worried, "what about Doctor Kent? I mean, if you speak on Saturday, Doctor Kent is going to think that you're—"

I pin my gaze directly on her. "He'll think I'm what?"

She seems to sense that she's said too much. "Sorry. I didn't mean—"

"Danielle, for the last time, let the Doctor Kent thing go. Please. Just leave me alone, alright?"

Danielle backs up for the door that leads to the stairs. "Fine. I'll leave you alone. Do what you want, Sav. I was only trying to help."

She pushes open the door and rushes into the stairwell. The door slams behind her, the sound echoing painfully in my ears before it dies away.

"Savannah, what are you still doing here?" Now Lynn is coming down the hall from the conference room with the stack of completed exams in her hand.

"Oh, I was about to leave."

"Good! Get out and enjoy some sunshine!" She cheerily continues by me. "Have a wonderful day!"

"I'll try."

As Lynn heads down the hall, the elevator chimes. The doors open. Brittany steps out and saunters into the foyer. She slows her pace.

"Hi, Savannah. Ready for your big speech?"

She doesn't wait for a reply before she brushes by me.

I crutch into the elevator alone and push the call button. Saturday. I just have to get through Saturday. Then all of this will be over.

Chapter Fourteen

Hello, my name is Savannah Drake. Why have you come to the emergency department today?"

The guy who is seated in a chair beside the stretcher starts to reply, but I'm barely paying attention. I glance at the clock for about the three hundredth time since starting my shift. It's only nine-forty. Thankfully, I still have nearly three hours before I need to be at the ceremony.

"And this one is from July seventh at four-twenty in the afternoon," I hear the guy say. He digs around in a container he brought, which is on the floor at his feet, and pulls out something to show me.

"I see," I reply distractedly.

While the patient continues talking, I go over my plan in my head again. Around noon, I'll pretend to have a flare up of ankle pain. I'll tell Doctor Kent that I need to lie down, and that's when I'll slip away to the ceremony. Everything will be fine.

"And this was a very interesting one from July ninth." The patient reaches again into the container, which I realize is a cooler.

I'll be gone from the ED for ninety minutes. Two hours, max. After I'm done, I'll return, tell Doctor Kent that I'm feeling better, and finish the shift.

"And this occurred about an hour ago," the patient remarks. "It's not frozen like the others, but I wanted you to have a recent one. Forgive the smell."

I snap to awareness. "The smell?"

He holds up a large freezer baggie, which has something inside. "Yes. It's quite fresh."

A horrible stench begins filling my nose.

"Sir, is that a *stool sample*?"

"Of course. That's what I've been saying. It's my most recent one."

I stare. This man has brought in a cooler full of his own neatly packaged stool samples, with each baggie meticulously dated and timed.

"It was fortunate that this happened right before I came in, don't you think?" He proudly holds the baggie higher aloft. "You'll have a fresh sample for comparison."

My eyes drop to the mound of baggies he has piled on the floor. Then I read the triage note on the chart:

65-year-old man here for ???

Slowly, I peer at the man again. Dressed in shorts and tropical-patterned shirt, he appears extremely comfortable.

I cough. "Sir, what made you decide to come to the emergency department on a Saturday morning with all of these?"

He carefully sets down the baggie next to the others. "My freezer was full."

I think I am going to vomit.

"So what do you think?" He motions to the collection on the floor.

"What do I think?"

"Yes. I don't know what to make of it. Some days they're hard. Some days they're soft. Sometimes they're light brown, and other times they—"

"Stop!" I suppress a dry heave. "You need to get those things out of here immediately."

He seems offended. He lifts the newest baggie and examines it once more. "But isn't the smell going to help you figure out what's going on?"

"No. Because we're not going to figure out what's going on." I use the chart to fan the air past my face. "You need to talk to your primary care physician about what's going on. He or she can refer you to gastroenterology."

"But I already have a gastroenterologist. I have an appointment with him on Monday."

I'm pretty sure that my blood pressure is tripling. "Then why did you come to the emergency department?"

"I had a few free hours this morning, so I figured I would come in here to chat with someone today, instead."

"Sir," I bark, "this is the emergency department. We deal with medical emergencies. We do not handle, examine, or test a month's worth of stool samples!"

He appears affronted. "This is not a month's worth. I make far more than this. This is only —"

"Emergency medicine is a specialty, not a catch-all." I exhale severely. "We are trained to manage certain conditions, the same way cardiologists handle heart problems, pediatricians care for children, and gastroenterologists evaluate stool samples."

This seems to be an epiphany for him. "Are you saying that you think it's better if I wait to see my gastroenterologist on Monday?"

"Yes! Unless you think that you are having a medical emergency."

He laughs. "Of course this isn't an emergency, sweetheart! My bowel movements have been like this for years!"

Stay calm. Stay calm.

"I feel great!" the man adds.

I tap the chart. "Then I recommend that you let the gastro-enterology experts handle your chronic gastroenterology issues." I start retreating toward the curtain. "I'll go get my attending so he can see you before you leave."

He motions to the baggies. "You want me to put these away?"

"Definitely."

While the guy begins gently setting each baggie into the cooler, I bolt from the room. Hadi and Doctor Kent are talking nearby. Hadi breaks off from what he's saying and contorts his face as he sniffs the air. Then he does a double take when he sees me.

"Hey, Savannah, you're kind of pale. Green, actually."

Doctor Kent takes a step my way. "Are you alright?"

I jerk my thumb toward the patient's room. "A cooler full of dated and timed stool samples, which are quickly defrosting. The guy only came in here today because his freezer at home was full. Oh, and he brought a fresh sample as a little bonus."

Doctor Kent doesn't move. Hadi begins laughing so hard that he can't stand up straight.

I can no longer hide a grin. "And I told the patient that my attending would be in to see him."

Doctor Kent rubs his forehead. "Why does it not surprise me that you'd get a patient like this?"

I shrug. Hadi is still laughing as he gives Doctor Kent a whack on the back. Doctor Kent resignedly heads off to see the patient.

Hadi eventually controls his laughter. "So I hear this is your last shift in here, huh?"

"Yeah." My grin fades. "My last one."

I pause to gaze around the department. Constant noise, exhausting hours, crazy patients, non-stop interruptions, uncertainty, lack of space and resources, intense emotional ups and downs—the pandemonium that I so dreaded a month ago will be over after today.

And, I realize, I don't think I like that.

Hadi goes on, "Wes tells me that you're going into pediatrics?"

"Yeah. Pediatrics."

"Well, we're gonna miss you. You've been awesome down here."

I look at him. "Thanks. I really appreciate that."

"You're welcome. And I mean it, too. Most med students are like a deer in headlights around this place, but you aren't. You fit in really well. All the nurses think so."

I do a double take. "They do?"

"Yeah, they do. So does . . ."

Hadi goes quiet when the curtain to the patient's room is pushed aside. Doctor Kent steps out with the man, who is protectively cradling his cooler of precious treasures in his arms.

"Enjoy your weekend," Doctor Kent tells him. "And don't forget to see your doctor on Monday."

The man obediently heads to the exit.

Doctor Kent puts an extra dollop of sanitizer on his hands before he rejoins us. "Just when you think you've seen—and smelled—it all."

I start to giggle but stop abruptly when I notice the clock on the wall. Nine-fifty."Doctor Kent, we've got a code coming in," announces the charge nurse.

Hadi starts for the resuscitation bay. "I'll go set up."

"Here's what I've got so far," the charge nurse says to both Doctor Kent and me. She refers to her notes. "Twenty-five-year-old male. Downtown at the pier. Fell into the water. Cause of the fall unclear. Rescued by witnesses and resuscitation began. Possible v-tach. IV established. Medics are still doing CPR."

Doctor Kent is more focused than I have ever seen him before. "ETA?"

"Ten minutes," the charge nurse replies.

I look up at Doctor Kent.

He sets his gaze on mine. "Are you ready for one last code?"

"Yes," I reply. "One last code."

We go together into the resuscitation bay, where the familiar, coordinated dance is already starting to play out: nurses setting out what they need, techs bringing in equipment and preparing to do chest compressions, the radiology tech moving into the corner to wait, and the social worker on standby near the door. Without breaking stride, Doctor Kent goes to the head of the stretcher and sets out the airway equipment. When he tosses on a protective gown over his scrubs, I grab another gown and start to do the same.

"What do you think you're doing?" he asks.

I freeze with my gown halfway over my head. "Getting ready to help with the airway."

"No, you're not. You're going to run this thing."

My heart slams. "But this patient is young. He may actually have a chance. You don't want me messing it up."

His dark eyes flash. "Savannah Drake, you know what to do. So save this kid's life, alright?"

And with that, Doctor Kent resumes setting up airway equipment. I slowly peer around. I'm running this code. I am in charge of trying to save this patient's life—a patient who is about my age—a patient who still has a lot of life to live. I can't let this young man die.

"Al-alright, everyone," I stammer. "I'm going to be running this code."

"What did you say?" a nurse at the other end of the resuscitation bay calls out, putting a hand to her ear. "Can you speak up?"

"I'm running this code," I repeat, my voice gaining traction.

There is a surprised break in the commotion, and I can feel my face getting warm under everyone's stares. I peek again at Doctor Kent, who just continues what he's doing. I take another breath. This really is my code. I feel that powerful sense of calm and focus settle over me. Now, nothing else matters. It's just me, the ED crew, and the young man whose life we have to save.

"Do we have airway?" I ask.

"That'll be me," Doctor Kent replies.

"And respiratory therapy is here," a woman adds from close by.

I nod. "Chest compressions?"

A tech motions to herself and the guy beside her. "We'll be alternating."

"Great. IV access?"

Hadi raises an arm. "All over it."

"Putting the patient on the monitor?"

"I'll do that," another nurse states.

"Who's pushing meds?"

"Me."

My eyes keep moving methodically around the resuscitation bay. "Someone to document?"

"Right here."

"Radiology?"

"Yup."

"Ultrasound?" I inquire.

"It's here for you," another tech announces, motioning to the machine.

"Okay. And—"

The resuscitation bay door is pushed open. I stand up straight, ready to take control. But it is not the EMS crew who enters. It's Erik, and Brittany is right behind him.

"What do we have coming in?" Erik demands.

I step forward. "Twenty-five-year-old male submerged in ocean water. Possible v-tach."

Brittany puts her hands on her hips. "Are you practicing on another code?"

A tense hush settles over the room. But it doesn't rattle me now. I'm in my element. This is my code.

"No, I'm not practicing," I tell her. "I'm running this."

For one moment, Brittany seems surprised. Then her smirk reappears. "Well, try not to take forever before calling this one, okay?"

The time. I forgot about the time.

I whip my head toward the clock and exhale with relief. It's only ten-fifteen. I have plenty of time before I need to be at the ceremony.

The door is slammed open again, and a new rush surges through me. The patient is here. My patient is here.

The EMS crew charges into the resuscitation bay, pushing a stretcher with the young man lying upon it. One of the medics is doing crisp chest compressions and another is managing his airway.

"Currently in asystole," the lead medic announces loudly.

The patient is transferred over to our stretcher. An ED tech takes over chest compressions as another starts peeling off the patient's cold, wet clothing. Meanwhile, Hadi begins working on placing a second IV in the patient's arm, and another nurse puts the patient on our cardiac monitor.

"Twenty-five-year-old male who was at the pier downtown with his friends," the lead medic reports over the din. "An object was dropped from a balcony above and struck the patient on the head. He is believed to have been knocked out, causing him to fall into the water."

"Second IV is in," Hadi states.

"The patient was pulled out of the water by witnesses. A bystander initiated CPR," the lead crew member goes on, his forehead lined with perspiration. "Upon our assessment, he was unresponsive, apneic, and pulseless. His initial rhythm was v-tach. He was shocked once. After that, he went into asystole and has remained asystolic since. Estimated down time since water rescue is sixty minutes."

"Thank you." I turn to the tech. "Hold compressions."

The tech stops pounding on the young man's chest. I watch the cardiac monitor and wait. But the only sound that the monitor makes is a steady, quiet tone, and nothing shows on the screen except for flat green line. Confirmed asystole. The young man's heart isn't beating. He's dead.

My thoughts remain crystal-clear. "Please resume chest compressions," I order the tech. Next, I address Doctor Kent. "Ready?"

Airway equipment in hand, Doctor Kent is completely businesslike. "Ready."

The respiratory therapist moves the bag away from the patient's mouth, giving Doctor Kent room to work. Within seconds, Doctor Kent has the endotracheal tube inserted. He uses his stethoscope to listen for breath sounds.

"Airway is in place." Doctor Kent takes the stethoscope from his ears while the respiratory therapist connects the patient to the ventilator.

I motion to the lead medic. "Anything else?"

"Friends are in the waiting room. Social work is meeting with them to contact his family."

"Thanks."

As the EMS crew packs up, I feel someone come up beside me. I glance over and see that it's Erik. He smiles flirtatiously at me.

"Glad you're running this instead of Kent," he whispers. "At least it won't take forever this time."

I return my focus to watching the resuscitation. "What do you mean?"

"Over sixty minutes of asystole?" he goes on. "You aren't getting this one back."

I shift on my crutches while my eyes settle upon the nameless young man on the stretcher. His heart isn't beating. He's dead. And he has been dead for over an hour. The chance of this young man's survival is basically none, and the chance of meaningful survival is even less.

But he's only twenty-five. He is not supposed to die.

"You want meds?" one nurse shouts.

I lift my head but hesitate. It feels like I'm missing something.

"Meds?" the nurse repeats.

I'm still racking my brain. "Um, one of epi, please."

"You're going to run a code on a guy who's been dead for over an hour?" Brittany frowns. "Great idea. Really good use of everyone's time."

Erik gives me a playful nudge. "It's okay, as long as we're not still here this evening. After all, some of us have a date to go on, right?"

Brittany glares. Out of my eye, I see Doctor Kent watching too.

But I don't care. That stuff is not important. Nothing is important but the patient.

I look at the nurse and say it again. "Yes, one of epi, please."

"You got it." The nurse promptly pushes the medication into one of the patient's IVs as chest compressions continue.

Brittany throws up her hands. "Seriously?"

A few staff members glance my way, and my confidence falters. I know what people are thinking, and they're right. There's no point in doing this—the patient has been dead for way too long. No one can survive without a pulse for over sixty minutes, no matter how young.

I turn to Doctor Kent, expecting him to signal me to call the code. But he doesn't. From the look in his eyes, it's almost like he's waiting for me to do something.

"Hey, do we need to keep these for any reason?" One of the techs holds up the patient's water-logged jeans.

I catch my breath. Water. This patient was submerged in water. Ocean water. Extremely cold water. Hypothermia-inducing water.

He's not dead until he's warm and dead.

"Hadi," I sputter, "I need a core temperature."

"You got it," he replies.

Doctor Kent smiles slightly.

Brittany rolls her eyes. "She has got to be kidding."

Erik slides closer to me. "Don't feel pressured to run a long code because your attending is here. Dead is dead."

"I don't care who's here," I retort. "We can't call this before he's been warmed up and we confirm that he's still asystolic."

Erik backs up without replying.

"Twenty-six degrees Celsius," Hadi announces, hooking up the temperature probe.

I speak to the whole team. "Alright, we need to raise his temperature. Where's the warming machine?"

"Broken," a tech tells me, gesturing to a discarded device that's sitting in the corner. From the amount of dust collected on a red tag that's hanging from the machine, I doubt the work order is going to be filled any time soon.

I sigh. We're doing to have to do this the slow way. "Okay, I want warmed O2 going, warm blankets and warm IV fluid, and bladder irrigation. And let's get an NG tube placed for possible warm gastric lavage."

The team springs into action while the techs continue the exhausting work of chest compressions. Everything is in motion. All I can do now is continue directing efforts until the patient is warmed up to at least—

"Savannah," Erik interrupts my thoughts, "don't you think this is overkill? Warming him was a nice idea, but it's been over thirty minutes now."

I blink. Thirty minutes? Thirty minutes have passed already? How is that possible? I check the clock. It's ten fifty-five. I have barely more than an hour before I'm supposed to clear out of here and go to the ceremony—or else Doctor Kent will lose his job. I glance at the temperature probe. To my dismay, the patient hasn't even warmed a full degree.

"There's nothing you can do for him." Erik starts reading a message on one of his pagers. "At this rate, it's gonna be a long time before he's even warmed up to where you want him, and then he'll still be dead."

I look from the clock to Erik to the patient. "We have to keep going until he's about thirty-two degrees Celsius."

Erik puts his pager away. "There's a difference between a textbook and real life. In the real world—"

"In the real world, he still has to be warmed . . . even if it takes a long time," I insist, though my voice catches.

He lets out a sigh, as if he's trying to be understanding. "Fine. Your call."

Erik moves away and says something to Brittany. She rolls her eyes again.

"Hey, need a break?" I hear Hadi ask the tech who is doing chest compressions.

"Thanks, man." The tech wearily steps aside to let Hadi take over.

I watch as Hadi starts pounding on the lifeless young man's chest, and then I survey the room once again. The place remains packed with doctors, nurses, techs, EMS personnel, social work, respiratory therapy, volunteers, and radiology team members. As I count the number of people in the resuscitation bay, I'm overwhelmed with guilt. Because of my decision, all of these resources are being devoted to one patient—one dead patient—while countless other people in the ED are waiting for care.

What should I do?

I drift my gaze to Doctor Kent. As if he senses me watching him, he looks my way. I search his face. He searches mine. Then he turns back to watch the team's efforts. For me, it's all I need. I am going to keep trying to save this kid's life.

Chest compressions continue. As more time passes, although the intense energy in the resuscitation bay remains, a palpable sense of doubt is setting in. It's clear that the mental and physical fatigue from the prolonged resuscitation is taking its toll. People are whispering. I notice a tech showing someone her watch. Brittany shoots Erik yet another aggravated look. And I overhear one nurse saying something about how I'm "just a med student."

"Twenty-nine." Hadi reads the temperature probe. "He's up to twenty-nine degrees."

"Fabulous. What's next?" Brittany feigns curiosity. "After spending another very productive twenty minutes on a dead guy, Savannah, what's your next step?"

My eyes leap to the clock, and my mouth goes dry. It's eleven-twenty.

"Please assess for cardiac activity," I instruct.

Tension is thick in the air as chest compressions are stopped. The line on the cardiac monitor remains flat, announcing to everyone that the young man's heart is still not beating. His heart hasn't beat in over two hours now. He's dead. Long dead.

Meanwhile, outside the resuscitation bay, countless other patients—some who are extremely sick—still remain uncared for. All because I'm insisting that we keep working on a dead guy.

Erik puts a hand on my shoulder. "It's time to stop."

I look away. What am I really trying to do here? How can I expect this patient to have a meaningful recovery—or any recovery at all—after being pulseless for so long? So what should I do now? Stick with the plan and force everyone to keep going until we finally get to a number on a temperature probe? Or, after repeatedly insisting that we keep working, must I suddenly admit that it was pointless?

I look again at Doctor Kent.

"You're running this code, Savannah." It's clear that he knows exactly what is going through my mind. "It's your decision."

Behind him, the clock on the wall ticks forward to eleven-forty-five. I have half an hour before I'm supposed at the ceremony.

The patient has been dead for over two hours.

But he's too young to die.

"They're not dead unless they're warm and dead," I can hear Doctor Kent telling me on that first day.

I put my eyes on the lifeless young man. I have to make a decision.

"Please continue chest compressions," I say.

There is murmuring throughout the room.

Erik remains at my side. "Savannah, we all have other patients to see."

"Thirty-one degrees," I hear Hadi call out.

"Yeah, don't be embarrassed to call the code," Brittany tells me. "It's okay that you don't know what you're doing yet."

"Thirty-two degrees," Hadi announces.

I catch my breath. "Hold chest compressions and check his rhythm."

The tech stops pumping on the young man's chest. The room becomes perfectly, nerve-rackingly still as everyone watches the monitor and waits. I clench my fists anxiously. Hopefully.

But the line on the cardiac monitor remains flat.

The young man is dead.

All of that work—all of that time—for nothing. I didn't save him. Devastated, I lower my head. I made an idiot of myself on my first day in the Emergency Department, and I've made an idiot of myself on the last. I cannot believe that ever thought I belonged here. I—

Blip.

A sound from the cardiac monitor echoes throughout the resuscitation bay. I whip my head up and stare.

Blip.

Blip. Blip. Blip.

As the sound picks up speed, recognizable waveforms start traveling across the monitor's screen. There's a collective gasp around the room. The patient has cardiac activity.

"Do we have a pulse with that?" I ask, shaking.

Seeming to be the only person in the room who isn't frozen with shock, Doctor Kent steps forward, reaches down, and palpates the patient's neck. "We have a pulse."

Every emotion in the world crashes over me. The young man's heart is beating. Nearly three hours without a pulse, and the kid is alive.

"Still at thirty-two degrees," Hadi adds.

I make myself breathe in and out while I try to process what's happening. The patient is alive, and he's right where we want him: warm enough to perfuse and benefit from our interventions, but still cool enough to continue receiving the protective benefit of hypothermia. This young man has a real chance for a meaningful recovery.

In a haze, I back up. "Doctor Kent, I'll go call the ICU, if you're good managing stuff in here."

He looks at me. "I'm good."

I turn to leave and nearly crash into Erik and Brittany, who are still hovering behind me. There's a pause. Brittany's cheeks get red, and she hurriedly spins away from me and walks out the door. Erik observes me for a long second, gives me a nod, and goes after Brittany.

I watch them depart and then head toward the door myself. But before I step out, I take one last moment to peer over my shoulder. From where he has now positioned himself at the foot of the stretcher, Doctor Kent raises his eyes and gives me a smile. I smile back.

He was right.

Chapter Fifteen

And we're maintaining him in therapeutic hypothermia ranges," I finish saying.

"Great," the intensivist replies over the phone. "I'll be down in five minutes, and we'll get him up to the ICU. Nice work."

I hang up, trembling more now than I was a few minutes ago. The emotions are starting to kick in fully. That young man is alive. And although he'll likely never even know my name, I will always remember him.

After another moment of reflection, I sit up with a start. What time is it?

I spot the nearest clock and jolt in alarm. It's twelve-ten. I'm supposed to be on stage in five minutes.

I burst out of my chair so fast that I knock my bag over, spilling my cell phone onto the floor. The phone promptly lights up and plays another distorted song. I pick up the phone, press a bunch of buttons to shut it up, and then jam it into the pocket of my scrubs top alongside my speech cue cards.

Using my crutches, I scamper toward the charge nurse. "When Doctor Kent comes out of the resuscitation bay, could you tell him that I wasn't feeling well, and so I went to lie down?"

"Of course," she replies. "Nice job with that code, by the way."

"Thanks!" I call to her over my shoulder, heading for the exit as fast as my crutches will allow.

I plow out of the building and rush down the sidewalk toward the front of the hospital. Noise and music from up ahead steadily get louder as I go. When I finally round the corner, I come to a halt in the blazing sunlight.

This is worse than I thought. Way worse.

The expansive lawn in front of the hospital is filled with people. There must be thousands of attendees here—men and women in business attire, parents with their kids, photographers, vendors, journalists, and hospital staff are everywhere. *Everywhere.*

I start venturing forward into the terrifying scene. I see that the perimeter of the lawn is lined with booths where visitors can get food, receive information about the hospital and its services, and participate in various family games. There are musicians performing on stages. Scents of hot dogs, cotton candy, and popcorn drift through the air. Children who have their faces painted run by me, carrying balloons shaped like animals. On the far side of the lawn, someone is making an announcement about a relay race that is going to begin soon.

Basically, an entire state fair has been set up here at the hospital.

Begrudgingly, I turn my path toward the front of the endless crowd, headed for a larger stage that's decorated with blue and white balloons. A humongous banner hanging off the front of the stage reads, *"Lakewood Medical Center: For the patients, for the future."*

As I get closer, I focus on the fancy podium that's on the stage. It has enormous speakers on each side of it—apparently, they want my speech to be audible on the other side of the ocean. Collected near the podium is a group of people who are all dressed in business suits despite the heat of the day. When I note Rick Gatz and Mark Prescott among the clan, my throat tightens. That group must include the other hospital administrators and the investors—the men and women whom Mr. Gatz lied to about the ED census numbers.

I see Rick Gatz check his watch, undoubtedly wondering when I am going to arrive. It's time for me to make my presence known. Tormented by the thought of what I'm about to do, I shove my way faster through the ever-growing crowd. I've nearly reached the stage when I come to another halt.

The media. I forgot about the media.

Right in front of the stage are rows and rows and rows of reporters. Further crowding the space are people who are setting up to record video and photographers prepping cameras with massive lenses. And each one of them is focused on one thing: the podium. The podium from where I will be speaking.

"Ah, Savannah, I was beginning to wonder if you were going to show up."

I nearly cry out in surprise. Rick Gatz somehow made it down from the stage and to my side. He's observing me with his creepy eyes.

"I came from the ED," I explain testily. "I had a sick patient."

He clucks with disapproval. "Ah, so that explains the rather *casual* attire you have on."

My attire? I hadn't even thought about that what I was going to wear for this shin-dig. I peek down at my wrinkled, faded blue scrubs. But instead of shame, I feel pride.

"Yeah. Scrubs." I say, pointedly glancing at his suit. "This is what you wear when you actually take care of patients."

His eyes narrow. Before he can reply, though, someone behind me calls out:

"Is this Miss Drake? Miss Drake, I have a question!"

I peek over my shoulder and seize up with terror. A legion of reporters is coming for me. They all start shouting.

"Miss Drake, I have a question!"

"Miss Drake, is it true that Wes Kent has been your attending in the ER?"

"How do you feel about the fact that Doctor Kent lied about ER census numbers?"

"Do you think that Wes Kent has been putting himself in the spotlight in hopes of advancing his own career?"

"Miss Drake, could you please describe to us your relationship with Doctor Kent?" The reporters all hold out their microphones toward me, waiting.

"I, well, I . . ."

A camera flashes. Then another. And another. Now everyone is shouting at me again.

"Miss Drake, please tell us what you think of Doctor Kent!"

"How does Doctor Kent feel about you supporting the elective surgery center remodel?"

"Does Doctor Kent—"

"Ladies and gentlemen!" Rick Gatz says over the ruckus, clearly enjoying every bit of it. "There will be plenty of time for questions with Miss Drake after she gives her speech. I'm sure that we're all extremely interested in what she has to say, especially about Wesley Kent. So please hold your questions until later."

There is a collective moan of disappointment from the reporters. A few more cameras flash, and then they begin returning to their place by the stage.

"Questions afterward?" I growl at Mr. Gatz. "You expect me to stay and answer questions?"

"Of course. Did I fail to mention that was part of the agreement?" He chuckles wickedly. "Must have slipped my mind."

"How long will it take?"

"As long as I want it to."

He has me completely trapped, and he knows it. I have to pretend as though I support the most evil, dishonest person I have ever met.

"You're on a smear campaign," I snap. "You want to destroy Doctor Kent's career because he threatens you. You're scared of him."

He laughs heartily. "Oh, Savannah, you're making this far too personal. This is simply business. This is the real world." He gestures toward the stage. "Shall we go?"

Without waiting for my answer, he starts leading the way forward. Under the growing scrutiny of thousands, I follow and gingerly crutch up the staircase to the stage. The investors break off from their conversations, observing me curiously.

"Savannah, how are you?" Mark Prescott comes over to shake my hand.

"I'm fine. Thanks."

He motions to three vacant chairs that are off to one side of the podium. "Please have a seat. I believe everyone is here, so we're ready to get going."

More cameras flash as I move to the row of empty chairs and drop onto the one in the middle. Mr. Gatz promptly takes the seat on my right. The empty chair on the other side, I decide, must be for Mark Prescott himself, who has now positioned himself behind the podium. The investors sit down in the rows of chairs that are behind us. The crowd comes to an expectant hush.

"Ladies and Gentleman, we welcome you to Lakewood Medical Center!" Mr. Prescott's voice booms out from the speakers.

The audience applauds. With an air of showmanship, Mr. Prescott waits until the noise dies down. Then he continues:

"Today is very special for this hospital and this community. Today, we are celebrating the start of our elective surgery center remodel!"

There are cheers from the crowd, and the investors behind me begin clapping, too. I shake my head. Don't they get it? Statistics or not, how do they not understand that while they're partying out here, people with medical emergencies are sitting in the ED without even a room to be examined in?

"To start off this celebration, we have someone very special here with us," Mr. Prescott is saying. "Miss Savannah Drake, a fourth-year medical student, has quite an inspiring story of how the surgical care at Lakewood Medical Center changed her life."

Changed my life? Is he serious?

Mr. Prescott gestures toward me. "So without further adieu, please welcome, Miss Savannah Drake!"

The crowd breaks into more boisterous applause, and the photographers and cameramen shove even closer to the stage. I drag myself to my feet and crutch over to the podium. Mr. Prescott steps aside, proudly leading the audience in another round of cheers before he takes his seat.

Alone at the podium, I stare out at the sea of faces before me. I don't bother reaching into my pocket for my cue cards. I don't need them. It was easy to memorize this speech. It covers each point that Rick Gatz demanded be included. No more. No less.

"Hello, everyone," I say into the microphone, startled by the way my voice reverberates from the speakers. I then proceed with rattling off my prepared remarks. "My name is Savannah Drake. I am currently a fourth-year medical student."

The audience is respectfully quiet. I hear more photos being taken. Reporters are scribbling notes and holding up small audio recording devices. Video cameras are pointed directly at me. So far, so good. Only twenty-nine minutes left.

"I'm here to tell you about an experience that I had this past month," I go on without emotion. "A few weeks ago, while hiking, I fell down the side of a mountain. I suffered several injuries, including a badly fractured ankle."

I wave my crutches slightly, as I planned to do. There is appreciative laughter from the crowd. More cameras flash. Out of the corner of my eye, I see Rick Gatz and Mark Prescott exchange smiles, clearly pleased with how things are going.

"My ankle fracture required surgical repair," I continue blandly. "But thankfully, I was taken here to Lakewood Medical Center, a place that is famous for providing excellent care."

The audience breaks into more cheers. I fake a smile, grateful for any reason to let extra seconds pass. As I wait for the audience to settle, a motion near the front of the crowd catches my attention. The white coat army has arrived. Erik and Brittany, accompanied by several other interns and residents from the surgery department, are merging into the throng with their aura of importance. Clearing my throat, I look out over the audience and resume speaking:

"While I was a patient at Lakewood Medical Center, I received wonderful care from the general surgery, trauma, and orthopedic services. I can personally attest to the amazing care that this hospital's surgery programs provide."

I let my words linger before adding, "After experiencing such fantastic care, I came to understand how important it is that Lakewood Medical Center's surgery department be supported. This will allow future patients to receive the same type of exceptional care as I did. And the importance of patients receiving the best care possible is particularly meaningful to me, for I will soon be starting my own career as a physician."

More applause. More photos being taken. Mr. Prescott continues to smile. Rick Gatz is beaming in triumph. But I'm only wondering how much more time I have left to fill before this stupidity is over. Suppressing a roll of my eyes, I go on to the next part of my speech:

"My experiences over this past month have changed me, and I have come to realize that . . ."

I trail off when I notice someone moving forward through the crowd. I blink a few times, and then my pulse starts racing. It's Doctor Kent. Ignoring the reporters, he is keeping his eyes trained on mine as he makes his way to the front of the stage. As always, his expression is impossible to read. I have to take a moment before I can resume my speech:

"As I was saying, my experiences over this past month have changed me. I have come to realize that . . . that . . ."

Again I falter, my memorized speech fading from my mind. I look again at Doctor Kent, and I realize that it's time for me to say something else. Something more.

"When I started medical school," I explain into the microphone, "I was certain that I wanted to go into pediatrics."

I have no idea what I'm trying to say, but I want Doctor Kent to understand the truth. Driven by something that I don't totally understand, I keep talking:

"However, this past month caused me to do a lot of soul searching, and I discovered that there was something else I wanted to do with my career." I am forced into quiet by another swell of emotion. Several seconds go by before I'm able to proceed. I discovered the place where I really want to care for patients. A place that's crazy, unpredictable, and challenging. That place is the emergency department."

I catch my breath as I realize what I've declared. Emergency medicine. I want to go into emergency medicine. It seems so obvious now. The specialty fits me like a glove. For some unexplainable reason, despite the madness—or, strangely, perhaps because of it—the emergency department is where I am at home.

Murmuring filters among the crowd, and expressions of confusion are appearing on people's faces. I need to get this speech back on track. But then someone waves at me from the audience. It's Danielle. She's standing beside Joel and watching me with happy tears in her eyes. Strengthened by her support, I lean closer to the microphone and go on:

"You may wonder what the emergency department has to do with what we're talking about here today." The image of the elderly woman lying in the walkway stretcher is now forefront in my mind. "You may not be aware that the emergency department is also hoping to renovate their facilities. Without funding to expand and update the ED, critically ill and injured patients may not be able to receive the care that they need and deserve."

Reporters are starting to fight to get right to the edge of the stage while holding their audio recorders up even higher.

"Many know that I have had the privilege of being supervised in the emergency department by Doctor Kent, who is the leading advocate for funding an ED remodel."

My eyes track again to Doctor Kent before I realize it. There's a wave of frenzied activity as the reporters follow my gaze and recognize him. The news crews are jockeying for position to take his photograph. But Doctor Kent doesn't seem to notice any of it. His focus remains completely on me.

I speak above the racket. "However, based upon recent ED census data, the determination was made that funding an ED remodel was not necessary. Yet I can attest that—"

A sharp cough causes me to break off and look to my left. Mr. Gatz is zeroed in on me, and he appears absolutely enraged. Mark Prescott is observing me closely. The investors have started speaking quietly to each other. Like a slap to the face, I suddenly remember what I'm supposed to be doing here. I'm trying to protect Doctor Kent's career.

I face the crowd to resume my prepared speech, but now I'm so flustered that I don't remember what I am supposed to say next. I hurriedly reach into my scrubs pocket for my cue cards. My hand hits my cell phone, which I take from my pocket and set on the podium under the microphone. Then I reach again into my pocket, fish out my cards, and shuffle through my written remarks to find where I left off.

"*Very well. But when Wes Kent loses his job and can't get hired anywhere else, be sure to tell him that it was your fault.*"

I jump when the unmistakable sound of Rick Gatz's voice carries loudly over the speakers. Everyone, including myself, glances around in bewilderment. Mr. Gatz is still seated in his chair, and he appears as stunned as I am.

What is going on?

A flash of light on the podium catches my eye. I look down and gasp. My cell phone has lit up, and it's playing an audio recording. I grip the podium for support as a one-in-a-trillion thought strikes me: is it possible that my phone actually recorded the conversation that I had with Rick Gatz the other day? When I thought I was pushing buttons to shut it off, did I actually put the phone into record mode?

I stare at my phone, hanging desperately on this insane hope. Please, please let there be more.

"*I can ensure that no respectable hospital will ever hire Wes Kent. A few words of concern from me—perhaps suspicions of stealing medication or poor patient management—will guarantee that he'll never work again."*

I clap my hand over my mouth in astonishment. My busted cell phone recorded the conversation alright. The crowd continues to wait in tense silence, ready to hang on every word.

"But you'd be lying," I listen to myself cry. *"You'd be slandering him."*

Rick Gatz's reply is clear for all to hear. *"Who could prove it? More importantly, who would want to take the risk of hiring someone whose previous employer had such significant concerns?"*

One by one, the cameras are shifting to Mr. Gatz. I, too, peer in his direction. He is seated on the edge of his chair, pale and wiping his brow. The investors are whispering with more animation. Mark Prescott slowly gets to his feet.

My phone makes a strange noise, and then the audio becomes too garbled to understand. I wring my hands, begging my phone not to die yet. Just a little bit more.

"If you refuse to speak, we're going to have a lot of investors wondering why you backed out. Significant questions would resurface. Questions that might make more investors pull out of the project. Questions I don't want to answer, since it was difficult generating false statistics about the ER census in the first place."

My cell phone flashes, plays part of an old ringtone, and then goes black.

Shell-shocked, I lift my eyes. The people in the crowd are still, their attention alternating between where I stand and where Mr. Gatz is seated. Mark Prescott remains on his feet, stony and mute.

A reporter raises his hand. "Miss Drake? Excuse me, Miss Drake?"

"Um, yes?" I say into the microphone.

"Are we to understand that this is a recording of a conversation between Mr. Richard Gatz, Lakewood Medical Center's Vice President, and yourself?"

Is this for real? Is this actually happening?

"That is correct," I answer. "But to be clear, I had no idea that our conversation had been recorded. It was also by accident that the recording played right now."

I am starting to wonder if I could go to jail for this.

Another reporter jumps in. "So Mr. Gatz not only threatened to slander Doctor Wesley Kent, but he also admitted that he falsified the ED census numbers that were presented to the investors and Mark Prescott?"

I gesture to the phone. "You heard it yourself."

There is an explosion of questions and camera flashes. I hear a clatter and look behind me. Mr. Gatz has stood up so fast that he knocked his chair over. After another panicked glance between the news cameras and Mark Prescott, Mr. Gatz scurries off the stage as fast as his stocky legs will carry him. He gets down to the grass, shoves past Erik, Brittany, and the other white coats, and forces a path through the crowd to get away while a parade of reporters goes after him like a pack of wolves chasing their prey.

I think my speech is over.

The gigantic crowd starts to break up amid excited conversations. I wrap my hand around my cell phone and put it carefully back into my pocket.

"Savannah! Savannah!" Danielle rushes up onto the stage with Joel right behind her. "I'm so sorry! I didn't understand! I didn't know!"

"It's okay." I give her a hug. "I wanted to tell you, but I couldn't."

Danielle claps her hands. "That was incredible! *You* are incredible!"

"Yeah, that was some fine undercover work." Joel has admiration in his voice. "How on earth did you manage to get that conversation recorded?"

"Dumb luck," I insist, still amazed myself. "One hundred percent dumb luck."

Joel laughs. Danielle shakes her head, at a loss for words. I just pat my pocket and smile. I love this phone. I'm never getting rid of it.

"Savannah Drake."

I turn around. Mark Prescott is approaching, followed by the investors. He goes on gravely:

"Apparently, there have been things occurring behind the scenes that I was not aware of."

"Yes."

Mr. Prescott seems upset but not angry. "Why didn't you notify me?"

"Trust me, I wanted to. But I didn't know that this conversation had been recorded. Without proof, I knew it would be Mr. Gatz's word against mine, and I didn't think you'd believe me. Plus, I was afraid of what Mr. Gatz might do to Doctor Kent in retaliation."

Mr. Prescott exhales. "Sadly, that is likely true, Savannah. I would never believe that my longtime colleague and presumed friend was so dishonest."

I venture a nod.

"So it is I who needs to apologize," Mr. Prescott continues. "I'm extremely sorry that you had to carry this burden by yourself."

"It's okay." I blink hard. "Thanks."

Mr. Prescott addresses the investors. "We shouldn't let this party go to waste. After all, we spent quite a bit of money on it. So how about we call off the formalities for the day, regroup next week, and discuss our options from there?"

The investors seem to approve. They begin filing off of the stage, some casting me looks as they go. Mark Prescott moves to follow after them but pauses to address me once more:

"Savannah, thank you."

I smile. "You're welcome."

Mr. Prescott leaves the stage. Now Danielle, Joel, and I are the only ones left.

Danielle speaks gently. "Sav, does *he* know? Does he know what happened here?"

I gaze out over the dispersing crowd. "Yeah. I think he knows."

And then I realize that it's past the time for my last ED shift to be done. I don't even need to go back there. It's all over.

Chapter Sixteen

Congratulations, Savannah. This is a big step in your healing process. Literally."

I look up at Dr. Briggs in surprise. I think she just cracked a joke.

"Thanks." I take a few more strides around the exam room in my new walking boot.

Dr. Briggs reassumes her usual brisk tone. "You're ready to transfer further care to your regular doctor. But don't hesitate to call us if there are any concerns."

"I will. Thank you again for your help."

Dr. Briggs steps out of the exam room. After making sure that I have my bus pass, I pick up my purse with one hand and my well-worn crutches with the other. And I walk out. It feels so good to be doing that again.

As I approach the lobby, I hear heavy rain hitting the roof. I pass the receptionist's desk and exit outside through the glass doors, where I hover underneath the awning. It's not just raining, it's absolutely pouring. I check the time. Luckily, the next bus will be here in less than two minutes. Clutching my things, I dart out from under the shelter and hurry across the parking lot, dodging puddles as best as I can. I'm completely soaked by the time I reach the bus stop.

Wiping water from my eyes, I glance behind me to view Lakewood Medical Center for the last time. I'm done with my medical care here, and the rest of my rotations will take place at University Hospital. Then it will be off to residency next summer, wherever that may be. I doubt that I'll ever step inside Lakewood Medical Center again.

I feel a pang of remorse and look away.

Soon, the rumble of a large engine reaches my ears. Brushing aside the hair that has become shellacked to my face, I peer down the road. The bus is approaching, its headlights on and its windshield wipers swishing fast. I raise my arm, signaling the driver. The bus begins to slow, its brakes screeching loudly and its tires throwing a wave of standing water over the curb. Finally, the bus comes to a stop. The doors open.

"Hold the bus!" someone yells.

I inhale sharply. It couldn't be him. There is no way. Still, I turn around. My heart thuds when I see Doctor Kent running toward the bus stop.

"Miss, are you getting on?" I hear the driver ask.

I blink and say over my shoulder, "Would you mind waiting for a second please?"

"You've got exactly sixty seconds." The driver militantly taps his watch.

"Got it. Thanks."

I face forward and resume staring in astonishment while Doctor Kent sprints the rest of the distance across the parking lot. He halts in front of me. His t-shirt and jeans are soaked. Pushing his wet hair back, he settles his eyes on mine.

"Hi, Savannah."

I find that I'm barely able to speak. "Hi, Doctor Kent."

"Excuse me," the driver calls. "Time to go. Are you getting on, Miss?"

"Say no," Doctor Kent says quietly. "Please say no."

The driver clears his throat. "Miss? Are you getting on?"

"No," I tell the driver, still gazing at Doctor Kent. For some reason, I'm trembling. "There has been a change of plans."

I hear the driver let out a sigh of exasperation followed by the sound of the bus doors closing. The engine growls and the bus pulls away from the curb, heaving frigid water onto Doctor Kent and me. We both let out shouts of surprise, which evolve into laughter as we shake the water from our faces. But when we make eye contact again, our laughter fades away into silence. There's a pause. What does he want? And why do I feel the confusing, exasperating, thrilling way that I do right now? I was finally coming to terms with what Doctor Kent really thinks of me and that I'd never see him again, and suddenly he shows up out of nowhere. Like this.

I can't stand it.

"What are you doing out here?" I blurt out.

"I came to find you."

"You did?" There's a spark in my chest, which I quickly extinguish. I gesture toward the building. "But why . . . I mean, did you run all the way from . . . I mean, how did you know—"

"I called Danielle, and she told me that you were at your appointment. I went to the clinic to find you but realized you had just left. I came out here to catch you."

"Oh." I try to think of something else to say. "Hey, good news: I'm done with crutches."

"That is good news."

More silence.

I brush the water off my nose. "So, what did you need to find me for?"

"I wanted to thank you in person before you left Lakewood," he explains. "Though what you did, and what you had to go through, is something I'll never really be able to thank you for."

Thank me. He's here to thank me, that's all. My heart crumbles with disappointment, even though it shouldn't. What else could I have expected?

"You're welcome." I manage something like smile. "I'm glad everyone understands the truth about the emergency department, Rick Gatz . . . and you."

He runs a hand through his hair. "Speaking of Rick Gatz, Mark Prescott fired him today."

"Really? Well, I'm glad to hear that, too."

"And Mark apparently discussed the situation with the rest of the hospital administrators, who then had a long meeting with the investors. There has been quite the fall-out over this." A light appears in his eyes. "The investors unanimously decided to fund the construction of a brand new emergency department. Not a remodel. An entirely new facility, built from the ground up."

"What?" I practically shout. "A new ED? Doctor Kent, that's incredible! Congratulations!"

Elated, I drop my crutches and almost embrace him before I realize what I'm doing. I stop, flushing furiously, and step back from him.

But he takes another step forward. "They want me to stay on at Lakewood to head up the committee that will design the new place."

"That's wonderful, Doctor Kent. Really wonderful," I tell him breathlessly.

His tone changes. "Well, this wouldn't have happened, had it not been for you."

"That's not true. This happened because of all you've done for the past two years." I glance away. "Congrats to Monica, too. She must be thrilled for you."

He draws his eyebrows together. "Monica doesn't know."

"What? You haven't told your girlfriend about—"

"Monica's not my girlfriend. Not anymore."

I take time wiping the rain from my face. "Oh. I'm sorry things didn't work out."

"Don't be sorry." He peers off into the distance. "It's been a long time coming. She has her life out there, and I have my life here. We grew apart. The reason she came out to visit was to convince me that we shouldn't break up, but her visit had exactly the opposite effect."

He starts to analyze my face, as if hoping to read my thoughts, and then goes on, "Remember that night when Monica came with me to work?"

My cheeks get hot despite the chill from the rain. "How could I not? That shift was one of the most humiliating nights of my entire life."

"What? Why?"

"Why?" I echo, equally surprised. "Because I did everything wrong. I backed out of running that code. I cried more than Vernice did. I called that patient to tell her about her husband. And, to top it off, I had a meltdown and went home early." I shake my head. "You must have thought I was the worst medical student on the planet."

Now he is the one who takes time before responding. "No, that's not what I thought."

Something about his tone makes my body tingle a little bit.

He steps even nearer to me. "That was the night when I knew I really was falling for you, Savannah. And that was the night when I knew it was unfair to Monica to try and salvage whatever she and I thought we used to have. That was the night when I knew that I couldn't keep pretending to care about D.C. when my heart was becoming settled here."

My head feels fuzzy. I'm breathing faster. Is Doctor Kent saying what I think he's saying?

Suddenly, he backs up. He appears stunned. "I'm sorry. I was not intending to tell you that." He shoves his hands into his jeans pockets. "Really, I only came here to thank you. I obviously know about you and Erik. I didn't mean to—"

"Erik?" I cut in with confusion. "Erik and me?"

Doctor Kent gives me a look. "Don't worry. Erik Prescott may not be my favorite guy on the planet, but if he treats you well, that's all that matters."

Hang on. Doctor Kent thinks . . . he's under the impression that . . .

"Doctor Kent, there is nothing going on between Erik Prescott and me," I say as firmly as I can.

He pauses again, and then his expression changes. "But that night at the restaurant, he was holding your hand. And in the resuscitation bay, he said something about you two going on a date. He—"

"We never went on that date. I cancelled." I sigh. "I admit there was a time when I tried to make myself believe that I was interested in Erik. But Erik was only a distraction. I focused on him because I was too scared to admit that I was falling for someone else." I stop abruptly, my eyes getting wide. "Sorry, Doctor Kent. You're my attending, and I—"

"I'm not your attending."

After a beat, I say, "Yes you are."

He steps so close to me that the water from his face drips lightly onto mine. "What day is it?"

"What? August fourth."

"Which means that your emergency medicine rotation is over. Which also means that I'm not your attending anymore."

I don't move.

Cautiously—gently—he puts one hand under my chin and tips my face upward. Then he bends down and kisses me. A wonderful shiver runs down my spine.

"But as one last attending comment," he adds, pulling his face back just enough to see me, "I can't tell you what a relief it was for me to hear that you chose to go into emergency medicine. The thought of you going into any other specialty has been making me crazy."

I gaze at him through the raindrops. "Really?"

"Yeah. You are a perfect fit for the emergency department, Savannah. Everyone could see that but you."

"But Monica said that—"

"Monica?" His tone sharpens. "Monica said what?"

"It's no big deal," I assure him, sorry that I brought it up at all. "It's in the past."

He puts a firm hand on my arm. "Please tell me. What did she say?"

"She told me about the low grade you're going to give me. But I don't care, Doctor Kent. All I care about is that you know I haven't been in this only for a good evaluation. I suppose it started out that way, but once I began working in the ED, everything changed. It wasn't about the grade anymore."

He is still holding my arm. "I gave you an honors grade. And my decision to do so was made long before I realized that I was developing romantic feelings toward you."

"Are you serious?"

"I'm completely serious, Savannah. Any student who will advocate for an elderly woman on a walkway stretcher, run a resuscitation on a septic infant, and stand up to a resident in the name of patient care deserves an honors grade."

Overcome, I can't reply.

He goes on, "Not to mention the type of humanity you showed Amy Nichols and Vernice Barnes, the baby you delivered in the middle of the ED walkway, and the way you stuck to your guns and saved a life by running a long code. You earned an honors grade, no matter what."

A warmth fills me that even the storm cannot stop. "So you really think that I'm okay in the ED?"

"You're more than okay. You're a natural. Of course you still have things to learn, but everyone does." He grins. "I should let you shadow other med students for a while. Then you'd get a real idea of how well you did this past month. At least you never tried to order three thousand grams of morphine for a patient."

My eyebrows shoot up. "Oh dear."

His chuckles, but his affect soon becomes serious. "So whatever Monica said to you, she was lying. While I can't say for sure, I'm going to go out on a limb and guess that she was jealous. I think she recognized that I was developing feelings for you."

I dare to lean into him. "Then please forgive the way that I acted toward you by the elevator the other day. That's why I was crying. I had just run into Monica, and I was pretty upset."

Understanding comes over his face. "I had no idea what I had done to hurt you. It was kind of tearing me up inside."

There is more silence, this time warm and comfortable. I sigh contentedly.

He wraps his arms around my waist. "So hopefully, we've cleared everything up?"

I feel a thrill from being in his embrace. "Everything is cleared up."

He pulls me to him. Suddenly, a weird-sounding song begins to play. With a giggle, I reach into my jacket pocket, pull out my cell phone, and hit a bunch of buttons until the music shuts off.

He watches as I put the phone away. "You're not going to get rid of that, are you?"

I shake my head. "No way, Doctor Kent. This is one very special cell phone."

He leans down and kisses me again. "It's Wes, by the way."

Acknowledgments

First, I am extremely thankful to the many team members at Cedar Fort Publishing & Media—past and present—for loving this story and helping me to share it.

To my fans, I remain deeply, humbly grateful for your enthusiasm and support.

I am forever indebted to the dedicated teachers, colleagues, and mentors who encouraged and instructed me over the years. This novel would not have been possible without you.

Nick, I love you. Thank you for believing in me. Thank you for everything.

To my family, I will never be able to fully express how lucky I feel to have your guidance, examples, and humor in my life.

Cookie, thanks for regularly taking me on walks so that I could clear my head and plan the next chapter.

And I'm incredibly appreciative to those dear friends who cheered me on and helped make this story better.

About the Author

TJ Amberson hails from the Pacific Northwest, where she lives with her husband and nutty cocker spaniel. Her most recent novels include *The Kingdom Of Nereth*, *Fusion*, and *Love at Lakewood Med*. When she's not writing, TJ can probably be found enjoying a hot chocolate, pretending to know how to garden, working in the ER, riding her bike, playing the piano, or surfing the Internet for cheap plane tickets.

Scan to Visit

www.tjamberson.com